YEARS OUT

YEARS OUT

ROSS FELD

ALFRED A. KNOPF
NEW YORK 1973

THIS IS A BORZOI BOOK
PUBLISHED BY ALFRED A. KNOPF, INC.

Copyright © 1973 by Ross Feld

All rights reserved under International and Pan-American
Copyright Conventions. Published in the United States by
Alfred A. Knopf, Inc., New York, and simultaneously in
Canada by Random House of Canada Limited, Toronto.
Distributed by Random House, Inc., New York.

Library of Congress Cataloging in Publication Data
Feld, Ross, date
    Years out.

    I. Title.
PZ4.F318Ye   [PS3556.E454]   813'.5'4   72–11020
ISBN 0–394–48138–0

Manufactured in the United States of America

FIRST EDITION

To ELLEN, *with love*

Pray that your griefs may slumber, and that the brotherhood of remorse not break their chain.
—HAWTHORNE

What is 'funnier' than forms which will not go away.—ROBERT CREELEY

OUT

NO ONE COULD HAVE KNOWN HOW SULTRY IT would be. Serena, since four in the afternoon, had been with Stuart and Marilyn in the apartment those two shared in Washington Heights, and, sipping No-Cals, had turned as woozy on a laziness and absence of pressure as she might have got from the strongest whiskey. When David and Joyce arrived at about six, they found a Serena so unlaced by the atmosphere, the runs of sunlight all over the plastic tablecloth, the funny things Stuart had been saying, that they stood for a moment like victims as she rushed up to David to kiss his startled face. "I love you," she said. She turned to Joyce and hugged her. "You, too. I love you too. Come."

David walked into the kitchen and picked up one of the glasses on the table to smell it.

Marilyn smiled and said, "Just No-Cal."

Stuart had hauled a footstool from near the sink and pushed out the extra chair at the table. He beckoned for Joyce and David to sit.

Serena sat down again and waited till everyone had a glass. "So, congratulations."

David nodded. "O.K."

"Listen," Stuart said. "We were thinking of pizza. How does that sound?"

David turned to his wife.

"Fine with me," Joyce said. "Just no anchovies on mine. I hate anchovies."

Serena made an exaggerated pout. "We have a problem, then. I love anchovies. All of that stuff I love: mushrooms, and perponi . . ."

"Perponi?"

She waited till the glassy laughter from all the rest settled. "Well, whatever it's called."

Stuart took her up straight-faced. "No, no, no, that's all right. I just have to remember all of this when I order. On yours you'll have perponi. On mine I'll have also some marshrums, a few anchinos, maybe a little mordantfella cheese."

Serena tsked and grinned. "You're making fun of me."

"No, I'm not."

Joyce interrupted. "To get back. I don't want anchovies. Serena does. Who else has preferences?"

"I don't care for the dough," Stuart said. "Mine'll just be the stuff on top, arranged neatly in midair."

David and Stuart went out and brought back the pies to the apartment, where the girls had set out paper plates, strips of paper toweling, and salt and garlic-powder shakers. Beer out of the can accompanied the meal. Stuart sat eating on the floor of the living room in front of the television: the first game of a twinight doubleheader was being broadcast from Cincinnati. The others ate around the table.

Serena lifted her beer. "I just feel like saying it again. Congratulations."

"Hear, hear!" Stuart shouted from the other room.

Joyce let go of her slice and quickly clamped a hand over her husband's mouth. "Don't. Please? For me?" She turned

to Serena and Marilyn with a martyred look on her face.
"Adolescent jokes." She removed her hand from David's lips.
"Where, where?" he blurted delightedly.
"See what I mean?"

Still they laughed. The whole apartment, especially the
kitchen, had been dunked into the fine beginnings of twilight.
Greys and pinks were strollers in the blue sky above the roof-
tops, mottling the inside air and working on smiles and actions
like slow motion. It was irresistible—the laughs, the expres-
sions: they were a soft and pliable tribute to each of them.
Serena's toasts of congratulations had grafted words onto the
feeling, but wordless, too, it would have thrived. If they chose
to, each of them could spend this night discovering with ad-
miration their friendship pressed into every little thing. The
light in the house simply helped it along, making the well-
being ember in someone's eyes like a mote caught drifting in
a bright slash. Every smile was powered to smooth the lap of
intimacy they felt so snug in.

The day before, they had all graduated. The actual ceremony was unattended—much too formal and unrelated to
whatever they felt—but the behind-the-eyes vision of it stayed.
The shuffling forth. The years released like a gay balloon. An
amphitheatre carbonated with possibility. Rather than ignore
the event, they seemed to have settled on finessing it, coaxing
it here, to what turned out to be brilliant calming rooms, and,
instead of dispatching it with one great binge of memory and
regret, marking it with a cool offhand indelibility. The best
way to never forget was to never quite remember.

So they laughed, ate with their hands, played rock-'n'-roll
on the record player, then Irish folk songs, which Marilyn
sang along to in a nice calked voice the others had never
heard before. The sound of the ball game went off but the
picture stayed, and then there was a record of organ music
that David had slipped on the changer: Buxtehude, dense with
cathedral resonances, impish reedy sounds, crashingly deep
bass notes whose loudness filled the air like another tempera-

ture, and then, lingering, seemed to harden like a crust. When Marilyn mentioned the party they were all invited to downtown on Ninety-sixth Street, it was almost like a violation, but Stuart thought the least they could do was call there and get some idea of what was going on. He was on the phone first, convincing one of the revelers at the other end to hold his receiver to the celebration in progress, and then the others gathered around to hear the transmitted soup sounds and the slappy yells and the purée of gurgled and distant festivity. They listened for only a minute; then Stuart hung up. In winter they might have gone: the evening would, as expected, pitch off into night; faces would begin to glare off the windows made mirrory by a darkness outside like pudding; and the night, like a thick, resistant challenge, would be scraped through in subways and taxis until they arrived at another lighted place. But now it was different—graduation always also means raw summer. Now they would have to abandon a night that had looped in on them rather than collapsed. Without yet having to turn on lights, they'd been sitting as the sounds from the streets rose up against the apartment buildings and came through the open windows like a somnolent insect chatter. Quirkless, feathery dusk was in every room, around every head. To leave now would be to leave somehow insultingly, a rude disturbing of the half-light that had made their hours so far a warming bath. They needed a firmer, less solicitous night, but this one was without nerve or decision; it just had a heart, and the heart was like a stomach—full and in repose. So they stayed where they were; they played a game involving a dime, a napkin, a glass, and a cigarette; the pink in the air disappeared in time, leaving the buzzing grey and the puffs of May breeze warping the room with cool extra space. Stuart joked; Joyce was sentimental talking about how David would sometimes, late at night and in bed, sing old songs—Gene Autry songs—each absolutely recalled off some scratchy red plastic disk from his childhood; David's smile was canted by embarrassment; and Marilyn, at a moment

when the games and the jokes and stories seemed to be stretch-
ing up to twist off the finest plum of their friendship, cried—
a privately confused swirl—until Serena's smile, so open, so
aware, seemed even more apt and to the point.

It continued until midnight, when Joyce and David left.
Serena stayed on till the end of the Charlie Chan movie that
had followed the ball game: Stuart's cracks about Number
One Son, her own hectoring but fizzy glances shot back to
get him to shut up and let her watch it in peace. When it
was over, she also left, moving through the foyer and to the
door, propelled by kisses and thank-yous. Marilyn then har-
vested the empty cans and glasses and napkins with the cheer
of exhaustion, and when Stuart finally clicked the lights, they
also felt as if they were leaving, though it was only into another room.

FIRST

SHE WAS WATCHING THE SUMMER SUN LAY TO her side of the street, the rays separate and defined, almost a violence to them, those not fluidly snaring on the white curtains left to smash abruptly on the worn wooden floors. One of the air vents on the roof of the hospital across the street was scorched with light. At moments like this, she thought about her papers, her assignments, about their impossibility in view of the crazy light around her. Marilyn Dissman went to the phonograph and put on the Mendelssohn she had taken out of the library to chart sonata form. The record was old and badly scratched; she would learn nothing from it and maybe wouldn't even eat supper. Lumba-lumba, lumba-lumba. Reformation symphony that made her feel so awful, hating to have to go back downtown to return the record—it was worthless—having to hate to go downtown, hating to go, to leave, to hear someone say "Where did you go," and to say to them "I went here." Lumba-lumba, dah dee dump.

Stuart's sock on the chair was hers, was manna, was a form, a Gorky shape, was a piece of uranium drilled from a salty place, and not his—big-deal universe, big deal. Someone opened a window on the top floor of Columbia Presbyterian and nothing could be seen inside. She grabbed the advertisements she had clipped from the Sunday *Times* Magazine and let them flutter out of her fingers and flap gently till they almost stacked on the floor. She hated them—whoever they were—for making her invariably think of Chinese food when it came to six o'clock Sunday: the worn fathers needing shaves, the kids—most to be felt sorry for—in frazzle that only got more and more annoying in the bedrooms, then the living rooms, then the kitchens, and then the bathrooms, until they, along with everyone else, wanted to flee into the quiet streets of Sunday and discover Monday.

She walked into the living room, bending down to the coffee table to finger the dial of the telephone. No one had called; if she kept her hand on the phone, would someone? Not Serena—she hadn't paid her bill, and they'd disconnected her. Told with a laugh. But Marilyn's anger was inexpressible; that is, if she wanted not to go to pieces herself. Don't say, but somehow get across, Why don't you pay the bill? Why are you so lazy? How come you have such a good job, neat life, and no dish drain in the kitchen with prongs to hold glasses? Why don't you buy Endust, why don't you go hysterical at roaches at least once in a while, for purgative value? Why are you living in that perfect little bachelorette apartment? Where is your husband and where is mine? When will you stop fucking and live? When will I? And stop all this thought about what? The Interborough Parkway, the High School of Music and Art, condoms, "We Shall Not Be Moved," Walt Disney, Chinese food, Chinese food! Marilyn was backing from the parts of the living room that the late sun was charcoaling. All of this damn black and white. The objects of her love: the singular, resonant nostalgia of even a brand-new folk song; the Winnie-the-Poohs carefully set one on top of another on her dressing table; the taste of gin-and-tonic when they all went to a bar after a softball game; falling asleep in the tall grass of Harriman State Park; the smell of barbecue—nothing was rescuing her from the moment. A whole afternoon of dull, dull leather, seems rotted, and now the threads moving out of the holes. What's the fucking matter? And if she yelled that out, here, alone: WHAT'S THE FUCKING MATTER?—what difference?

Out in the hall, someone was unlocking a door and stepping into a better universe. Marilyn pulled on a cardigan, slipped into her sandals, and grabbed her keys from the dresser in the bedroom. Once she had closed the apartment door behind her, facing four doors, she paused, her motivation spiraling away into nothing. She walked across the vestibule to the door directly opposite hers and rang Mrs. Díaz's bell.

A heavy step was coming down the long hallway inside; not carpet slippers, not housedress, not "Ah, *sí*, come in, *sí*" that she felt she wanted, but a man, and Marilyn backed away a step as the door was opening. Facing her was a short man with a lot of hair combed straight back from his low forehead. He was wearing a cheap sport shirt and had a piece of celery in his hand.

"*Sí?*"

"I'm sorry. I just wanted to ask Mrs. Díaz something. I'll come back later. Sorry." She took two steps backward but the man followed her out a step.

"No. Come in, she's here." His accent was not very heavy.

"No, really. It's nothing. Later." Marilyn began to push her open palms toward him, although he was a good three feet away.

Firmly, even a touch annoyed, the man said, "I understand English."

Marilyn stopped retreating. "Yes. Well, just tell her that I'll be back. I know you're eating." As she spoke, she peered for a moment over the man's shoulder into the darkened apartment, from which a heavy, lardy air was sifting. She couldn't see Mrs. Díaz or the form of anyone else coming out of the three rooms that angled off the long hallway of the railroad flat. "Tell her Marilyn, her neighbor."

The man made a quick gesture for her to come in. "No, it's fine. She's here. Carmela!" He then turned, keeping the door open for Marilyn with his elbow. She followed him in. The apartment's odor got stronger as they neared the kitchen, and it brought on an instant of peace in Marilyn—the cheap upholstery badly holding the summer heat, and the television blaring the ball game. Mrs. Díaz still had not come out to greet her, and Marilyn followed the man into the living room, standing up after smiling away his gesture to sit. She heard a toilet flush and saw old Mrs. Díaz come out of the bathroom on the other side of the kitchen. She was wearing a dark blue dress, the hem ragged over her stockinged knees. Above her left breast was pinned a corsage made up mostly of dyed pink netting, with a small plastic Easter bunny set in its center.

"Hello," she yelled, stopping her walk toward Marilyn for a second to push a pot back over to an unused burner on the stove. "Eat with us."

"No, I really didn't want to disturb you, but I wanted to know when the exterminator comes. It's getting very bad in my house."

Mrs. Díaz shook her head. "Never good, I see everywhere. Supposed to come on the Monday, the second week in the month. You never know, though." She lifted her eyes and raised a finger. "You know, maybe Ralph do it for you." She motioned with a half-closed fist at the man, who was standing by one of the two open windows of the room. He made no acknowledging gesture except to stare straight at Marilyn.

"He's not charging you too much money," Mrs. Díaz said.

"Well, it's not that bad. I can wait. I just"—she smiled for no particular reason—"wanted to make sure I would be home when he came. Otherwise they won't open the door themselves, right?" Her question was unfortunate; it was prolonging the talk, which had gone sour for her when Ralph was suggested to kill the bugs.

The man spoke up. "I do it for you this afternoon. I go home and get the stuff. This afternoon. I have a car."

Mrs. Díaz returned to the kitchen, then re-entered the room and held out to Marilyn a can of Rheingold and a dark-green glass. Marilyn accepted both and held them at her sides before sitting down on the couch. Her right thigh was chilling from the cold beer can.

Ralph nodded at Marilyn. "Cool you off. Hot as hell today." Then he strode out of the room, down the hallway. Mrs. Díaz sat herself down on one of the armchairs and slipped a finger into her right shoe. She had on a fancy sort of slipper—on the toe Marilyn noticed the sheen of plastic vinyl. "Ralph my nephew. He works as a policeman in the projects—who knows? Maybe he gets me in. Is cheap. He do the bugs when he's not working. He do it for you, not more than—not much."

Marilyn stood up, taking a short sip of the beer first. "No, Mrs. Díaz. I didn't know you had company. I really just came in to see how you were. And thank you for the beer."

"I'm fine."

"Well . . ."

"Ai, good—beer on hot day is good. Not too much." She gave a harridan's laugh. "But on hot day is good."

Ralph was now back in the room, wearing a jacket which, as he bent down to give Mrs. Díaz a kiss on the cheek, Marilyn could see had embroidered on its back a yellow and pink map of Korea, the words BACK FROM HELL sewn across the shoulders. He turned and faced Marilyn. "You stay here with Carmela and I be back in half an hour. How many rooms in your apartment?"

Marilyn was about to sit down again, but checked it. All her hemming and false starts had grabbed away most of her control. "I was telling your aunt that I appreciate it, I really do, it's a hot day and all, but I'd rather wait for the exter— I have things to clear up in the house. I'd never be able to do it today."

"I'll do it all."

"Yes, well, I also have company coming over. The smell."

"Takes a half-hour—it's summer, the smell gets out the open windows," the man insisted. He continued to look straight at her, which did nothing to allay her discomfort.

"How about another time?"

"When?"

"I'm not sure. I'll have to speak to my roommate."

"A girl?"

Marilyn finally found her self-possession. "Well, I'll let Mrs. Díaz know when," she said, brushing aside the question. She put down the beer can and the glass on top of the television set and smiled farewells at both the man and the old lady. For a second, as she turned her back on them, leaving the room, she expected to be grabbed by the shoulders. Not wanting to turn around and chance a continuation of the conversation, Marilyn increased her gait down the long hallway but could not bring herself to run. At the end of the corridor, she turned, goose-pimpled. Ralph stood at the other end. He waved at her almost effeminately, and stupidly she waved back. Only then, with the short motion of her arm, did she recognize her terror. When she slammed the door behind her and ran to her own door, an unbearable thirty seconds of digging in the pockets of her shorts for the keys brought it home. Getting the door open, she wondered how many inches behind her Ralph was, what he'd grab first. Her leg braced outside in the hallway, she executed the maneuver of both swinging open her apartment door to safety and then kicking the braced leg up behind her to where she was positive his groin was. The horselike kick went through air—nothing—and it propelled her forward so that her forehead hit the door. She hurried in and slammed the door behind her and looked out the peephole to the desolate landing. Her heart wasn't pounding, she thought, nor was her breathing ripped, but her thoughts, like ships in the lock of a canal, rose from one level to another: annoyance to fear, fear to terror, terror to a boiling. Her forehead hurt; she slapped at what she definitely thought would be an open wound, bringing her hands close to her eyes to see the blood. She saw nothing; she started to sob. The beer came up in her, and for a moment she thought its bitterness was the tears in her throat.

The phone was ringing. She ran to it, and only as she was about to put the receiver to her ear did she think it might be Ralph.

"What?" she answered unusually.

"Marilyn?"

"Yes. What!" Her head was throbbing.

"Joyce. What's the matter with you?"

"Nothing."

"We're taking a walk. I thought we'd come over."

"Don't. I don't want to see anyone." She felt herself settling slightly. "I've been bored all day. And bitchy."

"Me too."

"I'll call you back."

"Sure, but wait. I called to tell you that we saw Serena, and we're all going over to the New Yorker tonight to see that old horror movie *Freaks*. You and Stuie should come."

"He's not here. He went to see his parents for the weekend. Who'll take me home?"

"David and I'll drop you."

"No." There were times when an afterthought, a forethought, a shade of contrast, an extra consideration translated themselves into huge boulders of complication. Like now. "What'll you do then?"

"We'll walk home. It's only six blocks."

"It's not the safest neighborhood to walk through late."

"Come on, we used to live on the lower East Side, remember. This is paradise."

"Except for the Cubans who hang around drunk outside of the bars on Broadway."

"I'm not worried."

"No."

"No what?"

"I'm not going to go."

"Because we're going to take you home?"

"Because I'm tired. Being bored makes you very tired."

"All right. I'll speak to you tomorrow."

"Joyce, could you say one more thing to me?"

There was silence on the other end of the line. Then: "You all right?"

"No. Not that. Say something positive."

Joyce chuckled. "How about 'They're the best pieces of equipment for the money.' That good?"

"Good. Goodbye."

After she hung up, she went into the kitchen and took out a frozen beef pie and put it in the oven. Like a damaged sand-and-shell painting, each action she undertook now jarred and chipped off another small part of her upset. She looked at the real-estate section of the newspaper, concentrating only partly on the house and property sales in Vermont and New Hampshire. She wished Joyce hadn't called. She had forgotten about the telephone since she went in to see Mrs. Díaz and Ralph, forgotten the thin but real possibilities it had for pocking her boredom. Suddenly she thought of calling her father, or Stuart's parents to see if he was still there. But as Joyce's call had demonstrated, that little black machine was a strainer, a generalizer. She felt in no mood to be reduced.

She ate her beef pie along with a glass of milk. Afterward, there was the Ed Sullivan Show for as long as she could stand it—enough for the first acrobatic act and Myron Cohen. Marilyn dialed Stuart's mother, but there was no answer; she assumed they had driven him to the station. About nine, she finally put down the paperback Lewis Carroll she was reading to wash her hair, taking a long plain cotton nightgown into the bathroom with her and donning it when she was done. It didn't stick to her body, and there was finally something a little wonderful to the day. Ten-thirty she got into bed, after closing all the windows in the bedroom facing out onto the fire escape. She got up once more to check the window in the kitchen. While she was there, she took a glass and filled it with the cold water from the bottle always kept in the refrigerator. One of Stuart's habits.

Sleep was not difficult; maybe six or seven minutes and a few deep breaths and she was down into it. The next morning she would think, for some reason, of a waffle iron, and later on in the morning would connect it vaguely to a dream of which she only recalled that fragment. Later still, when she put on a Jean Ritchie record before she left the house and heard the line "Oh, fare thee well, my house carpenter," she was hit with the image of a house looking down over the Palisades—another stray from the night before.

Stuart had come in about one o'clock, a suitcase in one hand, in the other a shopping bag filled with a whole roast chicken wrapped in foil, two frozen Delmonico steaks, ten oranges, and six greengage plums, courtesy of his mother. He quietly put the food away and switched on a light in the living room to see if any phone messages were left on the coffee table. Finding none, he went into the bedroom. In the inadequate light, he could see Marilyn sleeping diagonally across the bed, one of her arms tight against her eyes, her nightgown pulled around her hips. Stuart undressed, opened the windows, hearing Marilyn shift beside him. When he got in next to her, her eyes were open.

"Don't open the windows," she said heavily.

"It's hot as anything in here."

She put the other arm over her eyes and slid her head off the pillow and onto the sheet, even with his waist. "We'll get robbed."

"We're in here."

"That doesn't matter."

"Go back to sleep." Stuart smelled his hands as he arranged a pillow: they smelled of paprika and garlic from the chicken he had just put away. He felt hair on his thighs, raised his head, and saw Marilyn close to his leg. He brought a finger down and traced her eyebrows.

"How are your parents?" she said, her voice the low, grainy chock of sleep.

"My sister is going to have dental surgery."

"Is she upset?"

"No."

There was no breeze coming in the room. As he moved his foot over the sheet, Stuart picked up a little relief from the cooler, unslept-on spots of the fabric. He sat up to bend down and kiss Marilyn. Her forehead was wet. She shook her head after the kiss. "Too hot."

Stuart settled back. "You out today?"

She moved up on the bed so that she was facing him. "Just to get the paper. Then I was drunk all day."

"*Drunk?*"

"No, I wasn't. I just said that."

"We went to the pool. You could have come, you know. Even this morning."

"No. I had things to do."

"My sister wants to know if you know where to get a certain kind of sandal. She said she'll call you, since she has to come into the city this weekend to go to the dentist."

"Uh-huh."

"No one called?"

"Joyce this afternoon. It was nothing."

"Nothing what?"

"To go to a movie at the New Yorker. A horror movie."

"Oh, I know. David mentioned it Friday when I saw him in the supermarket. *Freaks* or something. I forgot to tell you then. Did you want to go?"

"I didn't."

"Did you get any work done on the music paper?"

"I want to go to sleep." Marilyn drew off the nightgown and sat upright for a second at the side of the bed, looking out the window toward the lights of the bridge. Stuart fingered her backbone. She lay back, on his hand. Withdrawing it, Stuart hoisted a leg over her middle. "It's too hot," she repeated.

"I just want to stretch."

"Look, it's *boiling* in here. Your leg is heavy." Her sounds had clarified out of whisper. Stuart touched her the right way for both of them, and they began to make love. When they were done, Stuart still in her, she told him the story, down to the detail of the BACK FROM HELL jacket, her tone modulating with matter-of-factness, sure that he'd see through it and kiss her again.

It was the nice sense of regularity that was holding best in Stuart Lapin as he stood on the corner and looked at the office buildings lining the street, people issuing from the doors steadily, the streets temporarily slick after the rain shower the way only midtown streets can be, the traffic out of which he was trying to bag a cab ceaseless and homogenized. An hour before, he had jumped up from his desk and rushed, along with the woman whom he shared a cubicle with, into the managing editor's office to watch the storm come swiftly and without deliberation over the Hudson from Jersey, a thick bar of shadow chopping down at the Jersey shipyards first, then the raw green river, then the hotels of Eighth and Seventh Avenues, until it came to them and washed through the street with a thrilling preciseness that everyone who had crowded into the office to get a look commented on. The managing editor had said that if you were born in the Middle West, as he was, this thing became nothing special, happened all the time. You could see it coming over the fields, marching toward you, and then past. Stuart felt elated as he walked back to his own office afterward, sensing a closeness with the people here that was new after six weeks on the job. All their "wow"'s and "man"'s as the sky darkened overhead. The hour remaining until he'd leave went quickly, and now he stood thinking it was too bad he had to meet Marilyn at six; otherwise he'd have had a drink in the bar on Sixth Avenue frequented by some of the people in the office.

He walked a block or two uptown to the hotels, where he

thought he might have more luck in getting a cab. He opened the door of one waiting in queue before the entrance to a hotel driveway. The cabby, who looked like a confined and dumpy version of Stuart's own father, asked where the fare was to before Stuart even got a chance to sit down. When he was told, the cabby said "No" simply, and from inside pulled at the door that Stuart held open. Stuart said, "Go fuck yourself," and the cabby, shaking his head, replied, "Nice talk."

Walking to Fifty-seventh Street, Stuart caught sight of Gloria, one of the secretaries, half a block ahead of him. On her arm was a shopping bag from a health-food store, and close to her elbow a plastic tote bag with the word "schlep" printed in mock-Hebrew letters on its front. She walked quickly, too fast for Stuart to reach her. At the corner, though, she stopped at a newsstand and Stuart legged a few steps and was standing directly behind her when she turned away after getting her paper.

"Excu—Stuart! I didn't see you."

"You were walking ahead of me. I'm going to buy a paper too." He picked one out of the middle of the pile, looking with almost instinctive though groundless guilt at the news vendor in the shack. The man stared at his palms clasped before him, then slowly freed them to put one out toward Stuart. His eyes were vacant. Stuart arranged the pile of papers again before turning to walk away a few steps with Gloria. "I wonder how many people cheat him. Take a newspaper very quietly."

"I'm sure he hears. That's all he can do. When you're blind, your hearing gets very sensitive. Do you live around here?"

"Oh, sure," Stuart said.

"It's expensive."

"Do I look like I live around here?"

"Well, *I* didn't know." Gloria was a small brunette, just recently married to a sales representative for General Electric, living in Flushing with a cat, a dishwasher, and a bigger air conditioner for the living room than the wiring of the building could handle. These were the facts of her life she most readily revealed to anyone waiting outside her boss's—the production manager's—office, and they were imparted with a sequence of such meaningful looks that one naturally took them for the pillars and posts of her existence.

"Where are you going?" Stuart asked, snapping the paper under his arm, the pit of which was announced wet with the pressure.

"To get shoes. I had so much to do at lunch—Fitz and I are going to the Virgin Islands in three weeks—and I didn't get a chance. You?"

"I've been trying to get a cab since the office, but so far nothing. Supposed to meet someone at Third Avenue at six. What time is it now?" he asked as he shot his cuff to read his watch. "A quarter to six. I might as well walk."

Gloria turned her head at the window of a furrier they were passing and, sensing the break, Stuart said, "I have to run. I'll see you tomorrow."

Gloria turned back toward him. "Right. Have a good time."

While he stood at the corner of Fifty-seventh, a cab pulled up and let out a small fat man carrying a long yellow mailing tube. Stuart pushed his way through the people waiting to cross the street and got to the taxi just as the former rider was lifting the last few inches of the tube off the back seat. Stuart held the handle of the door, politely, selfishly, then slipped in the cab himself, closing the door with a weak slam that did not catch the lock. Opening the door again, he closed it securely and told the driver, "Third and Sixtieth, please."

The knack of riding in taxis completely at ease had never been his. Never ignored the drivers, though he rarely spoke to them; watched the traffic and the meter the way the kind of people who would no doubt be comfortable in a cab watched tennis matches; invariably went for his wallet too soon, oftentimes making the driver who caught the move in his peripheral vision or rear-view mirror tighten with the expectation of robbery.

A smart, easily elegant long-legs was at the curb before Bendel's, and her lunge for the cab made it look as if she were waving to Stuart. Her arm dropped quickly as she saw his outline through the window, and she faced away and looked down the street with a frantic emptiness. The women Stuart never knew. His knowledge about them was something like his knowledge of Africa: pulpy and much too far away. He stuck with that; who would contradict his feeling that these girls *lived* in Bendel's, or Saks, pushing out the doors of those places for presentation in his own street cotillion?

As he paid the driver, he saw Marilyn on the line outside the theatre. When he reached her, he said, "I'm sorry. No cabs."

"It's all right. I bought the tickets already." She took a puff of her newly started cigarette.

Stuart stuck his head to the side of the line and surveyed its length: half a block of utterly predictable faces.

Marilyn put her head on his shoulder. "I'm tired," she said, freeing a cone of smoke that died shortly in the fresh after-rain breeze.

"What'd you do?"

"I had my class, then I went down to the library to return the records, then I went to the park. Also shopping." She took her head off him, leaned back the other way until she rested against the window of the store they were in front of, and smiled nicely.

"Get caught in the storm?" he said. "You should have seen it from the eighteenth floor."

"I was in Bloomingdale's. It got dark very quickly. I was trying on a skirt, and there are windows in the dressing rooms. Well, really it's a storeroom near the dressing rooms. When I stepped out, it looked like night, and then the thunder."

"It was something. We watched it from Howard's office, saw it coming over from New Jersey like this solid line advancing."

"I love that darkness suddenly."

"You didn't buy the skirt, I see." Stuart lifted a fold of the one she had on, a summery cotton with small pleats, a skirt he really liked; a little square, it made her look, as he always said when she wore it, like "a Communist."

"No. I didn't *buy* it."

He was going to say it out loud but caught himself and leaned to her by the window. He made large mouthings. "You didn't *buy* it. Which means that you . . ."

"It's in my bag." Marilyn pointed down to the large burlap tote she now swung who-little-ole-me-ish between her slightly parted legs. "I tried it on and I was going to buy it. But then I thought I really wanted to *have* it, not to buy it." There was no defensiveness in her voice. "I once did it with a whole dress. You know that navy knit? In the Village, before they started to put in those monitoring systems. But the department stores are still safe."

Stuart flustered. Which was more disconcerting—her stealing the skirt or the way she told him about it? "You're lucky."

"That what I've been telling you for months. Finally you see."

"You know what I mean. How did you get it out of the store?"

"Under this skirt."

"Is it a miniskirt?"

"Yep. Slipped it over me, over my midriff, too, so it wouldn't make a bulge. It's light, so the material wasn't bulky."

"Didn't the saleslady say anything? Ask for the skirt?"

"A saleslady in Bloomingdale's? I could walk out with a washing machine under there."

"You think so."

"I know so. I'd say I was six months overdue and the father was a beautiful buffalo." She smiled, throwing her head back against the window. "But I'm going to only wear this skirt on sub-rosa occasions."

"Is that when you wear the dress you also stole?"

Marilyn continued to smile and dug into the tote for another Newport.

"Did you steal that lighter, too?" Stuart asked.

"I've stolen everything I have."

"Including me."

"Owh, poor, poor baby." She patted his cheek. He had to smile. On tiptoe, she said, "The line is moving. Thank God."

In the lobby, they headed up for the balcony and the smoking section. The theatre was quickly packing and individual seats holed strings of couples and triples seated randomly throughout. Marilyn whispered, "We better find two together. For three bucks, at least that."

"Why are you whispering?" he whispered to her as they climbed the stairs looking carefully at the rows.

"I always whisper in movies."

"Sounds like you're in church."

"I am."

"Bullshit."

"There's two in the middle here."

A cloying antiwar cartoon first. A trailer. The spiel for Colombian coffee. The nearest chain theatre. The movie.

A group of mountain climbers set out to scale a Himalayan peak. There is seeming harmony among them until a woman journalist, sent by a French magazine, is helicoptered into their camp to follow and report on their attempt. Each of three climbers, in turn, falls for her; the added tension she has brought confuses the precision needed for the climb, and for days, despite favorable conditions, they do not start up the mountain. In one scene, an airplane zooms low over the camp, leaving a black engulfing shadow.

Someone in the row behind them whispers, "That's pure Hitchcock. This guy has nothing of his own." Marilyn stares into the darkness for who has said it. She is bothered by and attracted to the quick verdict.

There is a scene of a thin saffron line of monks threading through the wildflower fields near the village close to camp. The Sherpas hired for the climb are mystified and impatient with the delay, and they begin to drink great quantities of the local beer. The sight of the line of monks appears to one of them as an omen. The woman journalist is murdered in her tent that night. Stunned, the climbing party buries her the next day, and, as if to leave the muddled and awful complications behind, they set out for the climb immediately after the burial. One by one, each of them is threatened by the others as they scale the icy walls: there are slipped ropes, loose pitons, badly placed ladders. Left at the end is only the Englishman who's been filming the climb; the others are dead. As he orders the Sherpas back down the mountain, one of them, accidentally on purpose, knocks the camera off the Englishman's brace, and it hurtles down silently through the air.

As the lights in the theatre come on, the same voice behind Marilyn says dryly, "The son of a bitch broke the wrong camera. If he'd used his head, we would have been spared this piece of shit." Stuart smiles; but Marilyn is careful to show no reaction. The movie was, after all, three dollars a throw, and besides, after seeing a movie—six-o'clock showings in particular—they liked to postpone talking about it until they got to sit down somewhere, preferably over a drink. They decided, as they moved slowly out of the theatre, to go to Cobbie's, at least for two gin-and-tonics.

In a booth, having ordered, Marilyn said, "I don't know."

"It was slick. There were parts, though."

"She was beautiful. I had mixed feeling about how real her motives were. Sometimes—that part in the camp where she goes walking in the dark—you weren't even sure she had any motives." Marilyn sipped her drink through the thin plastic straw that served as the swizzle stick.

"A lot of the visual stuff was good," Stuart offered. "Actually, it's hard to go wrong with the Himalayas when you want impressive imagery. Why don't you drink like a person, out of the glass? You look like a jerk."

Marilyn smiled at him and took another sip through the straw. Cobbie's was a small place on Second Avenue she had first discovered when she shared an apartment on York Avenue with Serena. Up to seven o'clock or so, it was filled with hookers and drinkers; then it emptied, and a few people who knew that there was a fairly decent Italian kitchen came in for dinner. She hadn't been here in six months. In one of the booths near the back, she had once suffered a bad scene with a guy she'd met in her Asian History class, who had begun a political discussion by calling her "a normal Jewish dilettante," and then couldn't wait to steer her into bed. She had sat there, controlling her anger enough to have one more drink from him, a drink that she desired out of nothing but spitefulness, then told him to take a flying fuck, and walked out on him, reaching the apartment fifteen minutes later after throwing up in the doorway of a Chinese laundry. That and a few other incidents, and there was something to the bar that was unsavory, softened by spoilage, yet strangely comfortable. She had made a point of bringing Stuart here on one of their first dates, slumping that night in the booth, saying hello to the waiters and bartender, talking about how much she felt at home here. But since they had begun to live with each other in Washington Heights, Marilyn had never mentioned Cobbie's and, sensing a cue, neither had Stuart.

"I think I'd like a Margarita now," Marilyn said, swirling the ice cubes in her empty glass. "You?"

"I'll stick with this. You know, when you mix—"

"That's a myth. I read it somewhere."

"It's your stomach. See if you can catch his eye."

The waiter brought the fresh drinks. Marilyn played with the coarse salt on the edge of the glass. "Do you remember when I worked at that advertising agency for a week, I said I met this girl Joan there? Remember?"

"Nope."

"Oh, c'mon. You do. She was coming to dinner one night, and then she couldn't come because she was getting sick. She got hepatitis."

"Vaguely." Marilyn made friends quickly, a trait for which Stuart balanced a share of envy against an equal share of distrust. The friends she made, all young women, were like herself; they all gave the impression of being orphans of the world, waifs thrown awry on the smooth surface of how things were. The friendly attraction stemmed out of shared interests —pottery, folk dance and folk music, children's books—but then moved off subtly from the original sympathy to a common inability to make do with the world. These girls would often arrive for dinner looking stunningly beautiful, then disintegrate before his eyes into a congregation of tics, dogmas, and fears, their limped sexuality melting to a discouraging ooze. They were never married or living with a man; Stuart had thought once that they waited, like a vast lost answering service, for those women like Marilyn—who knew men but could have lived without the knowledge—to walk among them, a client giving them precious access to the world of "normal people." The tenure of the relationship was always brief— three or four weeks, on the average. Then they saw each other no more, stopped going folk dancing or to Clancy Brothers concerts, and Marilyn spoke of the girl rarely, if ever. A card might come at Christmas from Santa Fe, New Mexico, or Portland, Maine, reading, in mournful diction, "I've got a job teaching underprivileged children here in the black section of town, which is very small. I do hope you and Stuart are fine. Have an extremely good year. Best, Norma Kantor."

"I spoke to her on the phone this afternoon, before I left the house. She works in the jewelry department of Brentano's and she's leaving at the end of the month to work with an archeological research group that's getting started in Turkey. I mean California. They're *going* to Turkey. Isn't that fantastic?"

"Why'd she leave the ad agency?" Stuart had finished his drink, and looked at the new one before him without desire. He was hungry.

"Why did *I* leave the ad agency."

"Right. Go on. Why'd you call her?"

"I met her in the street two weeks ago. I think I told you this."

"You didn't. You don't have to, either. We've talked about this, telling me everything."

"I'm *not*, I'm *not*. I'm just telling you this one thing. I met her and she said she might be leaving"—Marilyn's voice hooked onto the singsong she used to list a summary of facts that led to her point—"and where she was going and when, and where she was working. *Then* she said that maybe I'd like to take her job."

"Low pay, I think. But it's easy."

"Sure. I think it's at night, until midnight."

"Uh-uh."

"Why *not?* The subway's right there. I'd be safe. You could come and meet me at the station at home, or some nights you could come down there at twelve and we could go out."

"At *midnight?*" Stuart asked. "I work during the day, remember."

"I'm stronger than you are, then." Interest flew commando-like over her face, her eyes blinking bright then coy, lips firmed then slack-cute, her hand coming to her cheek and reassuring the small wart there.

Stuart changed the subject. "Do you want to eat here? I'm starved. What time is it? Ten after eight."

"I have no more money on me. I was going to cash a check, but I had to rush to the library."

Stuart took out his wallet. "Twelve. Until Thursday."

She nodded understandingly. "Tomorrow I'll cash the check. Let's eat downtown."

Stuart pulled a few bills from the wallet, then stopped when he saw that she hadn't begun her Margarita. "I'm sorry. No rush."

"I don't want it. Take it."

"Screw it." He got up, walked to the bar, and paid for the drinks. Marilyn met him there.

"I hate to leave the drinks," she said. "We paid for them."

"What should we do, have them poured into containers to go?"

"Sure. A Margarita to go, Jake. Easy on the Triple Sec."

They were out the door and on the street, which had now lost most of the ozoned air from the afternoon's shower. "How do you know about Triple Sec?" Stuart asked her, shoving his fingers in the belt of her skirt.

"I worked as a waitress once, I told you."

"I thought there wasn't a bar."

"They called it one."

"But that kind of place generally doesn't even have Bourbon."

"You never can tell." She knocked her hand against the small of his back.

Cobbie's was far from a subway, and Second Avenue was boring both of them as they walked south. Rather than take a bus across town and get the subway down, they decided on a cab. "It won't be more than two bucks," Marilyn said a moment before Stuart stuck his hand up in the air.

They ate in a Tex-Mex restaurant in the West Village. When they got in a cab to go home—too tired to maneuver the subway—Stuart had $3.77 on him. The fare came to a little over three dollars and Marilyn made the tip. They climbed the stairs slowly; just how tired they were was now apparent. Before the last flight, Marilyn stopped at the landing and rested her head against the steel bar bolted on the window to prevent children from falling out. She stared out the open six inches of the bottom part of the window, watching people and cars four stories below. Stuart had reached the apartment, but turned and went back down when he realized she was not with him. He watched her from the landing above.

"What?" he said.

"It's just that I'm tired of us having no money." Marilyn was diffident; her interest was not money, but why not? They didn't have anything, if having meant holding, keeping. If it meant that, they didn't even have each other, but stayed together out of fear of not doing as well without. Sure, that was the way she felt. They had money and look what happened

to it, like tonight, when it had streamed from them effortlessly.
More would be there, but the point was . . . The point was
more money. Getting rid of it gracelessly. There were people
who spent and, spending, received things in return which were
almost tokens, appreciative tokens, of their act. But what she
and Stuart did was just give the money and grab the stuff,
always worried about whether the chili was good enough to be
paying a dollar-fifty a bowl for, whether the Margarita sat untouched on the black lacquered table of the booth, whether the
skirt would wrinkle too quickly and immediately equal its cost
in cleaning and pressing. And now, when they didn't have any
money, what was the use of the chili or the Margarita. To feel
better? To be happier? That you had these things exactly because you had the means to pay for them? Stuart's job didn't
even mean money; it meant that he went to an office and lived
seven hours with people who didn't know how his breath
smelled at five in the morning. He could come back from work,
but where was she ever coming back from, instead of coming
to? Coming to here, coming to there, coming to hate having
to cash a check tomorrow, buy chopped meat, three luxurious
cab rides in one day. She heard Stuart's footsteps coming down
to her.

"I'm not going to have you stand here in the hall. Think in
the house. Look, I'm going to get paid."

"I want to take that job."

"Do." He was backing up the steps. When she turned to
him, his expression was nearly unerring: *I understand this as
well; I have no money either.* But what was missing in his face
was *I get this way also.* Because he didn't get this way; no one
did except her. If she started to cry now, it would change—he
could comfort her, making believe he knew. Marilyn followed
him. How could he understand if he wasn't hurt? He couldn't.
As she stood in the dark foyer of the apartment and watched
Stuart go to the kitchen to turn on a light, his form level and
sure in the spurious darkness, she began to cry—yesterday,
Mrs. Díaz and the nephew and the roommate and the bugs—
making for herself a cloud to hang low and shield her.

"Are you crying?" Stuart said from the kitchen as he opened the refrigerator door. He came out into the foyer and waved the water bottle at her. "Drink some water. You'll feel better."

"No." She walked to the door and turned the lock and fastened the chain. A small map of cracked plaster had started near the door; Marilyn picked at it, making it larger, holding the slivers of flaking paint in her hand. She walked across to the living room and dropped the paint into the Maxwell House can that served as a jumbo ashtray which they rarely emptied. The chips garnished the butts and ashes, making the mulch look almost gay. She sat on the couch and stared into the can, hearing Stuart entering rooms, switching on lights, and turning them off. She heard the diminutive click of the television and then its unfolding brutish blare, louder than he wanted it.

Stuart returned to the kitchen, opened the freezer, and tugged at the ice tray. The chili had killed him—his mouth was molded over the tingling arc the spices had left on his palate. Water had done just so much good; now he thought about iced tea. He set the water on the stove, jiggled out three tea bags from the box and some sugar, and found that the ice was so thick in the undefrosted refrigerator that the tray was beyond extraction. He couldn't complain now; it would only veer from her, and possibly touch a more sensitive nerve. The fragment from a book—what book?—"in keeping us from grievous harm." The garbled, hacked-from-the-whole sense it made for him came back as he closed the refrigerator, giving up. That maybe it meant in the variety of her travels he was the oasis. Or that the slide in Marilyn, her own constantly available and ready elevator down, was what was really important to her: not why she sometimes bowed out, but how she did it. Whatever it meant, it had a way of being his as well: ". . . in keeping us from grievous harm . . ." He turned off the flame beneath the water, and went into the bedroom, taking off his clothes and then watching the news. A funny commercial for a bank made him think the world was too serious.

Stuart was dozing when Marilyn came into the bedroom. She undressed and put on a nightgown. In the bathroom, after putting on her skin cream, the odor of which was getting more potent as it got older and sediment grit formed to occasionally burn a pore, she decided on a shower, bothered that she had nearly forgotten how hot she had been all day. She washed torpidly; the water bored her. Afterward, she put the cream on again, hoping that was all right, and brushed her hair. A steady alternation of loud and soft music came from the television as the commercials broke up what Johnny Carson and his guests talked about. It was difficult to recognize clearly, but as she hit thirty-nine strokes Marilyn thought she heard a guitar and a voice all by themselves. She rushed into the bedroom. The folk singer, a blonde girl who looked somewhat like Serena and whom Marilyn had heard of but not yet actually heard, was ending "Crow on the Cradle." Saying "Shit" quietly to herself, Marilyn waited hopefully for another song. Hairbrush in hand, she sat there as the singer began "Don't Think Twice, It's All Right." Marilyn raised the volume a little, then lay back on the bed and closed her eyes.

But she had missed it, even though she heard the whole song. Applause was sizzling and there was a station break, and she had missed it. All the calm that struck down ridges in her when a voice sang accompanied by a guitar had not unfurled. What was the goddamn matter?

She got up in the middle of the night. A light out the window, a screech, the caracoling of an ambulance siren as it entered the emergency driveway of the hospital, a chafe near her thigh. After a deep tug out of sleep—she was even more wide awake than she cared to be—Marilyn searched for what she fell asleep to. She thought about the job in terms of a room: glass display cases, order books, locks and keys. *This is jade, a pre-Columbian replica. That's a little higher; it's still goldplate, but the stone is genuine. Yes, we'll ship it.* It gave her a nice secure feeling. She anticipated the camaraderie between the salesgirls, their working hours spent handling small smooth things, their talk proportional.

She was wedging back in, the filament of restlessness dimming until she was almost there. What she would bring home would be crisp bills, money that would wing away a little at a time. Roast beef, shoes, movies: just the fact of living and knowing that the well replenishes. Buying time: was that what it meant? She wondered whether or not she was mercenary, but that wasn't the point. Accumulation, like the first wet flake, began with the gift, then piled softly, roundly, covering. She slept again.

Her second awakening was a bad hoist against her nerves. The sheets were rucked and gratingly stiff. The luminescent face of Stuart's watch was buried under his cheek as he slept on his arm. She couldn't be sure, but the stillness that she gathered from the streets made her figure it to be three or three-thirty. At four, the growing roar of the trucks coming over the bridge and down Broadway to make early deliveries began; after that sleep would be difficult. Marilyn slipped her nightgown over her head, folding it into an approximate square and flinging it toward the night table. It lost its shape in flight and, like a cartoon ghost, landed on the table, over her hairbrush and books, in its own strange way. She got up and toed for her zoris at the foot of the bed. Then she walked through the house to the living room, where she kneeled on the couch before the window. Careful to keep only her chin resting on the back, her nude form covered from view, she looked out for a while. On a swing of her foot she encountered her tote bag left near the couch and remembered that she hadn't removed the skirt she'd taken from Bloomingdale's.

She held it to her, seeing little of it in the dark. She put it on. Walking around the room, the material hitching to her skin, she smiled. *Oh, yes, we'll deliver. We have a whole line of pendant jewelry. Small Greek coins. That'll be twenty-eight seventy-five with the tax. No, I always dress this way.* On her second turn around the room, Marilyn felt a sticking in her side. She groped for the area, feeling the pin that secured the price tag. Keeping it free from her, she eased the skirt off her bare hips and took it to a corner of the room where there was a desk with a Tensor light, which she clicked on, keeping herself out of the range of its illumination. The light sent her eyes deep into her head, but in a few seconds she got sufficiently accustomed to it to gaze cockeyed at the offending label. Seventeen dollars. It hadn't seemed too expensive when she tried it on, but then she wasn't thinking about prices. Seventeen. She folded the skirt over the back of the chair at the desk, put off the light, and went back to bed. She heard a truck on Broadway. She thought about her parents for a while, then slept as the morning began to cool the room.

    At nine she awoke. Stuart was already gone, having awakened with a pinched morning lust that, when he touched her, had received no response from her sleepy body. He had dressed, shaved, and left, planning on breakfast in a coffee shop near work. Marilyn got off the bed quickly, her energy carrying her halfway across the room until a residue of weariness caught her sharply, puttying her arms as she grabbed at the dresser handles for her clothing. By the time she was dressed, she was ready only to sit on the couch in the living room and look out the window, watching the nurses go to work. She took the skirt she had left there during the night into the bedroom and placed it on a hanger. There was a check to be cashed; she toyed with the urgency of the act, not wanting to slip back into mood, much of which was still with her.

    She made herself a fried egg and two pieces of whole-wheat toast. As she was smelling the butter for freshness, an afterthought, the phone rang: Ellen, Stuart's sister.

    "No, I'm just eating."

    "Well, go back and eat. I'll call again."

    "Go on, I'll eat as we talk. What's doing?"

    "I want to get a pair of sandals. I'm not sure exactly what I want, but I like those you have, the ones with the thin strap on the heel, and without the thong over the toe."

"They're expensive."

"I don't care."

"You'll have to go downtown. I could meet you. There are a couple of things I have to do first, but . . ."

"I have to go to the dentist anyway."

"Stuart told me. Fun."

"Oh, loads of it. Maybe I can meet you about three?"

"Perfect. How about in front of . . . Well, I don't know where." Ellen did not respond, clearly leaving the decision to Marilyn. "All right, I know. Meet me in front of the drugstore on Eighth and Sixth Avenue."

"Fine. Three."

"Right. See you."

At the bank, Marilyn cashed a check for thirty-five dollars, grabbing a payroll envelope from a stack near the teller and putting the bills in that. She was scrupulous about the account, balancing it the day the statement came. She walked from the bank to 168th Street to get the Seventh Avenue I.R.T. down to Eighty-sixth.

Because she had some time, and the West Side had never been a pleasant neighborhood to walk through at that time of the morning except on Sundays, she headed for the park, planning to stay there for twenty minutes and then go to her aunt's.

The park, over a number of years, had changed for her. For a long time, it had been a maw of corresponded pleasure: a nice day and a walk in the park; a moving Russian film and a walk in the park; a walk in the park and then up to her friend Steffie's to listen to the album of *The Fantasticks*, wrapped in the accepting glitter of thirteen years old and romantic. It had become less vivid—maybe it had something to do with moving from the neighborhood. When she lived on York Avenue, she never got around to walking west to the park; it was something you walked east to. And now it meant a subway ride. But, above that, she suspected that there must have been a day when the park withdrew its festive meaning

in her and stood for a moment an open question. She had
not answered. That was the day she hated. It could have been
the day when she told her mother she could drop dead, the
day she worked a single morning at the optometrists' center
and left crying, never to return, or even yesterday. What was
the difference, really? Marilyn sat herself on a bench at the
first lane into the park. A brindle boxer pup took a piss against
one of the stone outcrops, his muzzle small and baby-tough.
A group of young girls, about six of them, were coming down
the walk singing "Hitchhike" in chorus. Marilyn turned to
her side, then all the way around to the windows of Central
Park West. The girls passed singing. Russet afternoons, the
first ones in October: she and Steffie sat on the good furniture,
in front of the pulled-open drapery, and let the restoring sun
play on their arms as they swayed and sang along to "Try to
Remember." A complete feeling. They were sensitive, they
were drinking in fine malt and thick romance on those afternoons, with a strength she could feel in her arms as she would
prop them against a chair or the piano, contented. She turned
back to see the girls, who had stopped singing, scrambling
onto one of the outcrops. Steffie's father, a nice man with a
triangular burn on the side of his face suffered in the Philip-
pines during the war, had always sneaked a look in, with a
comment about how they were both so "classy." Marilyn got
up and walked out of the park toward West End Avenue.

Her aunt's apartment house had stuck to an unraveling re-
spectability. The doorman, Jack, had stopped wearing a cap
ten years ago but still remained, his functions now more police
than posh. Marilyn stopped and said, "Hello, how are you?"
When he asked what she was doing, she answered, "Going to
school." That had served for as long as she had spoken to
people socially on West End Avenue; a decent thing to say,
it brought not exactly a smile of approval but a facial arrangement in which the eyes widened and the lips pursed: sucking
in a locally acceptable answer. Serena might be more honest,
saying "Nothing" or "Living with someone and having a good

time" or even "Sleeping around." But Serena had never lived in this area, nor did she ever know an apartment building in such detail and familiarity that it was one's own safe little fiefdom. "Going to school" let you out of their interested lives gently, a taut and fragile twine attached, the responsibility strictly yours to see it didn't break.

The door was slightly ajar to her aunt's apartment and Marilyn came in noisily, trying to avoid startling her. Betty heard, and yelled from one of the back rooms:

"Marilyn—that you, honeybunch? Don't close the front door. The super's coming back up to replace a screen. I'm just straightening, I'll be out in a second. Sit in the kitchen. I'll make coffee."

At least half of Betty was too small. Her frame, thin and hooking, was not up to her voice, a full and lifey *de gustibus non est disputandum*. Her mouth was dwarfed by her eyes, which were excited and generous. Her apartment was too small for her tinkering; she was her own decorator and while Marilyn hated her taste she appreciated it as a rare sign of life in the family. Even her grief had been inadequate to fill up the time and the great deal of money that had been left her when her husband, Marilyn's Uncle Sy, had died of throat cancer six years before. Betty and her sister—Marilyn's mother—signed up for courses at the New School: World Religions, Theories of Psychology, and Betty even took Introductory Calculus, which she dropped after the second meeting. The two sisters, manless on account of death and divorce, spent a year whipping themselves to shared pursuits, borrowing from each other even for their troubles. From that time, Betty had become accustomed to calling Marilyn twice a month, once a week when Marilyn and her mother stopped speaking to each other. But her concern was not espionage; all that was related by Betty to her sister was that Marilyn was fine. To Marilyn's knowledge, there were never any coercing schemes toward reconciliation. A trust had developed, one that gave Marilyn the opportunity to dip, when she liked, back into the family. Betty had two dresses for Marilyn from one of the men she dated, a manufacturer named Mac Felscher. Marilyn was there to try them on.

Betty came into the airy kitchen. She was wearing a flowered shift, her hair under a red bandanna, in her hand a large turquoise sponge, the middle of which was splotched with dust. "Hello, baby. Let me just rinse this first." She held the sponge beneath the water tap for a moment. "Now we can talk." She gave Marilyn a hug around the shoulders and a kiss on the left temple. "He's putting in a new screen, and to take out the one he had in there made such dirt. How are you?"

"Fine. The house looks nice. You having company?"

"When you live by yourself, the least you can do is make the house nice. You have that responsibility, at least to yourself. No one is going to say anything, of course, if it doesn't look right, but still. And there's a reason in that, even. Because no one will criticize, you have to be your own best critic. I'm going to make coffee."

"Not for me. It's too hot. I don't drink much coffee."

Betty stood suspended near the refrigerator. "Well, you're better off without it. Ginger ale, then? I can make iced tea in two minutes."

"Ginger ale. Put an ice cube in."

Betty brought the glass of ginger ale to the table along with a box of Social Tea biscuits. She seated herself opposite Marilyn, moving up the sleeves of her shift. "How's your music course? I'm going to take one in the fall. Introductory, right?"

"It's all right. It's almost the same course I took in college. When it gets very hot, and the classroom really gets stifling, I don't know why I took it in the summer."

"The point is you wanted to. You graduated and you thought there was a gap in your knowledge. I applaud that. It shows you're interested. I'm doing the same thing. I haven't done it for a few years now, since your mother and I took courses at the New School, but this year I think I'm going to go back. You know, you can get caught up in nothing—a job, whatever—and you stop living in the world, which is bigger than a job. So whatever you do—a course, lectures, discussion groups—it keeps you aware and interested."

Marilyn took one of the Social Teas. "This apartment is so cool. It's a pleasure."

"How's yours?"

"Hot. We get the sun in the afternoon so strongly that sometimes I can't stay there. And we're on the top floor, so the sun bakes the roof."

"How's your boyfriend. He working?"

"As a production assistant in a trade publication. *Food Today*. I've never seen a copy, but I guess you don't wait at the newsstands for it."

"It must be interesting work. I'm sure he likes it."

"I guess."

"And what do you do with yourself on the days you don't have the course?"

"Nothing. I'm thinking of taking a job at Brentano's, selling jewelry. Something to keep me off the streets."

Betty waved a disbelieving hand. "Go away."

"I've been getting very rattled. The job sounds nice. I don't know what I want."

"I'll get more ginger ale." She returned with the bottle and filled Marilyn's glass again. "Have you thought about looking for a permanent job, something to build a career on?"

"I haven't," Marilyn answered simply. It sounded abrupt. "You're an English major, but everybody else is an English major. So you become a secretary. Who needs that? How much will *Barchester Towers* help me in taking steno?"

"It's a problem."

"And anyway, the way I've been feeling lately I'm in no mood for anything major." Marilyn saw her aunt struggling to keep her face from falling into a serious pile. "I've just been feeling very low lately. I don't know what I want out of anything, or if I want anything."

"You remember that song, 'Que Será Será'?"

"I know, but I've never had to face myself without some sort of institution to back me up, like school. And now it's supposed to be different. But nothing's different."

"Maybe you should travel?"

"On what?"

"Work for a while, save, and you'd have a little. Stay there, I'll get the dresses."

Betty returned with two knits, one a lively yellow and red stripe, the other a solid burgundy. "Mac has nice stuff. Of course, there isn't much summer stuff now, because it's summer and they work two seasons ahead. But he had these two and I grabbed them. Nice?"

"They're beautiful. Here, let me." Betty handed over one of the dresses. Marilyn kicked off her sandals, pulled down her jeans, unbuttoned and removed her blouse. "Am I too close to the windows?" she asked.

"I'm standing in front of them. Go on."

The dress fitted perfectly, hugging her form. "I love it. Very sexy."

"The men will go wild."

"Stuart, at least. But I drive him crazy on general principles."

"Want to try the other one on?"

"If it's the same"—Marilyn had her head caught under the dress as she pulled it off—"wait a second, O.K.—no, if it's the —wait a second, I can't get this off. All right. If it's the same, I don't have to."

"It looks very good on you. You lost some weight."

"I've put some on."

"You can't tell. So I can tell Mac you liked them?"

"You can tell him I *loved* them. And, Aunt Betty, I can pay for these. I still get money from Daddy, so I have." Marilyn put her clothes back on, shaking out her hair before fastening it with the barrette.

"Stop, it was a gift from him. I told you, these dresses he

can't sell; they're last season already. I wish I could live my life that way, two seasons ahead."

"I do. It gets confusing when the snow is falling in late August, but you get used to it." They both smiled.

"Well, I'll tell him you liked them."

"And thank him."

"You know, you and Stuart should come over for dinner one night. I'll invite Mac; he's a nice man, very literate. We'll have dinner, we'll talk—we can even have a few drinks. Do you drink?"

"A little."

"If you're like your mother, you can't hold your liquor. She's terrible. A little sip."

Marilyn turned to look out toward the hallway. Now she wanted to leave. This was natural; she was being a little unfair. But invariably the knot came slipping down the rope. Reminiscence became chase: who could get to the breaking-down point first.

"All right, enough," Betty continued hurriedly. "I'll get the box for the dresses. You can carry them in that." She walked past Marilyn and, in passing, lightly dropped two fingers on her neck, which if they had remained there would certainly have had Marilyn starting to cry.

"Here," Betty announced loudly—nervous-loud—as she walked back into the kitchen. "Don't worry about folding these. They're knits. They'll crease, but carrying them in the box won't do it." She busied herself with folding the dresses into the beige cardboard box. Betty walked past Marilyn once more to a shelf above the refrigerator for some Scotch tape. "I'll tape it a little, just in case. Here."

Marilyn took the box. The only way to stave off the tears was to laugh. Putting on a British-*cum*-Boston matron accent, she said, "Pleeuhs chaage it. My man will be around tomorrow to settle the account."

Betty attempted to reciprocate with "Delighted," but it came out "Deleted," and both of them laughed.

As Betty walked with her out to the foyer, Marilyn asked, "Isn't your super coming back?"

"Eventually."

"Maybe I should stay. You know."

"No." Betty waved a hand. "You should see him. You should see his wife. I have nothing to worry about. So take care, and listen, call me or I'll call you and pester you about that dinner. It's all set, understand?"

"Of course. I love you, Betty."

"You should, sweetheart, I'm a wonderful person." She giggled girlishly. "I love you very much. And I don't want you to worry about things so much. Everything gets taken care of." They were standing at the door, near the breakfront that displayed a complete selection of family pictures, those of Sy, of Betty, of Marilyn's grandparents, her mother, father, and herself together when she was less than a year old, along with those of cousins and other relatives she barely knew. Marilyn stared at it for a second. Betty went on, "And if you need money . . ."

"I'll come to you. But I'm all right now."

"Good. Let me know if you get that job. And I'll have Mac look out for more dresses."

"Oh, you're having him do things already, huh?"

"I mean I'll ask him," Betty replied smilingly.

"Don't tell my mother about the job."

Betty shook her head slowly. "I don't tell your mother anything else but that you're all right. It puts me in a very strange position; I'm not telling you anything you don't know. But as long as it's this way, that's the way it'll be. You're fine, that's all, nothing else. It hurts her, of course."

"It hurts me, too."

"Well . . . look, I know. One day, when things settle down for you, we'll have to talk. Your mother can get hard. Maybe that's the family."

"I don't seem to have the talent," Marilyn said. "Well, enough of this. I have to meet someone downtown. And I promise to call you."

"Fine." Betty kissed Marilyn, then patted the box. "Don't lose those. I'll tell Mac you liked them. I'm going to lock the door. He'll just have to knock when he comes back with the screen."

Going down in the elevator, she hated herself for coming as close to crying as she had when Betty touched her neck. It was almost the third time in so many days. Little things she was losing—she was, she knew it as resolutely as she was losing them. The small refraction of goodness off simple talk—it blinded her. If hardness ran in the family, as Betty had suggested, then she was clearly the nick in the plaque, and nothing she did sealed the imperfection. A family of crusts and calluses, and she was something altogether different, her father's child. She felt better thinking about that. She walked to Broadway and took the train downtown to meet Ellen.

It was cooler in the Village. Marilyn strolled Greenwich Avenue looking at the clothes and the pottery, a smile skimming her contentment with the breeze and the uncrowded streets.

She passed easily. Summertime filled the area with girls like her, in ponchos and jeans, their Greek rope or leather bags only half filled with birth certificates, driving licenses, student I.D.s, Fems, surely in one or two a nightgown that had not been worn the night before. Also in their bags, but not so much in Marilyn's, was money with which to buy sandals, Jefferson Airplane records, books on D. W. Griffith, possibly even traveler's checks if the atmosphere became too chaotic and necessitated the long or short trek home to Grand Rapids, Azusa, or Parsippany.

Marilyn walked to Seventh Avenue and took a table at a sidewalk café-bar near Sheridan Square. She thought of the daylight as fierce, making everyone look more sensitive. She ordered a rare hamburger and searched in her bag for something to read. The Lewis Carroll had been left at home; now there was only a preregistration form from the music course she had signed up for and a flyer announcing an antiwar march

handed to her on Broadway and Eighty-sixth. She pulled out
her address book and a pen, laying them on the table, ready,
and thought about whether she should have a glass of wine
before her hamburger came. The waiter was swamped with
orders, but his good looks prevented his slinking into perplex-
ity. The smile he threw the way of all the prettier women and
the way he took the orders as if they were compliments made
Marilyn decide that his charm was a front for ineptitude, and
she dropped the idea of the wine. She opened the address book
and clicked down the pen. David and Joyce Abrams had
moved; the new telephone number had been hastily set beneath the lined-out old one, but now Marilyn inked in the
whole box and put them down in the first open "A." She knew
that if she concentrated she would remember the number of
the apartment house, and because she had no doubts about it,
she held it for a split second like a balanced ball above a water
spout, trying to keep it down and at the same time have it
irresistibly come to her. When it did, she puckered her mouth,
self-conscious at smiling to herself. She wrote the name, address, and telephone number in an even hand.

The "B"s were filled with people she wouldn't want to see
again. Mindy Billings had given up too quickly and accepted
the terrible job at the ad agency as if it were the zenith of
her life. Lester Baron was a history lecturer whose specialty
was the Merovingians; he fell out of her life at the end of the
term by the bland force of his own eagerness for "rapport."
Helen Berkowitz moved to Iowa and the Writers' Workshop;
Marilyn was still awed by the ease with which she quoted
Yeats at generally the right points in a conversation. Walker
Bennington was the stockman at her mother's haberdashery
store, a tall, heavy, demeaning man whom Marilyn could only
reach by abasing herself to his unformed opinions.

Serena Carlyle had occupied two boxes already. Marilyn
wrote in the number of the new apartment she finally knew
after months of getting there by the instinct of how many
flights up and how many doors over from the stairwell. She

wondered whether to add Jim's name to the listing now that
he had just a few weeks ago moved in with Serena, but she
was not totally sure of his last name. There were no other
"C"s in the book, which was just—one of Serena's gifts was
to occupy wherever she was placed. It was the kind of life that
Marilyn, to a certain degree, still responded to with her original feelings: outrage and envy; that cutting of figure eights
through self-created problems. Once, about a year ago, it had
changed. Not Marilyn's attitude to Serena's life, but the life
itself. Marilyn was used to it: perspectives don't shift, lives do
—what you think is a distortion of angle is actually the blur of
movement, the journey into place. Serena had become listless
and dark, and spent a lot of time listening to Brahms on the
stereo. It was followed by a succession of men, Serena popu-
lating this dark empty pan of her life with the right—or wrong
—performers. Serena and Rich, the first one, went back to her
parents' home in Colorado, then spent the rest of the summer,
or as much as there was of it, camping in the Canadian Rockies. She returned without Rich, who had left for San Francisco
—it was *that* summer, and to hear Serena tell it, they lay
awake in the Volkswagen camper and listened to the song
that urged hegira, howling at the blatancy of it, but he went
anyway. For months, she'd referred to him as a "gristle" and
Marilyn had cringed in exactly the desired effect. The first box
in the book contained the apartment she and Serena had
shared after meeting that summer at a party. The second box
the apartment where Serena now lived—she had moved into
it after she took the job on the teen-age magazine—a good
place on Lexington and Twenty-eighth, with a patio and air
conditioning. Much of the spring and summer so far had been
spent in throwing outdoor buffets; the medium-sized terrace
could hold fifteen people, and cold veal and ratatouille and
salade Niçoise and crusty bread with anchovies and *sangría*
and twilight, rich squares of chalky light held up by conversation, then let down upon them like a thin blanket, darkened.
The apartment had perfections: it was a great place to play

Monopoly or watch television or make phone calls. When Jim, the guy she worked with at the magazine, moved in, he installed bracket shelving in the tiny bedroom, along with a wall desk and a small wooden platform on which he placed slabs of foam rubber. Under the bed he built dresser drawers, which gave the room not only adequacy but a bracing odor of lumber. It was another just-right something added to the place.

When the hamburger came, she had turned the page to the "D"s, mostly Druggist, in three consecutive boxes: the first on the lower East Side, the second on York Avenue, the third around the corner from where she now lived, on Broadway and 172nd Street. She crosshatched out the first two, both of which didn't even contain the name of the store. A lot of money had gone to the one on the lower East Side; it was the year of first getting birth-control pills, the year of the severe catarrh in her ear and all that tetracycline, the year she had sun poisoning after falling asleep at the Newport Folk Festival, coming back in the car and knowing that pain bubbled beneath sensation until it would eventually bore upward and make her suffer unbearably. The two druggists in the store knew her by name and, except for the birth-control pills, followed with concern the ailments and conditions for which they filled the prescriptions. Marilyn closed the book over the pencil and dropped both back into her bag.

The hamburger was done medium, but she enjoyed it anyway; the food made immediate contact with the pearl of her hunger. Unexpectedly, Betty had tired her, and now she ate slowly and well, moving the chair opposite her which held the dress box with a back-and-forth motion of her foot. The bill came to $1.25. She didn't think about it one way or another.

After looking at dresses in a shop on Eighth Street—having to check her box at the sales desk, which made her remember yesterday's shoplifting with satisfaction—she walked back down to Sixth Avenue to wait for Ellen. Although Stuart had moved out of the house when the family jumped from Flatbush to Westchester, Ellen, five or six years younger, had stayed on, going to the suburban high school, and was now ready at the end of this summer to go to Antioch. She had a boyfriend who attended the State University on Long Island. According to Stuart, she suffered from a crisis of manners and mores—a third Brooklyn, a third Mamaroneck, a third coed-to-be. The rest of the family seemed to have the same problem. Sometimes Marilyn and Stuart would work themselves up to a screaming laughter on the train coming back from a visit, thinking about how his mother had tried to wear a terry-cloth playsuit or set out a rolling table of Tom Collins ingredients. For Marilyn, however, it was a limited laughter; she always felt moderately lousy afterward. The fact was that there were spaces large enough in the life of Stuart's family to be comically filled. They had never laughed at her own mother; there was nothing even to smile at. And her father—it was difficult just to think clearly about his ghosty ways, his checks, his girl friends, the towel rack he installed in each and every one of her apartments, never to visit again.

She saw Ellen crossing the street. She was a small girl, chubby-faced but lean-carriaged, her eyes, like Stuart's, turned up almost Orientally. She carried a leather bag similar to Marilyn's, holding it bunched at the top, letting it slap against her hurrying legs as she crossed. She wore a sweater and skirt, an outfit too warm for the day and one that Marilyn put down to nervousness about the dentist.

"Hi," Ellen said, close to winded, when she reached the corner and Marilyn. "I hope I'm on time."

"Uh-huh. Let me see your face."

Ellen turned her head back and forth, thinking her face was smudged.

"It's not swollen or anything. What'd he do?"

"Oh, you mean the dentist! I didn't know what you meant for a second. He only took X-rays. Next time, he says, according to what the X-rays show, he'll begin work. *Then* I'll look like a monster."

Marilyn started walking.

"What do you have in the box?" Ellen asked the question half to Marilyn, half to a window filled with rock LPs.

"Two dresses. My aunt's seeing a dress manufacturer, so. I think it's a peace offering."

"From your aunt?"

"*From* my aunt, but *for* my mother. It's subtle."

"Is it that you're afraid of getting indebted?"

"I am already. Oh, I don't know what I think about it. It really was very nice of the guy; they're good dresses, expensive. Talking about that, I hope you have at least thirty dollars for the sandals."

"Well, I have it, but"—Ellen's voice slid onto an exit tone —"it may be a little high. As I was coming in on the railroad, I saw an ad at the station for a new boutique that just opened in town, and they carry sandals. It's probably cheaper. I'm trying to save a little money so that Stan and I can go to Vermont for a week—that's if my parents don't make a stink. He bought a used Volkswagen while he was at school that runs pretty well, and he takes it to work—he works with the county Department of Highways—he's an assistant surveyor, just for the summer. So I'm trying to save pennies."

"Well, let's go down there anyway. Maybe you'll see something cheaper," Marilyn said.

They walked to Washington Square North and exchanged wishes to live in the red-brick townhouses, redolent, as Marilyn knew but Ellen didn't, of Henry James. They eyed appreciatively the well-heeled mothers pushing strollers, carrying bags of groceries into the carriage houses of Washington Mews, flipping back curls of tastefully cut hair, walking small-breasted under navy blue tennis shirts and hopsacking skirts. Then they cut west to the sandal shop.

Ellen saw nothing she liked. She handled the sandals and the long-haired salesman with the same impatience. Nothing was just right, nothing fit the way she wanted it to, nothing was cheap enough. The salesman gave up early and went back across the shop to pull raw leather thongs across a blunt slab of iron. They left, Marilyn smiling at the salesman, whom she felt they had bothered.

Once out on the street again, Marilyn asked, "What now? Do you want to go to another place?"

"No. Let's have a soda or something. I'm not going back on the train—Stan is meeting me and we're going to see a movie. Then he'll drive me home. So I have time. You?"

"I have nothing doing."

"What about Stuart?"

Marilyn looked at the younger girl blankly.

"I mean, what is he going to do?" Ellen spoke now with her voice column-like, suddenly stressed and solid. "I mean about supper."

"He can make his own. I'm not the cook."

Ellen mumbled "Uh-huh" very badly.

Marilyn continued, "Sometimes I can't get home in time. Your brother is not helpless. Sometimes he cooks even when I'm home."

"He does!" The voice kneaded out more.

"He cooks a good curry. We call it a curry; it's not quite. Chopped meat and onions and rice and green peppers, with a lot of curry powder. It's good."

"That's good, you know, for a man to know how to cook."

"He likes it, too."

"That's something I didn't even know about him. Wow."

They stopped at a downstairs ice-cream parlor on Thompson Street. The air conditioning was weak and Ellen was pulling at the sleeve holes of her sweater. "I thought it was going to be a lot cooler today." She ordered a black-and-white, Marilyn just iced tea.

"Have ice cream," Ellen said.

"No, I don't want anything that heavy. Although it would be cold. But, no."

"Have some. I'll pay."

"I can pay" came to Marilyn's lips quickly and with too much propulsion for her to dare release it. She merely shook her head, lips pursed.

"You're sure?"

"It would mess up my appetite. It's almost five." She
glanced at the clock directly behind Ellen's shoulder, its face
cut into a poster of Humphrey Bogart where the head would
be.

"I thought you weren't going home," Ellen persisted.

"I am. But I'm not sure when. How's your boyfriend?"
That was Betty's question.

"What are you smiling at?"

"Nothing. How is he?"

"Gee, that's right, I haven't spoken to you in such a long
time. We had a bad time around Christmas. He wasn't
coming home for the holidays; he said he wanted to study in
peace when the campus was empty. There was a scene with
my parents—maybe Stuart told you—when I wanted to go
out there to him. But I don't think he would have wanted me
to come. We were writing letters to each other every day.
A lot of them were absolutely fantastic—speaking about souls
and knowledge and faith in people. So anyway, one day—I
remember that it was a Saturday, because I was going into
New York and I read the letter on the train—one day he sends
a letter about the poem. We had both been reading Wallace
Stevens, and we included in every letter for a while that part
of the poem 'Thirteen Ways of Looking at a Blackbird'—
you know that poem . . ."

Marilyn nodded.

". . . the part that goes 'A man and a woman/Are one./A
man and a woman and a blackbird/Are one.' We both really
understood that—it's all complicated, I guess, but we did. It
became a real entity, something we shared, an outlook we
loved. Then, in this letter, he seemed to go back on it. I knew
that he cared about what the poem meant, what it meant to
me, but he said he didn't, and he took up about half the letter
making fun of it—cruelly, too. Like he'd write, 'I hope I don't
find myself in bed with the blackbird one day,' or something.
And then he got serious and started to attack the meaning,
that there is this equivalent. Toward the end of the letter, he

was saying things like 'Beware too simple linkage. Nothing makes any sense. Love is the bakery product of weak wheat. Sympathy means fear.' I wrote back one of those letters"— Ellen smiled—"that are like a great wail. What I should have done was call him up and just cry on the phone for an hour. But we were into this letter thing, so I wrote."

"You feel safer sticking to the pattern."

"Right. Well, then he didn't answer. I waited three days, which was very difficult in the state I was in; then I wrote again. I don't remember what, but it must have been pretty hysterical, and clear to him that I was upset. At the end of the letter I put the lines of the poem, underlined in red ink. He called the next night. It was very strange. First he sounded conciliatory: how are you, told me that the campus looked like something from a dream, all empty and snowbound, things like that, but then he sort of cleared his throat, like Winston Churchill . . ."

Marlyn smiled, as did Ellen before taking a scoop of ice cream from her soda.

". . . and he said 'I want to stop it. We're getting too hung up on symbols.' I asked him what he meant and he said the poem, other things. He never said 'love' once, except that time with the thing about the bakery product."

"But you're still seeing each other. Maybe being explicit isn't his way." The same tolerance Marilyn felt for Ellen she was applying to Stan.

"I don't know whether saying 'I love you' once in a while is unnecessarily explicit." Ellen chewed off the last word, protest hardening her fleshy face into something not very attractive.

"For some people it is."

"For men. There are no women I know who think that way."

Marilyn recognized and was, in a sense, enjoying the cool recklessness of the conversation. "You don't know every woman."

"True." Ellen had finished her soda and was wiping the foam off the straw on the edge of the glass. "But I do know women who want that. And most men won't give it. I think Stuart is that way. Does he ever say 'I love you'? You need that, right?"

"I'm not sure."

"You've been brainwashed, then."

"I think that happens in a relationship." Marilyn rarely used the word and it rose in her heavily. "Relationship"—its ungainly accuracy. "Well, look. Everything's fine with me just as long as he doesn't hog the covers. You want to go?" Marilyn tried to avoid Ellen's stare. She motioned for the waitress and ended up paying for both checks.

In the hour that they'd been in the ice-cream parlor, the day had taken on grey in the form of huge dirty plaster clouds diffusing in a strong wind. Like almost everyone around them, the girls rushed, talking about rain and the time, toward Eighth Street. There Ellen kissed Marilyn, thanked her, and hurried to the Sixth Avenue subway to get uptown and meet Stan. Marilyn walked north along Fifth Avenue.

It was not going to rain just yet. At Union Square, the last of the rush hour made a mess of traffic, and as Marilyn crossed Fourteenth Street, a bus horn sounding a half block away turned her head and she saw what was left of the brightness of the day sandwiched in pastels over the West Side, over the Hudson, over her father's New Jersey. The day there had gone hard orange, a line of tinged blue separating it from near night. She stood at the corner staring—New Jersey. In between the pitch and soothing shadows, her father might still have enough daylight to clean out the arts-and-crafts house, then walk quietly toward the dining room, sitting with the other camp directors in the soon to be gone peace of preseason preparations. His strong, lean arms thrusting out of the camp T-shirt; his high, already sunburned forehead throwing back toward the crown of his head his wavy and iron-flecked hair. Her father in sunlight—it was an easily natural way to picture him. Watching the bar of afternoon fire before her, Marilyn felt again her father swallowed by a net of wrong turns, missed chances, sour offerings. To stand there and think of him walking on the green and shadow-black lawns of the camp in a special rapture, the screwed-on peace of warmth and moment, a simple life made that way out of the indigestibility of its problems—nothing else was as clean as this. She would let him have the rind of light fleeing her now the way she had let him have her child's kisses when he called for them on leaving the house after his monthly visit. Now he'd have clay in his fingernails or small splinters from arranging the pine and the plywood on the shelves, making ready for the children he would firmly guide a plane for, tighten a vise, stroke a kiln, jigsaw a curve, glaze a pot for: small things and minute pressures—how did he, of all people, know how? Now he'd have the light.

Gauzy-headed, she cut through Union Square park and entered a coffee shop on Park Avenue South. After checking the time, she decided not to call Stuart—he was most likely on his way home. She'd eat. There was some problem in getting the dress box into the narrow shelf under the counter, but the thin waiter who approached told her to put it on the next stool—they were never busy at that hour. Marilyn ordered an egg-salad platter, $1.25, as she looked at prices carefully for the first time all day.

She was deciding on whether to eat the coleslaw when the air cracked outside and what was threatening to come down did. The waiter, who was standing nearby squaring a pile of menus, said, "It's about time." The drops smeared the windows in a hesitant drizzle, then increased as the sky got red-black and large sheets of water bounced off the sidewalk. The thunder had an abbreviated sound, like the stem of a pipe being cleared. The cashier up front bent down and raised the volume on the Muzak, sending "Our Love Is Here to Stay" into the largely vacant restaurant.

Falling away. She didn't want the coleslaw. Why couldn't

they arrange a divorce of anger and argument, as they
had a divorce between them? *Dear Daddy: Sorry. Dear
Mommy: What did you expect?* Marilyn thought of the
night Serena's father's car broke down on the Connecticut
Turnpike as he was driving down from Providence, and the
call in the middle of the night, with Serena out. Marilyn had
spoken to him—sure, he could come and stay there, since he
certainly couldn't make Philadelphia in time, anyway. "Of
course, come over when you can. Serena's out now, but I'm
sure she'll be back by the time you get here." The voice that
echoed "Serena's out?" was firm, disappointed, but not disappointed in a way Serena would ever be forced to notice. So
unlike her own father, or mother—why didn't they ever give
themselves a chance to grow up and keep adult secrets, valued
and private discretions? Serena's father had arrived about four
in the morning. The bell rang briefly. He said "Hello," put
down his bags, and, without carefully looking at the place in
which his daughter lived and which he had never seen, asked
where he could sleep. Marilyn showed him to Serena's bed.
He thanked her and said he hoped they would have a chance
to get to know each other in the morning. He sat on the bed
with his topcoat still on. Marilyn returned to her room, hoping
against but almost panicking with the thought that Serena
would return in the morning and see her father. In the morning, though, the bed was empty, remade, a note on monogram
paper left on the pillow: "Dear Marilyn, Had to scoot. Tell
Serena I will call her soon. Many, many thanks for the emergency lodgings and the sweet hospitality, Dan Carlyle." The
note had left her weepy all that morning; she still had it in
her sewing kit.

    "Oh, it was one of those quickies," the cashier was yelling
to the waiter.

    "At least it cooled things off." He turned to Marilyn and
nodded. "Right?"

    Marilyn smiled.

    "Right?" he repeated with the same dramatic nod.

"Right," she said. The waiter turned away from her, giving her a wry, placeless grin.

By the time she got home, her feet were wet from puddles on the pavement she couldn't completely clear. She headed straight for the bedroom, the bed, and was beginning to feel out sleep when Stuart came in the room. "For Chrissakes, I didn't even hear you come in. I was in the bathroom." He wore only a pair of dungaree shorts.

"I didn't know you were here."

Stuart lay down next to her, removing his shorts so that he was naked. Marilyn played with his navel. She helped him with her clothes. It was better than talking. Soon, as his motions came under the spell of home, drawn and enticed to release, he whispered, "I love you," in her ear, and Marilyn fell apart—steel and raucous, truncheon and holiday, sparks and saliva. She cried as her orgasm tipped. Take it.

N EAR DUNN, ON U.S. 95, DRIVING TO "SEE THE South as long as we're going to Miami anyway," Carl and Grace Abrams's car was the third vehicle to pile onto the already double wreckage. The first car, losing control on a mixture of faulty steering mechanism and very good bourbon, was registered to Leonard Frakes, economist for the Department of Agriculture, on his way to spend the first six days of his vacation with his parents in Lumberton, then planning to meet Millie Corbin in Charleston for a week of fishing and fucking. The second link of disaster was a gasoline truck owned by Claude Simmons Oil, an Esso franchise, driven by Tommy Lowder, who would have rather stayed in the Marines, even for another hitch in 'Nam, but whose parents protested. He never even saw the new shiny blue Fury until he was on it; the lights had been smashed when it hit the low double-cabled guardrail at the side of the highway. Half-standing, one foot on the brakes, the other propped against the door, Tommy would have been out of the cab and running through the pines, probably almost out of his mind, if the Oldsmobile had not hit him from behind and driven the top corner of the cab's door right through his neck. Carl had been watching the truck's rear-signal lights attentively, as attentively as Grace watched for nice-looking motels in the damp North Carolina evening, just dark. Carl had minutes before mentioned to her that oil-truck drivers were, as a rule, the most safety-conscious of anyone on the road; they had to be —can you imagine the problems of getting insured if that were not the case? Grace had nodded, weary from the half day in which they had crammed springtime Washington down— the Smithsonian, the Capitol, the Mint, the monuments. Carl was just bringing his right hand over to place it on Grace's for an appreciative squeeze when the truck before them stopped, its cab jackknifing and bringing the whole body around in a backward spin, the feeding hose stowed on the back shaken loose and swinging free. It was this black petroleum-caked snake they first saw flailing close to their windshield as Carl yelled "Oh, God!" and tried to brake. The whole truck had tipped, the left fender of the Oldsmobile directly under its fall. Grace screamed, "Oh, oh, oh, God, help! No, oh."

David didn't get a call until one in the morning. Even though he had been away from home for better than five years, the identification that the highway police removed from his father's pulped body instructed a call to David Abrams at their own address on Cabrini Boulevard. The police had called to no answer—the sole occupants of that apartment lay under their rubberized burlap in the next room. A patrolman went through the other cards in the wallet—restaurants, insurance men, piano dealers—until he came to the card of the dry-cleaning store, with the names Carl Abrams and Martin Sander listed small on the right-hand corner as proprietors. They went through the wallet again, enlightened a little, until they found a small sheet of notepaper with "business numbers," the first one of which was listed next to "Marty—Massapequa."

So it was Marty who called. He kept on saying, Sit there.
I'll come over. You're on the lower East Side, right? Just sit.
David wanted the number of the highway police. But his
father's partner insisted, Sit, David. I'll be there in an hour.
You can't do anything yourself.

So he sat. Joyce got hysterical, called her parents, who were
also coming over. David had to call them back and tell them
not to; maybe when he drove to the airport he'd drop Joyce
off at their house. Joyce's mother kept sobbing at him, Oh,
David, poor David, and he noticed that mother and daughter
cried similarly.

He had taken the address book and was going to make
calls—to his uncles first; he'd spare his grandparents, let their
sons tell them—when the phone began to ring. Evidently
Marty had made a few more calls before rushing out, and
David's Uncle Nat, his mother's brother, called first, voice
heavy with tears and cigarette cough. He'd come over. His
father's younger brother, Mike, then called. The plane to
Raleigh-Durham, the nearest airport, would be out of La
Guardia at nine-thirty in the morning, and the next one left
at twelve-fifteen. David said, The first one, and Mike responded, Fine, I'll make the reservations. David asked, How
many? Mike answered, Well, there'll be you, me, I guess your
father's partner—he said he wanted to go—and someone
from your mother's side. What's his name—Nat—did he call?
David answered, Yes, and Mike said, Then him, too.

In the twenty minutes between the last call and the first
arrivals—Nat and Toni, who lived in Murray Hill and had
taken a cab—Joyce had calmed down. She brought out the
two folding chairs and opened them at the table in the
kitchen. She also turned on all the lights and started coffee.
David sat at the table, leafing through the book, trying to
think of whom to call. He asked Joyce to be sure and remember to dial the call-in-sick number at the Board of Ed and his
principal, if he forgot.

Nat and Toni were crying as they came up the steps, and

it dissolved Joyce's calm. Nat came into the apartment huffing, tried to smile, saying, I'm glad you kids don't live on the sixth floor, and putting a hand to the back of David's neck. Toni touched her husband's back. Joyce announced the coffee, which Toni and David declined.

Who else is coming? Nat asked, sitting down. David said, Pop's brother Mike, and his partner, Mart . . . but at this Nat came apart, thumping against the table. Toni again administered a consoling hand to his back. Joyce became aware of neighborhood sounds: hubcaps falling to the street, glass breaking, cat shrieks, lust and anger yells—all of them entering the open-windowed house without strain. It embarrassed her. Nat shook his head for a few minutes, then, broken-voiced, asked about the arrangements, whether David had any ideas. David said, We should wait for Mike, someone from my father's family. There shouldn't be much problem. Didn't my father belong to a lodge? Toni said, Yes, I think so. Joyce added, Sure. Your mother—your mother mentioned that one time—a lodge.

Mike arrived wearing bedroom slippers. Toni's eyes moistened now more noticeably. Mike smiled at Joyce and kissed her. You both don't navigate this area at night, I hope, he said. David asked, Where did you park? On Fifth Street. David said, That's a bad street. I'm glad you got here all right. No one seemed to notice the remark, which was just as well. Mike took out a sheet of paper. I have some numbers— he turned to Joyce—which maybe you could call. David interrupted, No, I don't want her to do anything. Joyce was at the stove, removing the Silex. She said, No, I can help. But David stuck fast: I don't want you to. It's too upsetting. Anyway, you wouldn't know any of the people you'd be speaking to. He turned to Mike. I'm taking her to her mother's house. We can drop her off on the way to the airport. Neither of his uncles said anything.

David continued, I have no money on me, and began to explain, but Nat cut in. Don't worry about money. I have

enough for all our plane fares, expenses, enough for tomorrow. Mike nodded and said, There are other things to think
about. He was crying.

David asked Mike, How are the kids? Through his tears
Mike fished out, Fine. Judy's with them. They all got up.
Joyce smiled. There was a shave-and-a-haircut-two-bits horn
honk downstairs and David went to the window. Marty Sander yelled up, I can't find a parking place. I'm going to try a
lot on the West Side. Then I'll take a cab over. David yelled
down, Fine. Marty added, Anyone there? Yes, David replied.

Marty got there a half-hour later. He was the only one,
excepting David, who appeared not to have been crying. He
said to Joyce, We've never met. It's too bad now under such
circumstances. He hugged David. He told everyone that he
had already been in touch with the lodge officer and had
started the arrangements going for the cemetery. He asked
whether they had decided on the funeral, and David said, Not
yet. Nat said Manhattan, but Mike thought Brooklyn, where
he and his parents lived, might be easier on the old folks. Manhattan, David said. They have friends from the Heights;
it'll be more convenient. Nat said, The Riverside, on Seventy-
sixth and Amsterdam. When they all agreed, Marty got up
and asked where the phone was. Joyce said, You have to call
now? and Marty said, The sooner the better. They'll have to
meet us at the airport, remember. Joyce said, It's in the bedroom; please forgive the mess. She walked with Marty into
the small room, in which lay a queen-size mattress, an old
dresser piled with ashtrays and books, and the phone. Marty,
looking back into the kitchen first, whispered to her, How is
he? Taken aback by the unanticipated intimacy, she said, I
think he's too shocked yet to feel.

She returned to the kitchen and put on more coffee. Once
Marty got off the phone, both Nat and Mike made calls. Between two of the calls, the line cleared for a moment, Joyce's
father called and asked David, who answered, if he was sure
he didn't want them to come over. It would be no problem,

just hop in the car. David said, No, Mr. Cecere, my uncles
are here; the place is too small. We're going to the airport in
a few hours anyway, so we'll drop Joyce at your house. Her
father said, Sure, now? and David answered, Thanks. Sure.
So long. As he stood by the phone, he felt he should make a
call. He called Stuart and got Marilyn first. Wake him, he
said. When Stuart got on the phone and mumbled, Uhhh,
what, David said, I'm sorry to wake you up, Stuie. I don't
know why I called you, but my parents were killed tonight in
a car accident in North Carolina, so there'll be a lot of things
to take care of, just in case you'd be calling here. I guess I'll
call you—I'm going down there this morning—so when I get
back and things settle down a little, Joyce or me'll call you
and let you know about the funeral, if you want to go to that.
Stuart floundered, but finally said, Oh, *shit!* I'm sorry, man,
that's terr— Oh, *shit.* David said, Yeah. Well, I'll call you.
Or Joyce will. Go back to sleep.

It had been getting progressively lighter. Someone across
the yard had played Latin music without stop through the
night, and now it was especially horrible to Joyce: the tinny
sounds, the treble shouts and plinked drums, jostling the
morning without regard. As the dawn broke Toni looked hag-
gard. Marty said, No more coffee for me. Nat agreed: It's not
good for your nerves. Mike looked at all of them seated around
the table. I don't know, he said, I don't know, I don't know,
I don't know. It took Nat and, this time, Toni with it. Their
electricity, their jumped wires. David looked at the clock; the
spring daylight had come across its face in an early burn of
sun so that it obscured the hands. What time? Almost six-
thirty, Toni said, sniffling.

Joyce, who had started to get caught in the last jag, dried
out and said, I'm sorry there isn't anything but coffee for
breakfast. We were short this week and trying to improvise
until Friday. I can go down, Toni offered. Well, Joyce said,
there's a *bodega* on Avenue B near Sixth Street that opens
early— David interrupted forcefully, Are you crazy? You going

to let her go down there at this time? There'll still be junkies on the street! Use your head. Marty said quickly, We're taking Joyce into Brooklyn, right? Nat nodded. O.K., then, we'll take the Brooklyn-Queens to the airport. We can catch a bite there.

Before they left the house, Joyce made the phone calls to the Board of Ed and the school, explaining why David wouldn't be in. Mike called home. After putting Toni in a cab, they drove into Brooklyn in Mike's car, early morning traffic beginning to build going the other way. As they slowed to the curb before the Cecere's two-family house, Joyce's parents could be seen waiting on the steps in their bathrobes, waving stiffly to Nat, Mike, and Marty as Joyce and David got out. Her mother began to say something, but Joyce first wanted to tell David to call her when they landed in Raleigh and also when they got back to La Guardia, so that she could meet him at wherever he was going. He said, Probably Nat's. Why don't you come meet us at the airport? She nodded and touched his arm. Mr. Cecere, staring at the car, asked, You have transportation to the airport? David pointed. Joyce kissed him on the cheek, still holding his arm. She had something to say; she hadn't said anything, really. But she let go of his arm wordlessly, beginning to whimper as she walked past her parents and into the house. David smiled at her father, but the man didn't understand. He said, Have a safe flight. Her mother kissed him.

They didn't eat at the airport; they forgot. Instead they sat in the lounge, waiting for the flight. Nat asked Marty Sander, Where'd you finally park? All the way on the West Side, Marty responded. Sixth Avenue. You think I want my Riviera destroyed by the P.R.s on the East Side? You'll pay for a full day, then, Nat told him. So, Marty responded. Mike went over to the ticket desk to inquire about how long the flight would take. He also found out that he could rent a car at the Raleigh airport.

They boarded. It was not until then, sitting in the middle between Mike at the window and Nat on the aisle, Marty

across from them on the other side, that David felt something. The plane was all slick glare, filled with businessmen,
attaché cases, families with children, two nuns. A soft, anonymous music played over the public-address system, its fragile
nonsense ineffectively straddling the massive hum of the jet
engines buzzing and shaking the cabin. As the plane began
to taxi, the stewardess, blonde and petite, got on the P.A.,
replacing the music: Good morning, welcome to Eastern
Airlines flight 348, flying from New York City to Raleigh-
Durham, North Carolina. We will be taxiing into a takeoff
position and there may be a short delay . . . above your head
can be used very simply. Take the mask like so . . . only if
we hit high-pressure pockets, which is not anticipated . . .
happy to take your breakfast orders once we're off the . . .
a good flight.

The first sensation hauling at David was the mixed-up time.
Looking out the window, watching the plane slowly move between painted lines up to the runway, a hulking shadow on
the tarmac, he felt the complete reality, the utter truth of its
being Friday, early May, nine-fifty in the morning—but with
everything different. It was a morning torn off, stuffed with
unusual actions, speeds, lights. It made his throat close up to
think that he commanded no time tricks that might reposition
him. He couldn't think about tonight to get through today;
he couldn't wait a few hours and call someone; he couldn't
square himself around a lunch hour. The airplane might as
well have been taking off into another dimension, and he felt
completely at its mercy, weak and docile. As they began to
gain speed, a crest of panic touched him, a panic strangely
fearless. No grip, no hold. They rose up over the water and
the houses and up over everything that could expect to be
the same in an hour, two, three, a whole day. It got worse as
they gained altitude: the roads and houses below gave way to
water—they'd fly off the coast.

Marty was ordering juice and eggs; Nat nothing; Mike just
coffee; David nothing. Then came the feeling, spored off the

first, that they were going to something merely reported but completely believed. If his parents were not dead, if, by some freakish exclamation of luck, they still were breathing, piped and bandaged, what would he do? Feel grateful, of course, but the surprise might be too much for him, too much for feeling. Could he or any of them back-pedal that far, back to nervous hope? The fact was that they had killed them sitting in the kitchen all night—Carl and Grace had had their accident there, in the minds of brothers and son. Their lives, the words "my parents" lost all color there; David thought of them already as beneath a stone. His sweet mother, his good father. His hurt was in their stand-in pairing with death, their introduction to it without preparation, without the progressive coaching that might have come with serious illness. It was less that his parents did not live any more, wouldn't come back—or would: they'd bring them back as freight—than that he couldn't turn the key of his imagination far enough to *see* them dead, dead gracefully, peacefully, professionally. It had been done all wrong. There were no suggestions for him to make.

Nat pushed his tray away and took David. He said softly to him, Go. Did you think you'd be able to hold it in forever? Go, go.

But David stopped. The nuns bothered him; he was afraid that they'd come to him, a natural attraction to a self-control so scored that it flapped in the pressured quiet of the airplane. I'm all right, he said to Nat, who was again filled with tears himself. David looked around but saw only the antimacassar against his seat. Mike said, Have something. Coffee at least. You've been up all night. David said, I'm fine. He thought about Joyce and tried to guess how she was feeling. It was impossible: he didn't know anything. The hope that he hadn't cried loudly, that no one had heard, took on weight in him. He summoned up convictions that were already shrinking, so that they were momentary and precise: that they would be able to take care of everything without too much trouble; that it wasn't going to rain on the day of the funeral; that people would not call him every night and push condolences; that dreams in the next few days would stay clear and unscarred.

Selfish, he thought, and it calmed him. The suspension was just what he wanted, a shuttle that would never quite get to either place. Then the pilot said, Weather in Raleigh-Durham is good—nice sunny day . . . I hope you've had a good flight . . . Marty leaned over from the other row of seats and, loud enough for the three others to hear him, said, This is the part I hate.

A patrol car could be seen waiting beyond the gate when they taxied to the terminal. David went into the exit corridor first and, once in the terminal, waited for the others. All four of them then stood there, without baggage, waiting to be approached. Two cowboy-hatted officers, one David's age and the other about thirty-five, got up off a couch and walked toward them. The older one, scanning them, his gaze and address unspecific, said, Mr. Abrams? David said, Me, and took a step forward. The highway patrolman extended his hand: Officer Eaton, and this is Officer Barth. I suggest you folks rent a car; we didn't quite expect there'd be so many of ya. Mike said, Fine, and Eaton said, Be right outside. You just follow us.

In a yellow Chevrolet, they followed the light-flashing police car until they reached the downtown section of the city. They turned in behind a three-story building and into a parking lot filled with other patrol cars and county ambulances. The young policeman stuck his head out of the window and yelled back to them, Park here. You're on official business.

It had never occurred to David that he would be asked to view the bodies and confirm identification—and if it had been anticipated by his uncles or Marty, they had said nothing about it. He felt his head twitch and he began to turn to the other men. But he stopped and breathed deeply. Mike said, David? I'm all right, he answered. He followed Eaton down an antiseptic corridor.

They looked no particular way. David looked long enough to see one feature—on his father it was his eyebrows, on his mother her chin, which was pasty—and then shut his eyes. He signed something and was handed a copy of a preliminary report which he did not read, leaving it on a table. When he returned to the lobby, where Nat and Mike were handing money to a sergeant behind a desk, he asked Marty when the flight back was. An hour, he was told. Marty said solemnly, How did they look? David said, I didn't look carefully. He swallowed his surprise at Marty's question: why not?

They drove back to the airport, this time behind a nineteen-fifties grey hearse. The service provided was two plain coffins and transportation to the airport. Arrangements had been made with the airline, and Riverside would meet them in New York. Their flight was Number 890; they'd get in to La Guardia at four in the afternoon. In the terminal again, David called Joyce long distance—by mistake, at home—and got no answer, until he realized and called her parents'. She said, How are you? He answered, Tired, adding, Raleigh looks civilized. She said she'd meet him at the airport; her father would drive her.

Mike insisted he have something to eat. They got some chicken broth and ham sandwiches at a stand-up counter, taking containers of coffee to the window of the boarding lounge, watching their plane fuel. As the baggage began to be loaded, the hearse drove up to the back of the plane. The coffins were put on fork-lift, since the conveyor belt that brought the light freight aboard was both inadequate and unsuitable. Faintly nauseated, David accepted a Charm from Marty and felt better.

On the flight back, David sat alone. Marty said to Nat and Mike, We could have taken a cab instead of Hertz. They didn't tell us it was just downtown. Nat said, What can you do?

Initially, David thought of nothing this time. Disturbed by the vacuum, he strained to recover his thoughts of the previous flight. But they hadn't kept—maybe this was the numbness. Certainly his uncles and Marty were in the empty grip; look at Marty's question about how his parents looked. Yet David wished for a better anesthesia, one more adaptable, prepared for when he needed it, as he assumed he would at the funeral. Now it only hung on him, extra weight. He was even ready to cry again—it wouldn't hurt him; he had done it before, coming down. The only thing he would refuse to do was cry in front of Joyce—she wouldn't understand.

And then he thought that he ought to cry for his parents, and that he hadn't done that yet. He hadn't even cried for himself. He had cried for death itself, as if it were a thick and sentimental song, a song with bombastic chords and weepy choruses. His tears had been wasted, and he wanted to cry because of that. He didn't know how it was happening, but he sensed his emotions circling farther and farther from their source, taking wide turns to reconnoiter fake wounds and false solace. The understanding that he wouldn't cry again, at all, for anything, went through him like a rasping cough. Now he sought the numbness which a minute ago he had judged worthless and ill-timed. That was the way he'd act.

Joyce was there with her parents. They did not kiss; she just took his hand. Marty went off to make phone calls, as did Nat. Mike stood with the rest of them, looking at the plane unload. He said, There's the hearse from the Riverside, as the black Cadillac edged back toward the plane. The coffins came down and were placed in the hearse. Don't they have to speak to you, Joyce asked, watching the silent progress of the procedure, sometimes with her knuckles to her mouth. No, Mike answered, it's just a driver. He'll go back to the funeral home.

Joyce's mother held her hands out to them, shepherding. Come, she said, as Nat and Marty walked from the phone booths to them again.

Nat said, I called Riverside. You know, since it's Friday, the funeral can't be until Sunday. Mike interrupted, turning to

Joyce's mother and father, Because Saturday is the Jewish Sabbath and no funerals or burials are allowed till after sundown. Joyce's father nodded and said, Yes, I know. So, David, Nat said, you can come home with me, whatever you want. Mike and I discussed where we'll sit *shivah*, and we thought at his house. It'll be easier for your grandfather; he'll be close by. The other way he'd have to traipse into Manhattan. So you decide if it's all right.

David said, First we're going home to our house. I'll call you tomorrow afternoon. Mike frowned. And if at all possible, David went on, please don't call us. I don't want to be on the phone all day and all night. Whoever you speak to, tell them please not to call me. I'll see everyone in due time.

You're the boss, Nat said, and David, who was looking at Joyce watch Nat, saw her involuntary grimace.

They split up: Marty and Nat with Mike, David and Joyce with her parents. Talk in the car was sparse; the Ceceres had enough trouble floating a conversation with daughter and son-in-law under normal circumstances. Joyce's mother, with David's plea to his uncles still very much on her mind, asked, Can we call you tomorrow? Joyce turned to David. He said, Of course.

They asked to be let off on Fourteenth Street—they'd walk down to Seventh. Joyce's mother kissed David, her grip on his arm heavily imploring. She said to Joyce, We're glad you came over. Joyce answered, Yes. Her mother added, And thank you for going to church with me. David decided not to ask her about that.

As they walked down Avenue A, David's impression was that the streets were filled with people with laundry, going in or out of laundromats, bundles under arms grasping boxes of Cheer and bottles of Clorox. He mentioned it to Joyce; she said, Clean clothes for the weekend.

They walked slowly. The neighborhood was beautiful in the late afternoon sunlight, beautiful in a way they both, having lived here a year, had learned to appreciate. It was a frank loveliness, the ravaged slum minced with coarse and dramatic shadows thrown as if by luck against the tenement fronts. Unorganized, scattered yet not incoherent, it would be this way on Seventh Street, David knew, as he passed Tenth—the same pointless chiaroscuro of hard metal car fender and horizontal sidewalk. Once in a while, they walked west to the Village this time of day. As they got to the better sections, the beauty toned out; the houses were smaller, less victimized, less vigorous. But walking back east, it seemed that the streets livened as they passed; faced with the same elements that made the neighborhood unexceptionally depressing to them at other times, they saw these streets decked with a splendid gift, a glow of poor things for an instant retrieved by light into quality. Like something shockingly overornate, it robbed imagination: the world was right here, and in an hour, as it got dark, there would be no world.

If I were a little less tired, we'd walk down to the river, David said. I'd like to go home, Joyce responded.

As they went up the steps, David asked her, Did you call your office? She said, I spoke to Don. He said to convey his condolences. I told him I'd call Monday, once I knew the situation. David said, You can go in Tuesday. You'd better. Someone has to have some money. Joyce was getting her keys out of her pocketbook. We'll see, she said.

Because the door opened into the kitchen, the first thing they were greeted with was the table filled with coffee cups and ashtrays. Joyce made quick moves to gather the dishes and clear the table, but they had both already absorbed the scene. David walked into the living room and sat on the low couch. Over the running water, Joyce said, Would you like to go to sleep. He said, Soon. How about eating? she continued. David stretched his legs out in front of him. Soon, too, he answered.

When she was finished with the dishes, Joyce came into the living room, made a motion to sit by him, but retreated from it, standing in the doorway. I'm going down to the supermarket, then; it's Friday, and open late. Anything special you want? I don't care, he said, staring out the window. He had a feeling, and when he turned back to her, sure enough, her face was blanked by estrangement. He said, Meat, some kind of meat. Fine, Joyce said, her face a little more characteristic. My father gave me twenty-five dollars to tide us over for the weekend, until I can go and pick up the paycheck. David commented, That was nice of him.

She still stood where she was. Some things would not have to be explained—like the coffee cups on the table when they entered—but some would. He put his arm out to her and she came toward him, her steps ragged and tentative. David made room for her and held her with one arm around her shoulders. Now say, it occurred to him, now say: *I have no clear feelings about anything.* And also: *I'm numb, baby. You understand.*

But David said, You must be as tired as I am. If we have the money, why don't we get a pizza or some Chinese food? You won't have to cook. Joyce shook her head. I want to, she said. If I couldn't cook, I wouldn't. David?

All right . . . all right, he said, and she got up and kissed him. Picking up her sweater, she said, I'm off. David remained as he was, sitting with his legs out, feet tangled in a shadow web of the fire escape outside the window. As she opened the front door, his eyes were intent on her progress and his mind was plotting the build-up of his solitude. A moment earlier, she'd picked up her sweater, now the door was slamming and he was alone for the first time since six o'clock the day before. He went to the bathroom, then returned to where he had sat. The gilt of the afternoon was receding. Whom to tell what? He made up a list of questions. None of them were any good.

Because this must be the payment. There had been times in his life when there was a certain kind of hole that he knew how to fill instantly, lining it with beliefs and seeding it with words. He lived there; he had pulled Joyce into one, and they had taken fingers and heels and hacked at the sides, not to destroy but to enlarge, so that they could look out across the shared rim and see the tops of the heads of others—fitful activity, life. It was their pit and home, and what made it that way was talk, slow, excited, petulant, hurting.

A memory came to him: going to see a friend who was hospitalized in Queens to have a knee ailment corrected. It had been late September; he and Joyce had walked the ten or twelve blocks from the subway through a stale neighborhood of ten-year-old apartment houses. The streets were empty, though it was a Saturday. Joyce's gesture at the sign in the butcher's window explained it. Of course, he had said, I forgot all about it. Rosh Hashanah. Joyce asked, Does it always make a place into a ghost town? Ugh, she added. And he had looked at her, at her distaste, and feeling had come rushing to his face, half anger, half blush. Those beautiful crisp, quiescent days when any neighborhood he had lived in as a child curled at its edges and lost its pulse; these days . . . He had said nothing. Later, back on the subway going home, he had talked about the High Holy Days, making a vicious kind of fun, recounting his struggles as an adolescent to get free of their mythic hold, the fights when he would wear jeans. Joyce had laughed, but not enthusiastically. Maybe, he thought now, she, too, had recognized in him what he himself had, the whited bar of unsaid feeling. It would not cough up; there were no words, like a burred tongue, that could work and work and then snare it, hoisting it out of him whole.

He had it back, filling him at every inch. He tried his questions again, hoping that they might hook and pull it free. What if she feels neglected? What if she takes the silence as a no to her availability? What if she leaves me?

Nothing.

He thought for a moment, I am a very cold person, and then felt better. Let the lie and the truth contend in the air. The thought of his mother, crazily upset when they began to crash into the other cars . . . She had no training for that kind of situation. Tears. He could still feel. He lay down. I wish I lived alone, he thought, which did it.

· · ·

It didn't rain on Sunday, the day of the funeral. David thought beforehand that the sight of all the people would put him off, but it had the opposite effect; there were too many personal greetings and ways to act to each individual friend and relative for him to slip into self-concern. Also, most of the people had not met Joyce before, and toward her they raised peculiarly tender smiles and handshakes, glad, as one or two even told David, that he "had someone."

He stayed out of school for two days, until Wednesday; then, over a look of mute disapproval by Nat, he went back. The first day went smoothly. One of the kids—Leroy Knowles —whispered to him as they went down the stairs at lunch, I missed you, Mr. Abrams. After school, he'd go to Brooklyn, sit with the family until Joyce arrived, then sit some more until all the visitors left. They'd then drive from Mike's into Manhattan with Nat and Toni. Exhausted, most nights they fell asleep the minute they hit the bed. Since David's principal had told him that it was perfectly understandable if he missed turning in the lesson plan, there was nothing pressing. The traveling back and forth from Brooklyn provided a wearying regimen that lulled them both. One time, with the paycheck she had picked up on her return to work Tuesday, Joyce had bought manicotti and ricotta, leaving the office early to bring home the food before going on to meet David in Brooklyn. That night, when they returned home, she had it ready to go in the oven, and they shared a midnight supper, commenting as they ate on what an awful cook his Aunt Judy, Mike's wife, was.

On Thursday, after he punched out, he called Joyce at the office to tell her that he'd called Mike during lunch and told him that they wouldn't be at his house till seven-thirty. David was going to the Metropolitan to see the Italian fresco show. Then he'd meet her; they could have supper out, and then go on to Brooklyn. She said, Great.

There were stares when they finally got to Mike's, a little late, about eight-fifteen. People had come to pay their respects and some had already gone. David felt close to excited; he chatted animatedly with the new husband of one of his mother's old girl friends, talking about the Democratic Party. Joyce, as usual, sat next to him holding his hand. Even Nat and Toni seemed in a good mood as they drove back; they all laughed at the evening's talk about nude plays and the audiences that attend them.

But when they got home and into the house, Joyce's demolishment, the tears that channeled her face into a grid of angry disbelief and rage, massacred all the pleasantness that had gone before. She didn't understand it, she just didn't understand it; the world was so fucking cruel! So fucking cruel! She wished *she* were dead as David put down on the kitchen table the Stuckey's Praline Bar his mother had sent them from Alexandria, Virginia, the morning before the accident—along with a line written on the mailing box that said, "For your sweet tooths, Mom and Pop"—which had just arrived in the mail.

S HE WAS DARK, NERVOUSLY BEAUTIFUL. SHE HAD long legs that were stunning, especially in white or yellow strap shoes. She dressed very well and preferred department-store clothes to hip or collegiate fashions; sometimes she'd come to school with an Indian scarf or a satin blouse on that annotated her taste so perfectly that she looked all assurance and one step above sex. In order to get through days when nothing worked as it was supposed to, she thought in stages, entering one and letting go the handles of the other. Any continuity unshared by her she shied from; she'd rather be lonely. What she liked about him was that he was perky, voluble. (Later on, he'd tell her that was a "particularly bad time" for him.) He made no immediate demand; three weeks of before-and after-class time was spent talking about their mutual distaste for the peace movement (on strictly nonideological grounds) and their mutual taste for French literature. He told her he was really impressed when he had first seen her, because she was carrying a Livre de Poche copy of *Albertine disparue,* and he had never got that far into Proust, even in English. She said that she always was partial—he'd never forget that she'd used that word—to the English translation of that volume, *The Sweet Cheat Gone.* They cut class one day, went to a bar near the campus, drank beer, and talked about tragedy. For the first time in his life, he was not aware of having hooked and caught; for the first time, she was.

Joyce Cecere was taking History of Education because she didn't like thinking about alternatives; she thought change introduced itself in urgency, not speculation. He asked her what she meant, and she said that if she wasn't going to be a teacher it would be obvious soon enough. She was not a guesser about her life; if she made a mistake—"a whopper" (she was comically grim, waited two seconds, then smiled)—she'd correct it. But no set of tarot cards for her; her mind operated on the old if-at-first-you-don't-succeed principle.

"I'm a square," she'd said, dropping her eyes. David had not known why, but he felt like punching her in the mouth.

She drank three beers; they walked back to campus. He told her that he was only taking Ed because of the draft. He was an English major. She said, "No kidding." Again he felt like punching her in the mouth. She had to go; she was also taking a lot of psychology and had a lab that ran the whole late afternoon and into early evening. He offered to meet her afterward, but she said a friend generally drove her home; as a matter of fact, it was the teacher.

What else, David thought. Normally he could get down without much trouble—stray hopes were easy targets. But he went back to the bar, had another beer, ran out for a paper, and over another beer read the sports pages feeling exhilarated. It was fantastic. He had kept on wanting to hit her!

Joyce was thinking that it was Tuesday and they'd have three more days to see and talk to each other before the weekend. She did not want to press steam out of it too quickly. She felt sloppy the next day, therefore, because they went back to the bar and drank beer again, talking this time about a friend of hers who had taken a round-the-world trip alone and was sitting in her room in Cairo one morning when she realized that she hadn't spoken a sentence containing more than six words, in any language, for more than a month.

David walked her home—they were both finished with classes for the day—and as they reached her block in the Columbia area, he said, "It must be nice to have a lot of students around. Lively."

"Not as lively as your neighborhood," she countered when he told her he lived on Twelfth Street and First Avenue.

The next day she had only a French class, which she skipped. She went to Ohrbach's instead, had a shrimp-salad sandwich in a luncheonette on Thirty-fourth Street, and returned home empty-handed. She was glad there was an interval. He called about nine—she had been sleeping, but she clawed furiously at consciousness so that after the first few words she was perfectly awake—and she told him what she had done all day. He said, "Oh."

Nice weather facilitated a truce between the general rush of the thing and both their hesitancies. They explored Riverside Park by the inch. David refused to go to the Cloisters— it was too close to where his parents lived and, as he explained, the broad promenade through Fort Tryon Park was so filled with people, too many of them familiar faces, that it had the neighborhood dubbing "Little Vienna" on Sunday. To his mild surprise, she understood completely.

She wrote a little. One Saturday afternoon, they had coffee and torte at the Eclair, on Seventy-second Street, and she said that she loved Jacques Prévert because he was simple and "unexpected." She tried to write a little like that. David was going to ask to see something, when she continued, "None of it was real, though. I don't do it any more." He felt a cool wave of perfection pass over both of them; already they seemed to be talking history, and all that was comfortable and intimate along with it. Besides, he, too, had tried to write— one story about a swimming coach—and had found it too tiring, feeling his perceptions hurry to the mark with earnest anticipation, only to find that they did not run the race, his own words thinning the flow that until then had been rich and deep. Still, though, he loved words, loved how they curved passionately so that they could, like a sanded stone, skip from meaning to meaning, catching heat. He liked Joyce not making a big thing about it; a companion who could appreciate on his level seemed much better than one who was taking off from it.

It was her first affair since moving from her parents' house. The other one had been defined by those strict walls, more spiritually than physically, and it had been maneuvered with dread and discomfort. Her primary memory, outside of the sex itself, was the way everything took too long: a self-conscious and excruciating prelude as they pulled at each other's bodies, time at best borrowed; the endless six-block walk from the subway station when Joe would take her home after a slice of afternoon spent in his apartment; and, in her mind, his solitary progress back to the station and on the train to his recently vacated rooms. Maybe, on the other hand, it was too short—everything was actually rushed instead of elongated. Perspective had vanished early; maybe because of that she let Joe get the idea that there was no time for real things—need and affection—and so had let him treat her like shit, which he did. That ended soon enough.

She and David studied for finals away from each other; the History of Ed test was the last for both of them, and after it they went and had a beer, then went to her apartment, there sharing a shower after their first love-making.

They both got summer jobs working for the Parks Department—Joyce in one of the playgrounds in Morningside Park, David in Central Park near 110th Street. He said to her, "My T-shirt'll never look that good on me." Weeks went by in which they saw each other only on Fridays. Joyce found the work exhausting but loved her kids, David just the opposite. He was robbed at knife-point in mid-August, and when, sweat-

ing and throat dry, he came to her house, waiting on the couch
in the living room for her return, his first impulse was to enlarge the story, say he was roughed up. He wasn't, wasn't even
touched, but she loved her kids so much, more than necessary,
and his fear had curdled quickly to loathing, including her.
When she did get home, however, he told the story straight
and without passion; he let her add that in her consolation.
They lay in bed for three hours, dressed, went out to eat scal-
lops at the West End Bar, then caught the late show at the
Thalia of *Citizen Kane* and *It Happened One Night*. He found
that he was not earning enough to save anything, but Joyce
told him she was filling her mattress.

It was a cool summer. One Sunday, they went along with
a cousin of Joyce's to an afternoon party on Fire Island. The
wind had blown the sea up to an attacking crystal, sun shoots
flung unerringly off the water and toward the glass-walled living room of the spacious house. People drifted in and out,
circles of those in shorts and sneakers, tanned legs and Paisley
sundresses forming on the dry sand, divining autumn in the
air. David found himself with the luxury of thinking slowly,
reflection and idea balanced on slides that tipped to and from
each other with the faint pressure of another sound of another
voice of another person in the room. It was like the introduction to sleep, yet he kept alert because he was having a good
time. Joyce ran out to the beach at about five o'clock and
David followed after her and sat on the high wooden steps
that led to the sand, watching the dusk sharply define her and
the others who were getting up a game of volleyball—figures
yelling, "Wai . . . wai . . . wai . . . wait, I got it!"—like
strings plucked by the diamond strength of the losing light.
They ate fish kabobs and glugged Budweiser, had watermelon,
and both of them joined in a small game held off to the side
of the outdoor buffet tables where you had to spell "FUCK"
by spitting the seeds in the sand. Joyce did the lower curve
of the U—"big deal," she said, delighted—and David the
upper prong of the K. He thought it looked pretty good, but

wanted to get it right, so he was slow and careful, letting each saliva-washed seed out of his mouth as close down to the sand as allowable, until he had spit them in a decent diagonal. Someone from the group called out, "You look like you're being sick." Joyce answered, "You have no idea how sick he really is," which allowed her to savor the resulting laughter and the knowledge that their identification as a couple was now declared.

On the ferry going back they sat up on top, breathing salt and darkness. Joyce couldn't get her eyes off the four people a few benches forward, who, as partial shadows, were finishing off a thermos of what she assumed were Martinis, laughing about someone named Tom. David fell asleep against her in the car, and she was the one who told her cousin to take them to her place. In bed, before they began to run hands over each other, he said, "I'll have to go home in the morning early. My T-shirt." She said, "You can try to wear one of mine. I'll lend you a pair of white socks that are big on me." He repeated it: "That's right, I can try to wear one of yours. And your big white socks," and then he sucked one of her nipples, touching her cleft with the back of his index finger.

She began to want to straddle him in the middle of the day. One afternoon in the playground, close to the beginning of September, she was holding one end of a jump rope and the idea became almost too impossible to deal with. *My name is Al-ice and my hus-band's name is George.* She grew frantic, surprised that she felt so horny. She rushed the kids into Simon Says, and the fluttering of her hand on her head, hand on her tummy, hand on her nose, fingers on her toes almost distracted her, until she thought, What would happen if I put my finger *there?* Would they follow? and she laughed to herself. All the children in the front row who could see her laughed too, in accordance with the rules.

In the fall, they decided not to register for any classes together, and were proud of it. Joyce read *Diary of a Country*

Priest as one of the first assignments for a course she was taking, and she was so saddened by it that she told David one
afternoon that she wanted to quit school. He began doing research for a long paper on James Joyce and Vico's influence.
They spent a day at the A.S.P.C.A. looking for a puppy after
Joyce and Deena, her roommate, swore they had heard someone trying the door one night. Depressed and headachy from
the yelping in the iron-grilled pound, they returned to the girls'
apartment dogless. There they half watched a variety show on
television which promised the Beatles but delivered a vertigi-
nous, camera-posted-on-the-hood-of-a-speeding-car travelogue
of London, here and there sprinkled with the backs of four
moppy heads, only one of which seemed to bear a resemblance
to a Beatle—Ringo. And shortly they agreed that a dog in a
small apartment like theirs would not only be too much trouble but cruel, too, to the dog. Deena played with the truth
when she said, "Besides, they were all ugly," and Joyce and
David had to agree, first with somber faces, then with second-
ing laughs.

They got to be very good with each other, her timing especially excellent; she was able to siphon him gradually on top,
then flip underneath and wait for his orgasm, like a relay
baton, to slip to hers. Better to read Heidegger on Time than
Masters and Johnson on premature ejaculation, he once said.
And then, in a gesture increasingly familiar yet still to both of
them vulgarly exciting, she'd yank at his penis in their own
special semaphore: one—yes; two—no; three—who cares? All
of which meant: again, come on.

Her friends all left the city; she cried one night because the
last "real" one—Jeff—left without calling and she had to hear
about him from someone else. She dug out a postcard from
Michael, who was working as a translator for the World
Health Organization, sometimes in Paris, sometimes in Sene-
gal, and showed it to David. "I met him in my freshman year,"
she explained, "when I used to go to the French Club. He was
the one who read Gide aloud. I think he's queer. He was

a terrific guy!" This added to other things, and she grew more unhappy. David was finding out she was not the fatalist she had originally made herself out to be; a good steamy heap of speculation still sat close to the middle of her meadow. He mentioned her depression; she gave him a look.

Things—she—got a little better around midway in the year, Christmas vacation. Someone in her Advanced French Prose Composition course was leaving his apartment, and the remaining roommate was desperate. She'd been there, she told David, and it was a beautiful place. Move, she said. Please. He did.

He was closer to her now, five blocks away. The rent was ten dollars more than he had been paying alone, but it was worth it. Incinerator, elevator, the other guy's—Barry's—TV and his record player, even (a little guilty about this) Barry's insomnia, his nightlong walks, weekend disappearances: all added up, his badly neurotic life. David and Joyce made efforts at first to include Barry in some of their plans, to the same extent that they included her roommate Deena. But it didn't take, nor did Barry seem resentful. Joyce was over every day, sleeping there every night at first, but they agreed between them that they should cut it down—David could always come over to her house, avoiding all the possible hurt the other way.

Suddenly, in ways unknown to them before, they were alone with each other. Past the stage of what David called "romantic scenery": rowboats in Central Park, lying in bed Sunday morning with sections of newspaper spread around them, ferry rides; they were getting to a point where Joyce, at least, felt them quivering at the lip of talk, serious discussion. It was just a matter of days, she expected, until they'd get down to something that would not leave them alone, a shared obsession.

In the spring term, they found they had to take an Education course together, but assured each other that they were well along with whatever they had to be able to risk seeing each other every day in that kind of situation. Joyce was introduced, around then, to Stuart, David's best friend, to Paul, to Jamie. On an overcast Saturday, they went to Riverside Park and David played basketball with Stuart, Jamie, and two kids they picked up at the court. After the game, the four of them went to the movies, Joyce draining of energy hour by hour, so that finally she had to lean over to David in the middle of *Duck Soup* and ask if they could leave. Outside, he looked at her worriedly, and she told him, "My period, I think."

When they got home to his apartment—Barry out, as usual —she removed her skirt and lay down on the sofa. "I didn't really feel like being with your friends."

David stood up and stared at her. She asked him whether he had ever felt completely alone when with other people, and he answered that he didn't know what she was getting at.

"I'm not 'getting at' anything. I'm there already," she said, and then she smiled because she had no idea it would come out that way, so well.

"I don't like you to play games with me," David said. He sat down again on the table across the room, knees close to his chin. He felt the afternoon wearing on in heavy bolts of grey, in lackluster. He got up and put a record on the turntable, the *Eroica*. The firm direction of the familiar music, its correctness, imparted a certain strength, felt most acutely in his fingers, and he turned back to her. "If you're going to pull things . . ."

"What does 'pull' mean?"

"You know, pull things, do tricks, tell me stories."

This was what she was waiting for. Talking, snared with each other, ready to understand a complexity, even a problem, the way no one else could. "I love you, and only want to be with you, alone, me and you."

"That's not always possible. There are other people in the world." David's hands now almost twitched with the desire to arc conducting gestures in time to the music through the room's stuffy air.

"There aren't other people in the world." The hub of it,

she realized, the central proposition, the *idée fixe*. And yet he didn't answer, didn't take it up. She looked at him and waited a few seconds for his eyes to get up to hers. He smiled. "That's true."

Joyce cried at the failure, swept over with everything masquerading as nothing.

They went to bed; David, sweaty from the basketball game, showered first. When he returned to the bedroom, Joyce lay on the bed, nude except for white panties; it really was her period. He got in next to her, and with their backs to each other they fell asleep.

It was ten o'clock in the evening when he awoke. He felt frantic; Joyce still slept. Sweat had formed a body outline on the sheet beneath him and he shifted off and away from it, closer to her. Her back to him, he watched. David couldn't remember ever seeing her in panties before; her underwear was something he got merely a glimpse of going on or off, two minutes of exposure at the most. Now he peered at her dark form banded by the whiteness, its rayon sheen dull and disconsolate in the room's brackish aura. From the waist, her body rose, back and shoulders in steady heaviness—all sleep—and descended, long legs twisted within the sheet. She turned, freeing her breasts as she got on her back. Sex was shooed away from her; David felt the vague pulse of the athletic from her frame, and at first he smiled, going to touch her, but then desisted. Sleep had moved in and she harbored it safely under each inch of her, a body, a sleeping thing. His thoughts of eagerness, of clean and supple reality, of soft flesh in innocence, were corrugated with the press of her knowing nothing, with her weight on the bed, with the queer danger of it. Stung, he thought that she had slept this way for years and years before, even with another man beside her, had slept in panties and held off the world of desire and sense the same way, lolling in the completeness of her body, countless times unknown to him. Here and now she was truly identified, brilliantly clear, her self dancing on her name and her voice and her thoughts—all these things tucked deep away. She was his stranger, and never before had he really had one.

Joyce woke a half-hour later, her mouth first tight and round as a grommet, then stirred more generously into something like a smile. "I had a dream about my parents," she said. "Have you been up all this time?"

Embarrassed, David said, "Just got up."

"My parents were driving me to Asbury Park, where we were going to buy fruit bowls. We hit a large bump on the highway and the scarf my mother was holding flew out the window. But instead of falling onto the road, it stayed up in the air, and—now this is really wild; it's so vivid—this scarf kept on sailing in the air in front of the car, all the way to Asbury Park. We just had to follow it. It was a beautiful, sunny day, cloudless. Wow. But my father was upset that she had lost the scarf."

"What are they like?"

"They're like in the dream." She lifted and arched a leg.

"That doesn't give me much to go on."

"They've never given *me* much to go on. You never speak about yours."

"That's because I never speak *to* them. We don't get along."

"Me, too. I hate them."

"Don't say it if you don't mean it." He shrugged neutralizingly. "It's not fun, and if it's not real, don't invent."

"Yes, Doctor."

"Sorry."

"I have nothing to do with them," she said, "because they don't have any idea of what I am, what I want. The old story. My mother got very upset when she got the hint that I might be sleeping with men—men! I mean a man—and she's infected my father. Of course, my mother got almost as upset when I told her that I thought nuns were dopey. That was what she secretly wanted me to be—I'm exaggerating—but I'm sure that if I had decided to become a nun, she wouldn't

have raised an eyebrow. It would have been an improvement
in her own purity. But anyway."

"You love them?"

"Of course."

Barry came to David one night and, looking at the ceiling
molding, told him that he'd found an apartment in Brooklyn
Heights with his brother, who was just out of the Army. Also
he was dropping out of school to deal with "a lot of ideas
begging to be worked out." David said, "Thanks a lot. That
screws me royally," but backtracked quickly to an amiable
cast once he saw the other boy's ravaged expression. Barry said
he'd leave the next month's rent. David felt the impulse pop
around in him to decline the offer, but he ignored it, nodding
his head, saying "I guess that's only fair," and getting another
unfortunate dose of Barry's acid depression. Looking as if he
were going to melt away, Barry told him that he was living
at the new place already, so in the next few days he'd be back
and forth picking up his things; he'd of course call first, he
added meaningfully. He offered his hand and David punched
him on the shoulder lightly, and said "Good luck, creep,"
laughing because Barry wasn't.

David called Joyce; she wasn't home and he asked Deena,
who was, to have her call immediately after she came in. Ten
minutes later, the phone rang and he said, "Come over here
now. We have to talk."

When she got there, he told her, and she said, "Absolutely
not." Pressed for an explanation, she continued, "Because it's
not the way I do things."

Within two weeks, having got someone to take over the
apartment after posting index cards on bulletin boards around
the Columbia area, and having found a new apartment for
himself, David was back on the lower East Side: Seventh
Street and Avenue A. The swiftness of the change: the night-
moving with Stuart's father's station wagon, the preliminary
extermination of the three small rooms before he could move
in, the cards to the post office about change of address—all of

this had him close to a watery swoon. That first week, he thought more than once that he wished he were sleeping, that he knew this was a very bad time in his life.

Because he had no phone for a while, the option was his to get in touch with Joyce. A week and a half after he had moved, two weeks and a half after her rejection of his offer, he called her. She wanted to know if they could meet, and with a deliberation that pleased him, he answered, "Not in this place," meaning his apartment. She wondered if the Library on Forty-second Street would be O.K. He said the subway entrance on Sheridan Square.

She was wearing bell-bottoms and a lime poor-boy blouse, carrying a copy of Sartre's *Words*. They walked west toward the little park at Abingdon Square.

Alternately sitting on a bench and standing with her back toward him, she wanted him to be able to see that:

1. He wasn't taking a lot of things into consideration, things he possibly wasn't even aware of, but which were very important to her;

2. She couldn't leave Deena in the lurch, the way Barry had left him;

3. It seemed a halfway thing, and she hated halfway things;

4. She had just moved out of her parents' house nine months before; she didn't know if she could take so many life adjustments in such a short space of time;

5. It was difficult enough for her to study now, alone;

6. Being a bachelor girl had its charms, not that she was running around particularly, but a smile here in the grocery store and there in the bookstore—it was nice; why not let her enjoy that for a while. . . .

He suggested that she was a fucking bitch.

"I'm not!" She sat down next to him, thrusting the growth of a mean and angry smile at him. It vanished when he stared back, impassive. "I'm a person. And people get run around sometimes and they don't know exactly what to do. So they stick to things that they know, hoping that soon they'll be

ready to change. And then they change—really change, make
a quick leap. You don't know what a person *or* a bitch is."

"I do know. Those 'people' also have a whole collection of
angles, excuses, which let them stay where they are and never
move, just give the appearance."

"You really don't understand, do you?"

"I understand enough."

"No, not true," she said. "You understand little ideas you
have, plans, and then you understand people in relation to
those. Living together—that's a big deal with you, and you're
judging me now in terms of that. Well, I'm not going to be
judged that way; I'm not going to be judged against any idea
I'm not completely comfortable with, because then I can only
come out looking uncomfortable—bad." She rapped the book
against her thigh. "Judge me, you judge me just as me, and
when I'm ready."

"Oh. When you're ready. Sure."

Voice up an octave, she charged. "That's right, when I'm
ready! Goddammit, I'm a person, I have feelings, I want
things. I want to be with you all the time. I do. I don't want
to be *vague*, I don't want that. I just don't want to be vague!"

"Am I being vague?"

"Oh shi— Forget . . . You don't see what I . . ."

"I see."

"What if it didn't work? Then what would I have? What
would you have? Having to find new places to live, reconstruct-
ing so much. I just want assurance."

"I give it."

"Oh, 'I give it.' Very good. That does it, right? Like 'Open
sesame.' "

"I love you and I'm very lonely now." He said it in a matter-
of-fact way that half prevented him from hearing it.

"We can get married."

"And that's different?"

She nodded.

"Why?"

"Because it has structure, a sense; it has history. I need those things, I don't like to be Raggedy Ann, a feather blown first here and then there. I like to know what's happening and what's going to happen, because then I can look whenever I want and know I'll see *something* instead of question marks, and possibilities, and all the rest of that shit. Because I'm tired of question marks. I want something definite, and if you can't give it to me—well, then, you can't. But I think I'm a strong person, and I want something equally as firm. You want to live your life swimming in dishwater, go ahead. And good luck. But that's not for me; I wasn't brought up that way, to expect things like that, and it isn't the way I feel now. I'll probably never feel it."

"And that'll make everything wonderful. 'I do' and 'I do,' and suddenly everything is peaches and cream."

Joyce dropped her book, went for it, but left it on the ground, coming back to sit erect with "Right. Exactly."

"Oh, bullshit."

"No, it's not. That's right, it makes it all peaches and cream. But if it isn't peaches and cream, then I'm to blame, or you're to blame, but not some dumb living-together arrangement that leaves us both in the dark whenever it feels like."

"Arrangements don't do things to people. People mess them up."

"You're wrong. I'd always be aware that we're together in-formally, and if something minor happens, and one of us is in a bad mood—well, then, the whole thing blows up. I don't want that. That sounds so terrible to you?"

"It does. Because it means you don't trust me."

"Maybe I don't right now." She raised her head, pulling a haughty chin up to him. Movie gesture, he thought. She held it steady, though, so possibly it wasn't a movie gesture at all.

"Well, who's the one who's judging people up against an idea now? You play the game both ways."

"You're so *dumb!* I—"

"Wait a minute," David cut in, sharply solemn. "I don't like that."

"All right, I'm sorry. But what you're saying is . . . it's all wrong. I'm not talking about some idea. It means being together in a pact. Not just some convenience. *That's* an idea and nothing but an idea."

"You're very selective."

"You better believe it."

A little more than a week after Joyce phoned her mother to tell her, she received a letter from Father Licata, the youngest priest at St. Jerome's, her mother's church. On Wednesday afternoon, having got the letter in the morning, she found it too personal to mention to David. On Thursday she thought it was funny. On Friday it made her mad, and she was itching for David to see it.

David held the letter, which was typed on onionskin, to the light.

"What?" Joyce asked, watching him.

"I thought maybe there'd be an imprimatur or a *nihil obstat.*"

"Huh?"

"Oh, you're a great Catholic."

Dear Joyce:

The first thing I think I should say is that I'm writing you merely as a person who has known you for a short time, but in that brief period has come to respect and admire your vivacity and thirst for life and knowledge. I am not the Church; no one man is. So what I'll say will stem only from my feelings and reflections. I feel this is an important thing to clarify, since it not only better explains my own convictions but highlights a facet of the Church easily overlooked.

There is much the Church does and does not do that alienates many, often myself as well. It is a mistake to think that once one accepts the collar, a young man suddenly ages to the point in which he cannot recognize his own youth and the youth of others. I am thirty, not much older than you. Many young people, including a number in the Church itself, have grave doubts about the future of our Church. It is important to remember, however, that the very fact that such doubts exist

*within the framework of the institution questioned says some-
thing about the durability and tolerance of that institution. And
so, in disagreement as well as in consent, I find there a base,
and from such a base I write to you.*

*Can I seriously expect to write a whole letter to an intelligent
young woman while masking my point in abstractions and philosophical musings? No. My attempt would be meaningless and
insulting. I am writing you about your plans for marriage, which
I have learned from your mother, at least those plans that you
have told your mother. You may be thinking now: "Oh, here
it comes. The speech about stay in the Church, against inter-
marriage, etc." I won't say that—I'm not sure what it means
to say "Stay in the Church" when the Church is changing so
rapidly. What matters more than the Church, whose existence
will remain against the transitoriness of yours or mine, is your
life, its balance, and the disturbance to that balance you are now
suggesting.*

*You are a lively young woman. You are attending college, a
time and occasion for exploration. Many life styles open up to
you. Some you try, some you don't. What seems attractive
today, tomorrow may seem unattractive. And now you propose
to stop this whirl of investigation and settle down. There is
nothing wrong with this impulse—what kind of priest would
I be if I thought that, how could I ever perform wedding
Masses?—and one can only hope that it will be an impulse you
will cherish and respect. But there is, as Ecclesiastes (and Pete
Seeger) says, a season for everything, "and a time for every
purpose under heaven." My primary question to you is: Are you
sure? Is this, in fact, the time for this particular purpose under
heaven? It is not for me to answer this. It can only be answered
by you, and only by your deepest and truest feelings, those that
come to you lying alone late at night, those that cannot be fast-
talked or compromised.*

*I won't speak about marriage, its difficulties, about the added
difficulties of a marriage such as the one you contemplate. These
things are on your mind already. All that I ask is that you ask
yourself the questions and meet the difficulties as they are every
day before you act. Because while my letter will end, and may
even be thrown away, those doubts and thoughts will, and must,*

remain. It is your life, really yours, no one else's, and no one else, except the Lord Himself, can see it as clearly as you.

If you're like me, you have a horror of blindness. Blindness to ourselves, in particular. I can see that you can see. Do not let that sight fail you.

Sincerely,

Father James Licata, S.J.

"You should write back," David said, laying the letter unfolded on the dresser. They sat on the bed in her bedroom.

"I will. Oh, and I know just what I'll—"

"That's meaningless."

"You don't even know what I'm going to say!" Joyce got up on her knees, held her hands around a foot or so of space, and began to gesture. " 'In the world of experience, there are many gradations . . .' " Her hands made loop-the-loops, quick jabs, long curves.

"Is that how he preaches?"

"Yep." She sat back down on the bed. "I really am going to write. You know, it's like the French aristocracy—the Church and the people like my mother. She sort of hires a philosopher."

"You should meet some rabbis. At least this guy can speak English."

"He can speak bullshit." She took the letter off the dresser and glanced through it. "I'm going to answer in the same tone."

"Can I do the footnotes?"

"Terrific."

She got up and sat herself at the desk, flinging back a clipboard to David, along with a piece of lined paper and a felt-tip pen.

"Should I wait for you to finish?" he asked.

"What do you think?" Joyce had begun and was scribbling quickly, her head down, a sliver of tongue vised in her teeth.

"I'll tell you what," he said to her back, which stopped

swaying for a moment. "I'll write the footnotes myself. You can put them in wherever you like."

"That'll be great," she countered sarcastically.

"Wait. You'll see."

Joyce wrote: *Your conception of a lively young woman— for that matter, life itself—I suspect is greatly different from mine.*

David wrote: *Those deepest and truest feelings that I get late at night, lying in bed alone, are really draggy. Why don't you come over sometime?*

Joyce wrote: *My faith is life. I will be truest to that by affirming and enjoying its opportunities. Doubts and fears and guilts prior to a particular part of life have no meaning to me.*

David wrote: *What are those grey stains near your cassock pocket?*

Joyce wrote: *Time is a relative creation, a term of reference. There is no time for something, only time when something occurs.*

David wrote: *The Church is having a bad time. Want a loan?—for you, only sixteen percent interest. We Hebes got a lot of dough, and I'll let you in on a secret: you know that little flap they take off our peckers, right at the start? Well, we just don't throw them away. We keep and package them in little round tins to sell as pastilles for priests especially, who make up most of the market. We call them "Cock Suckers."*

"Because it's not funny," she said, handing him back the footnotes, ripped up, after she had read them. David sat still on the bed, hands at his sides, unaccepting. Joyce stirred the small torn squares of paper in her palm with a finger. "I was trying to be serious," she said as she dropped the scraps of paper into the wicker basket beneath the desk. Before she'd look up at him again, she had gone to the desk, scanned her own letter, and destroyed that, too, ripping it into twice as many smaller pieces.

"I would at least have liked to see what you wrote," he finally said.

"It was nothing. The whole thing is not important. His letter was just a gesture." She lay down on the bed next to him, a minute later springing up to take Father Licata's letter and get rid of that as well.

Flurries of paper instead of rice—applications, tests, forms, change-of-address notices again—and they were married in a civil ceremony. Stuart and Deena were there as witnesses and sharers of the enormous Chinese meal of dem sem, duck, pork, chicken and peanuts, fried dumplings, and lots of tea they feasted with on Pell Street right after the marriage ceremony. The first night was to be spent in Joyce's apartment. Deena and Stuart returned there with them, bottles of New York State champagne under their arms, and until three in the morning, in a kind of accumulating trance, all four found that they could remember almost every word of the Dylan songs they sang out abandonedly to each other. Deena left with Stuart at four, to spend the night with a girl friend; Joyce threw looks her way as one might throw confetti off a ship. "Right away, tomorrow, we have to make moving arrangements," Joyce said to David at the door after seeing the friends out. "I wonder how she feels?"

At the edge of the bed, feet on the floor, he helped her get on. She stood over him, then lowered herself; David steadied her until she could flex her knees and be speared. He put his open hands beneath her armpits and rose, standing still to wait for the soft mechanism to start, then walking slowly around the dark room, her legs wrapped fast against the back of his calves, her arms around his neck, and her pelvis saying "hello" and "goodbye." They walked to the living room, then the kitchen, then the bathroom, and there, near the sink, her grip on him tightened and her belly moved faster, urging him to keep walking, which he did, rising on the balls of his feet and coming down in step with a thud, which made it better, more violent. She held his ear complete in her mouth and unstuck her chest from his to insinuate its softness back again, meeting nipples. In the living room once more, she began to bounce. He stood with his back against an arm of the sofa, ready, and as she began to become all pit and suck, and he something like a ghastly laugh, he waited to balance them. Joyce's hands dropped from his neck toward his waist, jiggling the skin, and now David leaned, driving himself out to her. He said, "Cha-cha, cha-cha-cha," and the glimmer of friendship waved clear in her eyes already filled with so many other churnings. He sat, Joyce landing with his motion, and, head swinging back, she trimmed, she sheared, she decorated, with no time-outs.

Stuart borrowed the station wagon from his father, and, along with Marilyn, the girl he had begun to see, and David, they moved Joyce down to Seventh Street—Wesson oil boxes full of Racine, Molière, Stendhal, Proust, childhood Salinger, a complete set of the Ditte books; Gordon gin cartons crammed with letters, term papers, notebooks, drawing pads; cheap cardboard suitcases stuffed perilously with lots of skirts, not so many blouses; laundry bags filled with underwear; Joyce herself with dresses draped over her arms which she laid flat on the back seat, forcing David to perch on the boxes in the back rather than chance creasing the blue, green, wine, fawn, lilac, tartan, and striped variety.

After waiting two jittery weeks, Joyce's parents finally called and asked them out to dinner at Lüchow's. It went beautifully. Mrs. Cecere made gentle fun of her daily routine: "You have no idea what intellectual stimulation you can get from standing on the express line at Bohack," and Joyce's father made interested, high-in-the-throat murmurs as David outlined his Vico project, which was almost finished—and which, Joyce tacked on, she'd type. The goose was delicious and they had two bottles of Moselle that made her mother kick a leg back as they left the restaurant, and reservedly squeal, "I think I'm *drunk!*" She put a balancing, dramatic arm on David's shoulder, leaving it there all the way to the parking lot around the corner. Because it had been discussed beforehand, there was almost no stammering as they declined the lift back to their apartment in her parents' car. They'd walk. "Anyway," David said smoothly, "I have to go to a bookstore on Eighth Street to see if they have anything." Joyce quickly corrected his imprecision: "He needs a special book for his paper. He ordered it."

Mrs. Cecere had a kiss for both of them, and her father's handshake and pat on the forearm seemed to David to carry an understanding, if not an acceptance, of the situation. David and Joyce took a cab back home, waiting a discreet ten minutes for her parents to have driven out of the neighborhood.

His parents knew, David swore to her, but, he added, it didn't matter how. They knew. They hadn't called because they didn't care. They didn't need him any more, and they wouldn't need her. Joyce was unfazed. "But why? I mean, just tell me a little. Why?" He would, but not now.

The principal at an elementary school on Lenox Avenue in Harlem liked him and told him he was interested. If he didn't mind doing "piecework" for a while—a class here one day, another the next, subbing, helping out in an overcrowded group—they'd definitely have a place for him in the fall. David agreed on the spot; before he left, he made sure the principal would write his draft board that very day, confirming his appointment. Joyce made a special *osso buco* for dinner and they got drunk on a bottle of Jack Daniels to celebrate. In the night, she looked at him from the vantage of a raised elbow and said, "You're fantastic."

"What can I do?" He stroked her side.

"Now I have to do something. I'll get a good job, too. Then we'll really be set, right?"

"Right."

"Right on the money," she said placidly.

"Uh-huh. How much are you getting for *this* today?"

"Today? Well, let's see. Ohhh . . . For you, I think today —ohhh . . . since it's a celebration, ohh, free."

"Get up on your knees."

Joyce lined up a job, for the summer first and, if things worked out and the firm could afford her, permanently. Don Sullman, who hired her, told her that all she had to do was keep her eyes out for the slightest hint of "flair" in anything: the way a person dresses, speaks, what kind of reaction he gets from others, the first favorable impression of a particular product, whatever. If she attuned herself to that, she'd do fine. Public relations was a fascinating science; even—and he didn't want to pour out crap she'd see as such in a second, but this was true—a profound one, because the whole world is based on action and reaction. A seesaw, and it had been proven time and time again that if you know how to do it, you can get that seesaw to tilt exactly the way you want it, putting weights on one end, subtracting them from the other. And her background in Education wouldn't hurt at all; she'd have a certain grounding in getting across concepts, which was the other primary facet of the business. She'd have nothing to worry about in this job if she just refused to accept facts as given. Don put clenched fists together, then slowly separated them. Because in the middle of the fact is something more valuable; that is, its motivation, its use. So she had to get herself used to investigating the potentials of even the dullest things. She could have a lot of fun doing it, too; there were interesting people to meet, things to do. He leaned over that fantastic desk. But mainly it's exciting and fulfilling because public relations is about freedom. Free will. You do with life what you want done with it. It teaches you that ninety-five percent of what you've been taught to expect is crap, and provides the same percentage of something new to take its place. She'd make a hundred and forty a week to start; there'd be two weeks' vacation in the summer, along with standard things like health insurance. Some traveling would be necessary: Chicago and L.A. mostly, but that only three or four times a year, mainly in winter.

She was a carnival of bright designs as she left the lobby of the building, far too excited to go back up to school, find

David, and tell him the news just yet. She walked for a while around the lake in Central Park, then rushed back down to Saks and bought herself a dress with a Mondrian-like print. She called her mother from a booth and was wished good luck and asked to call more often.

David got his job with the Parks Department back for the summer, this time working a little lower in Central Park, near Eighty-eighth Street on the West Side. "We look like something else," Joyce would say on the few occasions they left the house together in the morning. She had spent a lot of money—all saved in various ways from the summer before—on clothes, expenses David appreciated the instant he saw her in one of the new outfits. And he walked with her down Avenue A, in T-shirt, shorts, heavy white socks, and Converses, holding her hand. "If anybody stops us," he said, "tell them that you're taking me to day camp."

At first, she thought that the big corporate clients were the worst; she preferred the smaller concerns, she told Myra, the girl she shared an office with, over lunch one day. It was all too cynical, trying to humanize companies who didn't give peanuts for humans, just money. Myra said that the small companies were no different, nor were the industrial groups. But that Joyce couldn't swallow; the first project she had been assigned to was the Japanese record-player industry, and the equipment was good! She worked very hard, staying overtime three nights in a row one week to prepare and check out the itineraries for Mr. Kenzo, the industry's representative, who was expected to arrive in New York later that summer. David's question, asked the day she told him about the account, banged in her head: "You think you can get a free stereo?"

His first day of teaching in September coincided with an argument at home that had slopped over from the weekend, and the mixture blunted his excitement. She wanted to know, that's all, and what was wrong with that? Why? he had asked. Because, she seemed to have said all weekend, he was

her husband. What kind of question was that: "Why?" He
obviously had no real feeling for her, for her feeling for him.
By keeping things from her, he succeeded in folding himself
farther and farther away. One day she'd look for him and not
find him. This thing about his parents was probably just a
spat that both of them, uncomfortable with the thought of
the other's discomfort, let get out of hand. Was she right?

No, she wasn't. He was tired, really exhausted with it, yet
it had gone on, in throwaway barbs and mute vituperation, all
Sunday, Monday morning, and now, coming home in the late
afternoon, sitting by himself, David expected it to continue
when she returned. As it did. Nothing would be really theirs
—did he understand this?—until he was able to tell her about
the things he had done and thought and loved before she was
there. Hadn't she done that with him? And because of that
she didn't feel particularly moody or down when there was
something she felt to be private. There was still privacy, but
a privacy based on trust.

Going back to it. Twisting it into him. "Tell your parents,"
she said.

"I can't tell them"—they said this almost simultaneously,
although with different inflections. Joyce laughed and said,
"We really have a problem."

Mr. Kenzo, when he came back from Tokyo for his second
trip in December, asked her, sitting in the lobby of the Palmer
House in Chicago waiting for Don to come down from his
room, if she had a stereo at home. Joyce didn't get a chance to
answer, as Don was striding toward them, saying, "I have a
cab. Please—it's an eleven o'clock appointment." But when
they later drove back from the Merchandise Mart, she decided
to say it; why not? "No, as a matter of fact, you know you
were asking me whether I had a phonograph. I don't." Mr.
Kenzo shook his head regretfully, lit a Marlboro. "You *like*
music?" he asked. "Bach," she said, confident for a moving
instant that her life would turn out all right. "Especially."

They received a really expensive setup three weeks later,

and apart from its being a beautiful and well-made piece of machinery and free, they enjoyed it most as a fruit of her labors, a clear tangible floating suddenly up to them out of the sea of her excitement, the faintly abstract, too-good-to-be-true quality of her job. "I'd be a fool to give you up," David told her, adjusting the bass and treble to test the ranges. "Wait till you go to work for the Jaguar people."

And, too, he finally figured out a way to tell his parents, to tell them even if they already knew. Home for the twelve days of school vacation, listening to the record player, painting the kitchen a strong apricot enamel, he had strung together a kind of explanation, gouged beforehand, he thought, with the sort of holes they would bore into any excuse or frank admission he'd make. He had married without telling them, and now he was going to live his life for a while the best way he could. He had finished school, taken a degree, was now teaching poor kids in Harlem, and had a beautiful wife. He no longer wanted to threaten them with his words or his actions. Look at what I have now, he'd point out; isn't that at least something?

A few days before New Year's, on a Thursday, his father's day off when his partner took the store, David called. It was four in the afternoon, before Joyce was yet home. His mother picked the phone up.

"It's me," he said. A hair of silence, dispiriting, so that what he was afraid he might have to say seemed called for. "Dav . . ."

"I know. This must be some sort of occasion." Her voice was not stony, but was of a definite piece, and David wondered if this was the way their voices had permanently become, waiting for his call.

"I just wanted to say hello."

"Do you want to speak to your father?"

"Yes . . . of course. . . . I'll speak to you for a while, though."

"Uh-huh. Are you all right?" The same voice.

"Yes, fine. As a matter of fact, more than fine."

"Good. I'm glad. That must be a nice feeling." The ends of her sentences seemed cast into a long funnel, for David to catch and assemble as they jangled down.

"I don't know if you know, but—"

"We know."

Was there really anything more to say? "Her name is Joyce."

"You think we're stupid, don't you?"

"Of course not!"

"But you do. I'm telling you that you do. I personally think you think everybody's stupid except you. And if they're stupid, what good are they?"

"That's ridiculous!"

"That's ridiculous. Oh. Well, I'll do you a favor and tell you something—though, to be honest, I don't feel like telling you anything—but I will. We're not stupid."

"I never said you were. I never thought that."

"You did, but all right. You were living down around Columbia for a while, right?"

"Yes, for a little—"

"So that's what—sixty or seventy blocks from here? Not Paris, not Rome, not Africa. It's New York City. Stupid people, like you think we are, might have had trouble tracking down their son over a distance of sixty blocks, but we didn't. You see? We're not stupid. We saw in the street friends of yours from the neighborhood here who knew something about where you were, how you were; we checked with the college. We exerted ourselves to keep track."

"I *know*, I *know*. There was so much, though, that was difficult for me, so many things I couldn't approach just yet. I know that . . ."

"Yes. All right. I understand. This may shock you, but I do understand that you had these feelings. Because everyone has them. Everyone—even stupid people."

"Her name is Joyce, and she's working now in a public relations firm, and I'm teaching."

"I *told* you, we know. I think your father even knows what school you teach at. He told me; I forgot."

"There were a lot of times I was going to call. I mean, you should know that."

"But you didn't." He could hear her crying.

"No."

"That's right. You've told me something, and now I can tell you. One phone call is going to do very little. Even though we're stupid and worthless people, we have feelings, we have very big and real feelings. Don't you think your father and I *cried*, both of us, we *cried* so many nights because we hated ourselves? Don't you know that? Were you too *stupid* to guess that by now we'd almost be crazy? We finally got up and exerted ourselves to find out about you, but that was only after we waited and waited and waited, to give you the courtesy to let us know how you were yourself. During that time, we didn't know a thing; we didn't know if you still lived in the city, or whether you were still even alive. We simply didn't know. I hope for your sake you see now why this call is not enough. It'll never be enough."

"I know."

"You know nothing."

"All right, if we can't talk, we can't. I called because I thought I should."

"Of course you should!"

"I said that."

"The hardest thing was not to know. You slapped us in the face worse than any real slap. You never called!"

"We're saying the same things again, Ma. Let's not constantly repeat. This is hard enough."

"Then, what? If you want me to say congratulations, I will. Congratulations. If you want me to say I'm happy you're happy: I'm happy—"

"Stop."

"Why should I?" At intervals, her tears had reduced to a nearly silent flow, but now they crescendoed again with abandon, so that her words grazed him with a burning force. "I should stop because you want me to? *I* should do anything *you* want? No, I'm not going to stop, because you never stopped to let us know you were still on this earth, so why should I do what *you* want?" She was now clearly hysterical. "What *you* want! What are you? You're a little shit. *You're nothing but a shit!*"

He heard his father's approaching voice. "Give me the phone. Sit down and calm down. Here, give it. . . . Hello, David?"

"Hi, Pop."

"We're very surprised you called." His father's voice had a neat edge.

"I see that."

"I'm not going to go into—"

"No more, please, no more."

"You've upset us terribly. You know that. It's a shock, especially for your mother, for you to call out of the blue. I'm sure she didn't mean what she—"

"Even if she did."

"She didn't. We know about your marriage, about what you're doing. I'm glad you finished school. Maybe things will start to settle down for you."

"I hope so. You know, we're living downtown now." He mumbled out the address.

"Well, I think it's good for a person to find someone to talk to and be with. For a young man just starting a career, a wife can be a support. Companionship is very fortunate and important for someone who's aiming to make something of himself in the world."

"Pop, you're talking about me like I was someone you read about in the *Times!* Stop it!"

"We would have liked to have read about you in the *Times*. You get news however you can."

"Come off it, Pop, enough of—"

"I'm glad you called. So is your mother. O.K.?" His edge had by now been eaten into, and he was crying softly.

"Please, Pop."

"Call again." He hardly got it out, and hung up.

Forty-five minutes later, when Joyce had returned home and was changing her clothes in the bedroom, the phone rang. David bansheed, "Don't pick it up! I'll answer," and lurched past her for it.

"Your mother and I would like it very much if you and your bride would come to dinner, maybe on Sunday. How does that sound to you?"

"Of course!"

"You know, she's upset. She's still upset. But she wants me to apologize to you for what she said before."

David kicked around, unable to right the sloping conversation. "No no, that's all right. It was difficult. I understand. Tell her not to feel that way."

"So is that O.K.?"

"Fine. Sunday. About three?"

"We'll expect you. So long."

"Right, goodbye."

Joyce had come into the kitchen while he spoke, but now returned to the bedroom. "I wish you'd told me that you were going to call them. At least when you were going to. I knew it would turn out all right, and I knew that they'd invite us over. But you didn't tell me, and now I have to go to Los Angeles on Friday afternoon and I'm going to be there a week. I wanted to tell you that, but you were on the phone."

David turned around to her after staring at the phone as she spoke. "Oh, great. What am I supposed to do now? Call them up; say, look, I'll come over but Joyce—my father called you my 'bride'—she can't make it? Los Angeles? Why can't you cancel out? This is more important. Let the other girl—Myra —let her go, why not?"

"Because it's the account *I'm* working on."

"Oh, shit."

"Call them back," she said. "Tell them we'll come next weekend. They'll understand."

David stood up. "No. They've called again—I mean, you have no idea what kind of conversation we had *before*. Did you think they called me straight out with an invitation? No! I called them first . . ."

"I figured that."

"And what a conversation! My mother ended up cursing me, and *he* was murderous-sounding. Talked about me like I was dead, somebody else, not his son. So we got through that, and they called again. I can't call back and postpone. I can't do anything. This thing is so fragile I'm not going to chance upsetting it in any way."

"*You're* being fragile." She smiled, pointing into the kitchen. "Look, you got paint on the refrigerator. Which is an idea. Why don't you paint the refrigerator? It's an enamel paint."

"I don't know what to do," David said, ignoring her change of topic.

"Call them."

"I can't!"

Joyce walked out of the room, David following her. "You're making problems for yourself," she said. "But go ahead; I don't care if you want to be a baby. I can't possibly be there on Sunday. I haven't developed the knack of being two different places at—"

"Oh, shut up."

She went to the sink to peel the wilted outer leaves off the lettuce.

Three days later, almost a year and a half before and eight stories above where Bobby Kennedy was shot in the head, Joyce let Don Sullman go down on her, then hoist her legs onto his shoulders, he whispering "You tell me," as she pumped her hips to him and away from confusion and muddle. Safe, and cleaned out—she got this impression partly from the slightly camphorated smell of the hotel room—the better exhortations, the ones she felt she should really pay attention to, came to the top. See and hear, then do; and only then, say. But do, but *do*. And not worry about myths lying woolly in the head, not worry about life turned ashen at the edges and given up on so that the whole sheet burned, un-attended. No. Breathe into life. Out of a vast tangle you emerged weary, and the time for exhaustion was later. She moaned, "O.K., O.K., O.K.," and, barreling farther into this ace world, she even grabbed at Don's tightened scrotum.

Starting with brave and rigid fronts, which thankfully crumbled as the afternoon and evening wore on, they all had a decently good time at David's parents' house. Joyce explained and his parents appreciated all her traveling, and how did she like Los Angeles? Did she know that David had a cousin out there, a lawyer? They bet she got to stay in some places, and with an expense account, wasn't that great! David didn't talk much. Joyce was telling his parents things about her job that even he didn't know and he listened with interest. He put his feet up on the arms of chairs and found ashtrays with aplomb. Afterward, almost smiling, he said to her in the cab going home—another indication of his generous mood—that the dinner, even a week later than originally planned, seemed spontaneous enough, even pleasant. And then, as they were passing the big-liner piers around the Forties on the West Side Highway, he said that when he was in high school—for the first two years—he wasn't the intellectual he was now. Or maybe he was, but he didn't want to be, and the people he hung around with definitely weren't. It was a knock-around scene: up to Inwood to bowl, hanging around in Fort Tryon Park late at night, picking up girls and taking them to Long Beach before the season began—that kind of thing. One night, because cars were rare and maybe had assumed an in-flated premium in their minds, they stole one for a few hours and drove it through Fort Tryon Park, and when they stopped for a second in the parking lot of the Cloisters to wait for two girls to make up their minds whether or not to get in—which the guys were sure they would, since they looked like real nymphos—the cops, very simply and very quietly, drove up behind them, investigated, and pulled them all in. He,

David, had some marijuana on him; remember, it wasn't such a common thing then, and that was why he had it. It was his special quality, gave him his niche with that bunch of people; he supplied a joint here, one there, nothing like dealing. He only had two joints on him at the time. They booked them all, but when the charges finally came to court, for some reason he still couldn't totally comprehend, he wasn't tried on the car-stealing charge, and the grass they'd found on him merely remanded him to a probation counselor and a psychologist for a year. Then his record was erased. But of course that was enough; now she knew about the thing with his parents. He'd moved out, got into college at night, worked as a shipping clerk during the day for a year, and so on. Now he was writing about Vico and *Finnegans Wake* and was married and had seen them after three years . . .

"Three?"

"Uh-huh."

"I didn't imagine it was that long," Joyce said, a little shocked, and surprised that she should be, now of all times.

And so it was like a different life. And, wait, he hadn't told her this yet because it happened while she was away, but one of the teachers in his school, Sam, an art teacher—he'd told her a little about him—was involved in setting up a new college in Vermont, an experimental place that would have fifty students and twenty teachers, with the hope that the small ratio would prompt a truly worthwhile educational process. It was all a foundation's idea, so the students would be going on scholarship, and the teachers would be paid—nothing fancy at first, but at least six thousand—and be provided with a house. Sam had approached him about it, and he had said he was definitely interested. He wouldn't know more about it till June—they were still making arrangements with the owners of the land up there—but it looked pretty good. David entwined his index and middle fingers, Maybe? . . .

They were cleaned out three weeks later. The bastards had climbed the fire escape, and during the day. It must have been junkies—who else would be that daring? They took the toaster, the clock-radio, some of Joyce's costume jewelry, one of David's winter coats, and the stereo system. The cops, when they came, said, "Give us a list of what's been taken. Then we'll file it and you can take it off on your income tax."

"That's great," Joyce muttered.

"Well, look, Miss," one of the cops had replied, "you're not gonna get the stuff back. You might as well get something."

Joyce told David that Don had asked what had been robbed, and she had told him, though omitting reference to the stereo. She just felt funny about that in particular. David said, "I can see how you could feel that way. But don't."

The apartment now looked empty and depressing, and they went to a lot of movies on the nights that Joyce did not have to work late. Once she took him along to a screening, and introduced him to Don Sullman, her boss. They all had Black Russians at the Ginger Man afterward.

Joyce made another trip to Chicago, got sick and came back early, and stayed in bed and out of work for a week. David thought she'd been running herself too much. She burst into tears, but then agreed, saying that she always got a cold in the spring.

In May, on a Thursday night, David got a telephone call telling him that his parents were killed driving down to the Florida vacation they had spoken so enthusiastically about the afternoon he and Joyce had visited.

The insurance company would pay in a lump sum, but David, talking it over with Joyce and his Uncle Nat, decided to make arrangements with his father's lawyer and take it in monthly checks.

That everything should be removed—David's order. He made it very clear to Nat and Mike. Whatever they wanted to do with it was their business—no, it was his business, too, but he wasn't going to do anything about it now. The furniture should be stored in a warehouse, and the clothing and the books and the photograph albums and the dishes and the appliances could be boxed and kept at Mike's until he was ready to look at them and see what he wanted. He wanted the apartment empty, and also, if possible, painted in different colors.

In a quiet way, Joyce said he was being a little impractical. Right, he was. But that was the way it was going to be.

The management first had doubts. It was, after all, a four-room apartment with a river view. The rent had been the same for a long time—his parents had lived there sixteen years—and a new lease would up the rent to a higher, more profitable monthly base. The next time they spoke to the agent, Joyce and David had agreed between themselves to submit to a slight increase, but not the full fifteen percent. That was all right with the agent; it was a special case. But a paint job was not possible; they'd painted for his parents a year and a half before. David started to say, "But it's in the same colors as they always had, and I don't want—" when Joyce put a hand on his arm and he cut short. "If you like," the agent said, "you can paint it yourself—that's always allowable." David said, "Thank you"—softly, warmly. So confusing to Joyce: normally his manner would have been brusque and cynical. After all, this was a landlord, and how many times had he said that he hated landlords, the cheap lice.

The agent had only one more thing to discuss with them, and that was references. David gave the name of the insurance company. As they walked down the hill toward the subway, Joyce asked why he did that, why he couldn't have just given the name of his school and her firm. That would have sufficed. "You have to keep some self-respect," she concluded angrily.

"No, you don't." David answered in the same doughy way he had thanked the agent for agreeing to let them paint.

"You do! You're going to leave yourself with nothing if you act this way. Nothing—not an apartment—nothing is as important as keeping yourself your own person. Oh, you *know* that! What's the matter with you!"

"You're getting all upset over nothing. When it really snowed, we used to be able to sled down this street. You can imagine. Look how steep it is. With no cars, it was perfect."

"No, come back, come back." Joyce tugged on his jacket sleeve.

"Stop. Don't you see that if he writes the insurance company he'll be assured that we have a monthly income—a really big one, with the check—and he won't bother us?"

"But we have a decent income just from our jobs!"

"This'll clinch it."

"But it's *your* business." She let him continue walking. "Not his. It's money your parents left to you. It's your parents' money, not yours really."

"It's mine."

"You don't understand. What I'm saying is that, yes, it's yours, but it's not yours like your salary is yours."

David was looking at something across the street, and Joyce, in his moment of distraction, was able to censor out: "You didn't earn it."

"Don't you want to live in a nice place?" he asked, turning back to her. They had reached the subway.

"Who'll be living there, though?" How could he not understand? How could he miss all he had missed in the last month, and missed awfully, positives blackening negative, facts puffed ludicrous, clear gone muddy, obvious sullied arcane?

"*We* will," David said.

In late June, they moved into his parents' apartment. The A train got Joyce downtown faster than the bus took from the lower East Side. And David had only a twenty-minute, one-transfer bus ride to school. The breeze off the river cooled the apartment in what turned out to be a muggy summer, and when fall arrived they had Fort Tryon Park six blocks up to stroll and explore in. Shopping was good and they enjoyed spending time with Stuart and Marilyn, who lived twelve

blocks south of them, on 172nd Street. Joyce could hear the
silence of the streets that David gloried in, the safety.

But the problem was not outside. David had fashioned a
code that he ticked off the first night they were in the apartment. There were to be no drugs, no alcohol. People who came
to visit would come to dinner; there'd be no casual dropping
in. And now that they could afford one, they'd have a cleaning
woman once a month—that was absolutely necessary. They
weren't going to let the place get away from them, wake up
one morning and find themselves in the midst of a disorder
that only got that way out of their own laziness. They had
to keep this place *clean*.

For the first two weeks, their furniture sat huddled in the
middle of each room, except for the bed and the kitchen
table, which were placed in their traditional spots. Nothing
looked right to him. Joyce asked that he only live with an arrangement for a while; then, if he still didn't care for it, it
could be changed.

One night she slept over at Stuart and Marilyn's, after
running out of the house when she was unable to get a word
in as David yelled at and berated her for putting up a poster
of the Rolling Stones in the kitchen. A few days after that,
when he screamed like a crazed bird at Stuart on the phone,
who called to suggest a housewarming party, she threw down
the frying pan she was washing and ran into the bedroom,
depressing the phone cradle and hitting at him wildly with
her dishragged hand. "Are you crazy! What's the matter with
you? That's Stuart! I don't care what he said to you, how can
you speak to him like that? Have you gone crazy?"

"I think so," and he began to cry.

She had not been able to stop herself. A great decaying edi-
fice, and inside, those freaks there, that was them. "Oh, God.
Oh, God. Look what's happened to you!"

"I know." He was sobbing watery fists of confusion, faults
jimmied by each groan so that they opened to crevices.

"We should move. This place is driving you crazy. I'm feeling it too. I don't want it."

"We better get used to it," he said softly. He had stopped crying and now put his palms flat to his cheeks. He raised his head to the ceiling.

"You being crazy?"

"No." He smiled waveringly.

It was a game, she decided, a strategy. It was how he was getting through. So she played, and in a few months they were able to set the furniture up so that the house looked as if people lived there. He walked late at night, and she thought, Something he does. Maybe it helps. They finally bought a bottle of Canadian Club, then a bottle of Jack Daniels, and one night she called Marilyn, invited them for dinner, and suggested that Stuart bring some grass, if he had any. Serena came, too, with her boyfriend Jim. They had all smoked, David joining in without comment, either then or when they had gone to bed after everyone left.

She invested twenty dollars in a big Frank Stella print from the Museum of Modern Art, and it went up, framed, in the living room, without protest. Don had said to her that David was probably coming out of it. She hoped so, and knew that was possible. Don said, "You know, you're a very strong woman. Stronger than you imagine. He's very lucky. The poor kid."

The first winter night that it snowed, they went into the living room after dinner, put out all the lights, and watched from a window the river light fuzz with the grey constant fall, the George Washington Bridge flashy and beautiful across its width. They knelt together with their chins on the sill; then one of them would occasionally move back and lie flat on the wooden floor of the dark room, watching the other's shadow settle, place, and shade even further the winy night. David crawled to one side of the room and turned on the radio, searching through static for music.

"Find something classical," Joyce said as she opened the window and wetted her hand with the fine flakes. She went over to where he had been lying. On his return, she pressed her damp cold fingers to the tip of his nose.

He began to tell her how much he loved the winter here, when the radio broke into a frazzled shower of drifting voices and strong hissing. He jumped up.

The dial moved through Top Forty rock-'n'-roll, news, but no Mozart. He traversed the cycle again; the bulb that illuminated the dial of the cheap FM he had purchased on Fourteenth Street the day after they were robbed in the old apartment threw a yellow ribbon against his shirt in the dark. He stopped turning at the first clear signal.

"*Christian Call-In. Your question?*"

"*Is this Christian Call-In?*" A small, high-pitched voice: a boy, maybe ten or eleven.

"*Yes. Do you have a question?*"

"*My question is . . . is this Reverend Hanley?*"

"*Yes, it is. Go on.*"

"What?" Joyce asked, getting up. David waved her down again, saying, "Wait."

"*My question is, I wanted to know what death is like for a Christian. I mean, is it like a good resting, you know, like a peaceful sleep? You know, being unconscious?*"

"*Son, Saint Paul tells us in Philippians 1:21: 'For to me to live is Christ, and to die is gain.' And then he says in Philippians 1:23: '. . . having a desire to depart, and to be with Christ; which is far better.' So, son, the Bible tells us that we live now in Christ, and once we are redeemed of that gift of living, we are able to partake of a far greater gift, that of death: for 'to die is gain.' Far better, the Bible tell us. It would seem, then, that dying is not merely sleeping but something better than we know now.*"

"*Thank you.*" More distant, voice away from the phone, the boy can be heard saying, "Should I hang up now?" The phone clicks.

David turned the dial, got music, and returned to lie next to Joyce.

"Obscene," she said. She had dried her hand on her pants, and now, as it grabbed David's, it was wool-warm.

"Sounds like someone made him call."

"His mother. No, probably his grandmother. Scared the crap out of the kid about hell and damnation. So he decided to get it straight from the horse's mouth."

"What was the book?" David asked, holding her hand. "Philippians?"

"Oh, please, David. Stop."

AT SIX MONTHS, WHEN THE HAIR BEGAN TO COME in really heavy, Dan Carlyle knew that the new one was going to be a beaut, one of those shining daisy children, with a whole basket of problems ahead of her just because she was going to look like a dream. Marcy and Katherine were good-looking girls, and what they lacked in the way of a chin or a strong mouth they'd putty up with things to do with that soft chin and things to say out of that small mouth. Personality wouldn't have to compensate for anything with this one, though. She was going to have it all. To have produced such a trio of fe-males—all, there was no doubt about it, his, rather than Trace's —to produce such fruit there had to be a style, a controlling sameness that either molted microscopically off his genes, or possibly arched up from a more visible grace. The way he made love to Trace, perhaps. Then, of course, there were those soft inner thighs of hers, and the strange sensation he had when he first saw the baby's golden-downed head a few hours after birth; that yellow-dusted pate, soft as rime, reminded him so quickly of the skin of the inside of his wife's thighs. In a company of females now even greater by one, he still felt he had a hand. These were his. Even Trace. Maybe it was in the way he caressed those thighs. What a lovely thing it was for a dark-haired man to have his inner sun burst out in such a baby.

"Bow. Ay bow. Ay bowies."

"Go away," Kate said to the baby. The baby crawled over to where her two sisters kept their dolls. "Don't touch that," Kate commanded. She was busy trying to tie a knot on a bib around Mimi's neck.

The baby stopped crawling and, raising herself on her arms, fell backward with a thump so that she sat. She lifted a closed fist at her sister. "Bow. Ay bow. Ay bowie."

Kate put down her doll, bib still untied, and looked at her year-old sister. "What do you have?" she asked.

"Bow. Ay bow." She brought the closed fist to her mouth.

"What?" Kate got up and crouched down next to Serena. "Open up your hand."

The baby did, smiling.

"Mommy!" Kate screamed.

Daddy was coming out of the bathroom—it was Saturday morning—and was closest to the girls' room and Kate's shout. "What?" he asked, peeking in.

Kate stood up the minute she saw him and retreated to her bed, away from the baby. "Serena's got caca in her hand!"

The baby closed her fist over the small ball of turd, looking brightly at her father. "Bow," she repeated, bringing her shut fist to her mouth. "Ay bow." She gave a delighted squeak.

"Oh, dear," Daddy said, coming into the room, laughing. He opened the baby's fingers, and the turd rolled out on the rug.

"Ughhh!" Kate said, getting up on her bed.

"What are you getting so upset for," Daddy said to her.

"You do this every day; everyone does. Except you do it in the water of the toilet bowl." He was trying to keep the baby's hand away from her mouth.

"Oh moe *bow*, or moe *bow*," the baby chanted.

Mommy had by now come up the stairs. "What's going on?"

"Serena had caca in her hand!"

"There it is. A little ball of it." Daddy showed Mommy.

Mommy went over to it and picked it up with a tissue from the pocket of her apron. "It must have been the rice I gave her yesterday." She wrapped the tissue around the little brown pellet.

The baby shifted in Daddy's hands, trying to crawl to Mommy. "Bow," she said. "*Ay* bow."

"Oh, God," Mommy said. "She thinks it's a ball. She ate one."

Kate again went, "Ughhh!"

Daddy picked up Serena and carried her toward the bathroom to wash her tiny hands.

Mommy warned, "Be careful where you step. There might be others around."

Kissing the baby's head, Daddy whispered to her, "Come on, my little shit-eater."

You know who she liked? She liked Princess Summer-FallWinterSpring. And then she liked Clarabell. And Mr. Bluster. And next best, Howdy himself.

"I think it would look a little strange," her mother said.

"I've seen scaled-down cellos. I'll ask someone in the music department," said Daddy.

"I don't want a little one," Serena protested. "I want a big one. Like the lady had." They had gone the night before to Red Rocks Amphitheatre to hear Zara Nelsova and the Denver Symphony.

"You'll get one you can play, sweetheart. It doesn't make sense for you to try something you can't even reach."

"She's a big girl," her father said to her mother, who was driving. "She knows that her parents know what to do. Right?" They were driving through Englewood, having picked up Daddy at the University.

"I want a big cello."

"She'd be able to fit in the case," her father said, smiling at her mother.

"Shh," her mother responded softly. "Don't make fun."

Daddy grabbed Serena from the back seat of the Ford and pulled her into the front. "I shouldn't make fun of my little girl? What? I shouldn't make fun of"—he tickled her arm, then her leg, kissed her neck, then her head—"the cellist?" He sat her down on his knees and bounced her once at every word. "Am I making fun of you? Couldn't you fit in a cello case?"

Serena put her head back on his chest and banged twice.

"Sure you could. And then I'd go around the world in a ship, and say to the customs officers, 'No, just me and my cello,' and then when we'd be all safe in the stateroom, I'd open up the case and out you'd come. Then I'd have someone to eat dinner with, so I wouldn't be lonely."

"Where would Mommy be?"

"That's right. Where *would* Mommy be?" Mommy asked.

"She wouldn't want to be eating what we'll eat on our trip around the world."

"What?" Serena twisted around in his arms so that she could face him.

"Well, let's see . . . There'd be roast punctuation. And crushed questions. And we'll have some special pretty-please wine. And then, for dessert, sugared sentences."

"?"

Daddy hoisted her back onto the back seat. "Jack invited

us for a barbecue on—I'm not sure—something like the sixteenth," he said to his wife.

"Barbecued invitations?"

Daddy yawned.

It was "Shut up" from Marcy all the way through, but Serena agreed with Katherine that *Red Shoes* wasn't very good. They liked Cyd Charisse better.

An autobiography was the first fourth-grade assignment Miss Hile asked for.

My name is Serena Carlyle. I live at 38 Calley Drive in Littleton, Colorado. My fathers name is Daniel Carlyle. He is a doctor. He works at the University of Denver. He does not fix people. He is an administrater. My mothers name is Cassa Carlyle, but my father and my sister Marcy call her Trace. I have two sisters. Ones name is Marcy and ones name is Katherine. We call her Kate. My older sister is Marcy. She is 16. She goes to bording school in Maryland. My other sister goes to Euclid Junior High. She is 12.

My favorite things to do is to play the cello and to go camping with my family in the Rockies. I like Mount Evans the best. I also like a lot of people who play the cello very well. My favorite music is Bach, but I can't play it too good yet.

When we go camping the part I like best is right after we cook supper and eat it and I can lay down under a big tree and see the sky. Then it is very beutifull.

Someone Daddy knew had arranged to get Marcy a summer job working for the Senator in Washington after she graduated from Bryan School. She came back to Littleton for a week at the end of August, before she had to fly back East and register at Sarah Lawrence. It was really the same story that she had told everyone in the living room, but now she was up in their room, sitting on the beds, moving over to the doll chest. Serena had never thought her sister so beautiful. Marcy looked white as milk, while she and Kate were dark from camping. Marcy took out a Viceroy before she started to speak, one of her new habits. Serena promised herself that she would always smoke Viceroys, if she smoked.

"The first thing was that you kept on seeing people in the halls whom you've seen in the newspapers or on television. I was never all that interested, but you know, you see their pictures. And here they were walking right up to you, shaking your hand. That's because Michael—that's one of the guys who worked for the Senator—he was always introducing me to the other Senators. He was really sweet."

"Did you go out with him?" Kate, who would say that, said.

"Well, once." Marcy said "Well" like a cat purring.

Kate clapped her hands.

Marcy continued: "The most exciting part, though, was the quorum calls. That's when the Senate is called into session to take a vote, and a loud buzzer sounds, and all the Senators who are there have to go to the Chamber. And then, sometimes, the Senator would give a speech. I always went to hear when that happened. Because it was an eerie feeling. 'Cause here he was reading something—and you know that it's important, because he's an important Senator—and everyone's listening, and soon it's going to be in the newspapers. And it's the same thing I was typing a day ago, or part of it. That's eerie!"

"Could you read it while you were typing it?" Serena asked.

"Of course she can," Kate answered.

"Sure," said Marcy.

"Boy, you could have . . ."

Marcy smiled.

"That's really keen. You could have been a spy."

"Why says I wasn't?" Marcy said, looking ostentatiously at the ceiling.

Kate turned to Serena, annoyed. "She's just kidding."

Marcy went on: "And then when you read about it in the newspaper it was a great feeling. Here you were, knowing something important before anybody else did."

"He knew," Serena said.

"Who?"

"The Senator. He wrote the speech."

"Oh, you'd be surprised. He has a staff. Sometimes someone writes his speeches for him."

"Uh-huh," said Serena.

"Really?" Kate was wide-eyed.

"Did you meet President Eisenhower?" Serena questioned.

"No."

"He doesn't hang around there," Kate told her.

"But I did see Vice-President Nixon. A lot."

"You should have gotten all their autographs," Serena said.

"Don't be silly."

"I *know*, I *know* what it is!"

"You should. With two older sisters." Then Mommy sat on the clothes hamper opposite the toilet.

"Are you going to sit there?"

"I want to see how you put it on. Otherwise you'll mess yourself up something grim."

The napkin felt good and secure.

"All right, stand up. Walk a bit. See that it doesn't chafe."

"It's fine."

"Go ahead. Walk."

"It's fine."

"Good." Mommy took a hairbrush from the shelf and began to brush Serena's hair. "I'll spoil you a little. You're not that old. So you know what it's about?"

"Yes, I told you."

"You know why?"

"*Yes!*"

"O.K. Tell me."

"Every month there's a discharge . . . Look, I know. Kate told me."

"In that case, I better tell you, too. Your sister very often twists her facts."

Serena scowled.

"The uterus—that's the womb, where the baby grows—the uterus prepares for pregnancy when an egg is given off, which is every single month, and if there's no sperm from the father to meet the egg, the egg dies. The uterus, then, doesn't have anything to harbor, so it sloughs off the material that it has collected to nourish and feed the egg, which would have been the baby. And that's what you see, that material."

"It whats the material?"

"It sloughs it off, gets rid of it."

"I like that word. Ow! You're pulling, Mommy."

She stopped brushing. "And I think that now that you're a woman—not strictly, but biologically you are—you can call me what grownups call me, all except for your sister Kate. Call me Trace, like your father and Marcy. Kate won't, but she's silly."

"Why?"

"Because . . . well, I don't know. Maybe she thinks that if she calls me by my name, I'm not her mother any more. And that *is* silly. I call you all by your names, and do you think that I forget you're all my daughters?"

"Not really."

"Of course not. Anyway, there's one less syllable in Trace than Mommy, so it's less work for you. And for me—well, I like the name Trace."

"It's nicer than Cassa, I guess."

"You bet. Do you want me to make braids?"

"Sure."

"You know the story . . ."

"Daddy met you in a chemistry class in college, and you were doing an experiment and you kept on saying there's no trace of carbon at all and he said there is, and you kept on saying there isn't. He was your lab partner."

"Right."

"And when you began to go out, he kidded you about it, because there was carbon in the experiment, and he nicknamed you that."

"Right."

"I like nicknames. But I don't like Eenie."

"Well, I think you're stuck with it as far as your father is concerned. You could mention it to him one day. You know, we should have waited to make the braids. You're going to wash your hair tonight anyway. You'll have to do it all over again."

"That's right, Trace . . . I don't like it!"

"You'll get used to it. You call me Mommy meanwhile. What are you giggling about?"

"I thought what would have happened if, when you had that experiment in college with Daddy, he began to call you Carbon instead."

"That's worse than Cassa," Mommy said, laughing.

"Much."

"I wonder how many A & W root-beer stands there are?" Serena said.

Daddy turned to Cassa, "You brought the radio, right?" It was the day after John Kennedy had been nominated in Los Angeles, and Dan wanted to hear the acceptance speech.

"It's packed in the back."

They were taking the first section of Trail Ridge, and it was as fantastic to all three of them as it had been the times before. It was Serena's third trip to Rocky Mountain National; Kate had gone when she was five, but afterward her parents had agreed that that was a little young for a child to do such rugged camping. They started Serena when she was nine and now, four years later, she was an old pro.

"You mean you weren't sure?" Serena needled Daddy.

"No. Sorry. Look, look—look how far up we are. I would say about two miles."

The brightest clearest day.

"He was too worried about the important things, like the Bisquick," Cassa said to Serena, turning around in the front seat. It was great fun when Cassa made fun of Daddy like that; it was like the air coming into the car—cold, refreshing.

Serena bent over the back seat to where everything was stored in the rear of the station wagon. She grabbed a small gray-and-red tin box. "There's a roll of two-inch adhesive tape, and there's aspirin, Chap Stick—why do we need that?—and Mexsana foot powder, and Six-Twelve, and Merthiolate, and —where did you get this snakebite kit?"

"Any camping store," Daddy answered.

"And a package of gauze."

"If you don't be quiet and look at this fantastic view, we'll use that gauze on you now."

"Everyone passing us would think I was being kidnapped."

"Don't we just look the type," said Cassa.

"Your sister Kate should have come," Daddy said. "What weather."

Cassa leaned over and arranged her headband in the rear-view mirror. "She's a big girl, Dan. I can see why she didn't want to come."

So could Serena. She could feel that same feeling creeping up on her. But it wasn't full yet, and she was glad she was here.

One of her biggest problems was changing position on vibrato. At first, she couldn't get her thumb to hang on to the neck and her intonation suffered. And then, ascending regis-

ters, her hand would tense too much. She had to remember—
as Mita, her cello teacher, had taught her—that going into
high-register vibrato from low-register vibrato is like climbing
one of the bigger mountains in Colorado. The air gets sharper,
chillier, and harder to take in. Serena thought of Longs Peak.
She played six or seven bars of the first movement of Bocche-
rini's A-Major Sonata until she thought that she'd puke at the
sound. But she got it right; at least she thought she got it right.

       Very rare. Everyone in the house—even though there
were only three of them now—hadn't watched the Ed Sullivan
Show together for years.
       "You have to sit through the whole show just for them?"
Trace asked.
       "It's always that way," Serena said. She got up and scooped
Cheez Doodles from the bowl on the coffee table.
       "Finally," Daddy said with a sigh.
       "How can they keep singing and still pay attention to how
they play the guitar when everyone is screaming like that?"
       "I didn't think they'd be wearing suits. What do you think,
Eenie?"
       Serena put a forefinger to her lips.
       "It is a funny-looking hair style," Trace commented.
       "Can't anyone be quiet around here for a second?"
       Daddy said, "Oh, they just love all the screaming. Look at
Sinatra—remember? He kept on singing, too. He must have
enjoyed it."
       "It's catchy," Trace said, tapping her fingers on the chair
arm.
       They sang another song.
       "Look at the one on the drums," Daddy said, reaming his
pipe. "What a schnoz."
       "Which one do you like best?" Trace asked her daughter.
       "Be quiet, I'm listening!"

"She likes . . . Nope, she wouldn't like these guys. She's in love with Pablo Casals."

When the camera panned out over the audience, Daddy continued, "Mass hysteria. Some of those girls look as if they're going to fling themselves off the balcony."

When they were finished, with the curtain closed and Ed Sullivan trying to speak over the last ammoniac wisps of screaming, Daddy turned to her:

"Well?"

She actually liked Bach better. That was music that went deep into you. But this was all right, really. Yes, she liked them; it was those faces, all four of them; they looked really happy and dazed, as if they couldn't believe all the attention and yelling. "Oh, I don't know," she said to her mother and father.

She wondered . . . yes, of course Kate had watched in Maryland. The whole Bryan School probably watched. It must have been fun with all the girls watching together. Maybe it would dull Kate's anger about having to be there. Serena still didn't understand completely. There was a boy named Pravda in the high school; he had lent Kate a book called *Howl*; Daddy found the book. But maybe Daddy had a point. Kate was falling in love with this beatnik. One day, in Serena's room, Kate told her that Pravda had said in French class that morning that he'd had "a faceful of Ferlinghetti." "Who's a poet," Kate explained. "Sounds like Italian food," Serena had said. "I know." Kate answered, "he's fantastic." Pravda had small fawn-colored pouches strung to his garrison belt when Kate and Serena met him on the street one day. A thin, ratty beard, for which he was in trouble with the principal, grew on his chin. Serena couldn't imagine kissing someone like that, but that was exactly what Kate did upon seeing him. It went on for a month or two, and suddenly, in the middle of November, Daddy had yanked her out of Littleton Senior and sent her off to Bryan. The night she left, when they returned from the airport and sat down to dinner, Daddy said, as sort of an announcement, that public education in Denver

was fine, but only up to the secondary level. There were too
many characters with too much freedom running around. In
a private boarding school, Kate would get, as Marcy had already, a sense of community. "You," Daddy said, pointing to
his remaining Denver-based daughter, "will also enjoy it."

Maybe she would. It would be fun to watch them in a room
full of girls. Did they scream?

Mita suggested that Serena make up a list of her reper-
toire for her cello teacher at the Bryan School, in order to give
the teacher some idea of what she knew. A needle-like sadness
flickered through her when he said that, and it was a sadness
she would begin to live with as the days before her flight East
would be used up. She typed it out.

ROMBERG: *Sonata in C Major, Opus 43, No. 2*

SQUIRE: *"Danse Rustique"*

WEBSTER: *"Scherzo"*

MARCELLO: *Sonata in A Minor*

BACH: *"Arioso"*

GABRIELLI: *Sonata in G Major*

FAURÉ: *"Après un Rêve"*

GLAZUNOV: *"Sérénade Espagnole"*

CORELLI: *Sonata in D Minor*

BLOCH: *"Prayer"*

Working on: SAMMARTINI: *Sonata in G Major*

MILHAUD: *"Élégie"*

MAX REGER: *3 Solo Suites, Opus 131c*

She showed it to Mita the night he took her to the Hungarian restaurant after her last lesson.

"The next time I'll see you will be at the Famous Artists

series at the University," he said to her, smiling that kind, washy way. "Your father said I could let you drink a glass of wine for the occasion. What kind would you like? Here's the list."

She waved it back. "Anything. But maybe I shouldn't have any wine. I think it'll make me cry."

"I knew you were a cellist," Mita said.

In front of her was everything unfamiliar: long giant meadow, pouring off from its green an air that became grey, then white, like a breath. Soft. A giant meadow that was green, and the low earth—different from the flamboyant walls of the West; here foggy and verdant and sleep—reduced to a giant magical meadow pouring off its green. On her skin, between her sneaker and the cuff of her pants, moisture had miniaturized in cool beads. The earth a great lid, a growing tray. And a long giant sleepy meadow meandering beneath its grey breath, and the two of them shifting and rolling on its dusky motions. Trees, darkening the white breath of air on the green growing tray, standing still against the sway of the sleepy and foggy long giant meadow.

On a walk with Pamela, her new roommate, half an hour after dinner and an hour before freshman girls' curfew.

With their hands on the wooden fence, a distinct feeling in her that nothing could echo, nothing sharp enough. Purr. Night and purr. So fantastically and softly alive, a long growing green tray of a meadow.

How in the world did she ever miss this? Villa-Lobos. For hours on end.

.　　.　　.

"Carlyle," said Mr. Hammond, the extraordinarily beautiful green-eyed science teacher. "Wait, it'll come to me . . . a sister. Carol?"

"Kate."

"Kate! Right!"

"I have another sister who came here. Marcy, about six or seven years ago."

"Before my time. Your sister isn't a blonde like you, is she?"

"No."

"I didn't think so. Sure, she was in my class three years ago. A senior."

"Right. She's going to Sarah Lawrence. My other sister went there too."

"Well, Miss Sec—*Third* Carlyle, welcome."

. . . going from Bryan to Sarah Lawrence, one girls' school to another, makes it very clear to you that the best part of your sexuality has been blocked by lack of contact with men. You have this energy and don't exactly know what to do with it. For freshman English, we've had to read D. H. Lawrence's Women in Love, and that book—which is great—really shows the incredible power and creativity that sensual impulses have. It's destructive to deny them. And it has made me think about Bryan and all the ways the girls dealt with it there. The best thing, Serena, is not to deny urges, even if they often look like they are Lesbian urges. I hope this doesn't shock you; if it does, I think you're not being honest with yourself. Now there are some men around, but at Bryan, I remember, because there were none, the girls formed close relationships, and they were close enough to always hint at physical bonds. No matter how it reveals itself, sexual impulse is never anything to be ashamed of or blocked. Sex is a beautiful, creative part of life. It should be used, not felt guilty over. . . .

Lesbian? Sex. Who said anything about sex?

. . .

The Piatti Caprices that Mrs. Seabrook, her new cello teacher, was working on with her were easy as cake. And when they went on to the Bach-Kodály Choral Prelude, *"Ach, was ist doch unser Leben,"* her left hand's pressure was so uniform that she was producing a sound that she had never quite heard herself get. No vibrato at all. Clear and white.

"Don't cut deeply. Then you'll ruin the organs. O.K.? You should be seeing the stomach, and to the left of that the liver. Now, I know that it doesn't look too pleasant—that intestine looks like a little worm—but if we opened you up, your insides wouldn't look much better."

Serena and her lab partner Cissy couldn't get together on who would make the cut with the scalpel.

"Why should you be squeamish?" Cissy had said. "Your father is a doctor."

"He's a health administrator; he doesn't do this sort of thing. And besides, even if he did, I'm not used to it."

Mr. Hammond walked over to their table. "O.K. The first time." He took the scalpel from Serena's hand and split the stiff frog down the middle. "You can write home to your parents, both of you, that you're pretty sure you won't be heart surgeons."

Cissy said, "Oh, we were going to do it, but—"

"All right. Now just keep up with the rest of the class."

In her sophomore year, when extracurricular activities were permitted, she tried out for and was accepted on the *Bryan Buzz.* Her first article appeared, and she sent copies to everyone.

LIVERPUDLIANESE: A Glossary

me	possessive pronoun, my.
notches	inches.
Mod	clean-cut English kids.
Rockers	leather jackets, long hair, and motorcycles.
gear	great.
stuff shirt	a pompous person.
potty	crazy.
loco	train.
nut factory	insane asylum.
kicky	funny, offbeat.

Dear Eenie,

You and your sisters are going to have to pitch in and give the old folks some advice on how to manage being a Westerner transplanted East. Yep, Trace and I are leaving the great open spaces to pack in with you near the Atlantic. I hadn't said anything before, because these things take a great deal of working out, but for the last two months I've been talking to the people up at Pembroke in Rhode Island, as well as someone down at the Medical School at the U. of Pennsylvania, and two days ago, two letters came in the same mail, saying "C'mon, you cowboy," or words to that effect. I'll be the Administrator of Health Services at Pembroke (sorry about the capitals—I couldn't help it) and Associate Professor of Hospital Administration—part time—at U. Penn. It'll mean a lot of traveling; I'll be teaching just one day a week, so that makes a weekly trip. Your Uncle Donald has found us a place to stay in Philadelphia for this summer, and your mother and I will spend some of that time going up to Providence and searching for a house. We found buyers for the house here with little trouble—someone from the faculty, a new English professor with a wife and two little kids, so the children-ghosts of my three little pumpkins won't be lonely.

Of course, it's a little tough, and I imagine you have mixed feelings. Tonight I'm also writing Kate at Sarah Lawrence, so I don't yet know her reactions, but Marcy just happened to call last night from New York to say hello, and when I told her she started to cry. Since you're all about the same in certain ways, I'm sure that tears will be the order of the day for you too. But please don't cry on this letter; it'll spoil my great handwriting.

Don't worry about anything. Everything—and Trace has seen to it that everything means everything—is being shipped East. Nothing will be thrown away. We'll still have the same menagerie of dolls outgrown and birthday cards forgotten that we always had.

As you can guess, I'm pretty pleased. There are the positions, of course, but Trace and I are in a way very relieved that we're closer to all you kids. We both don't know a lot about the East—I guess we're hicks. (Can you imagine the chairman of the department at U. Penn introducing me to my class, saying something like: "Class, I'd like to present to you Dr. Daniel Carlyle, who'll be here in a moment, just as soon as he reins up his horse and removes his spurs"?) But we know for sure that we'll be able to see each of you girls a lot more often than twice a year, and that's comforting to us, at least. (Although from the tough-gal letters Kate's been sending us lately, I can't be sure how overjoyed she'll be.)

Well, enough for now. We've got so much to do in the next three weeks. Trace will write you tomorrow, for the woman's point of view on all this upheaval. Be free to call us.

Love,
Your Big-Shot Daddy

Summer:
Two weeks with her parents and Uncle Donald.
Three weeks with Margot and her folks in the Laurentians.
A week with Pamela in Oak Park, Illinois.
Two weeks back in Philadelphia.
A week with Cissy in Orleans, Massachusetts.
A week in New York with Cassa, buying clothes.

Back to Philadelphia before returning to school. She hated
Philadelphia.

It spread like oil among those who were interested,
which was everyone she knew. Some of the girls had come *that*
close to it during the summer. But the boys either were too
afraid or just didn't know enough. Lettie, the gangly gristle
who had played second violin in the abortive string quartet
Mrs. Seabrook tried to arrange the year before, found a boy
who did know what he was doing, however. And she wasn't
keeping it a secret. Serena wrote to Kate and asked her to send
"that D. H. Lawrence book you wrote me about last year."
Kate refused, telling her to buy her own copy. That was that.

What was curious, it occurred to her as she was getting
into her parka, was that she had sisters who had gone to Bryan
too, who had most likely played tricks and broken rules, but
had never confided in her about them, even while knowing
that she'd be in a position—especially as a senior, like now—
to carry on the tradition. Laurie had made it very clear, in the
first whispered suggestions over lunch, that this was something
done with great regularity; it was just the first time they themselves had got a chance to do it. Serena felt a little disappointed in her sisters, but that was no way to feel starting off
on an adventure, so she put it out of her mind.

Pamela was out in the hall, looking up and down the corridor. Serena watched her roommate's face register recognition,
and then Laurie and Margot appeared at the door, all bundled
up, a flashlight in Margot's hand. "Courtesy of Mr. Jukes,"
she said, flickering the flashlight in Serena's face.

"You stole it?"

"Borrowed. Borrowed."

Both girls had come into the room, and Laurie looked out at Pamela in the hall. "All right?" she whispered.

Pamela pointed a finger forward, and they all quietly walked to the landing, went down the steps to the second floor, and crossed the length of the hall so that they were at the back of the building, where Laurie and Serena opened the window, let Pamela and Margot out onto the fire escape first, then followed them out.

Their heels bit into snow on the steps. But as they descended, the steps were clearer, and by the time they were ten feet or so off the ground, where the ladder was, they had no real fear of slipping. The metal of the fire escape wheezed under their weight, and as soon as it was safe the girls jumped off the ladder to the ground.

They didn't wait to assemble but, single file, followed Margot's lead; the collar of her afghan coat was visible enough in the cold clarity of the night.

A low-hanging evergreen stood before the chink in the fence, but Laurie, directly in front of Serena, who was last in the file, forgot to hold out the branch as the others did, and Serena got a full face of wet tree as she approached. There was no whispering now—anything would have carried—but she couldn't help muttering "Ow" on contact with the slapping branch. She then looked back behind her, searching for the results of her exclamation: Mrs. Tambelyn or Mr. Jukes, or Archie, or Terry coming running toward the escapees—but there was nothing, only the freezing shadows of the dining hall willing to let them go.

Crouched, the girls passed the main gate and scurried fifty yards—Laurie had estimated that to be the count of about a hundred and twenty while taking long low strides. Standing on the road so as not to crunch gravel beneath them, they assembled for the first time since they had been in the dorm. Serena, last to reach the group, put out her mittened hand, and everyone shook the first of a round of silent congratulations.

It had been decided to walk awhile; the possibility was strong that the driver of any car on that immediate stretch of road in front of the school wouldn't pick them up, sizing up the situation without much effort.

Just as they passed the far boundary of the school, with its stone post and the maintenance shed set twenty yards in beyond it, a light shot buttery over the road, and they looked back to see a car taking the turn in front of the main gate without reducing speed. Laurie whispered "Should we?" but by the time Pamela was able to say "Too close," the car had passed them. It was ten o'clock.

"It looked like a woman anyway," Serena said. They had agreed that they'd try to ride with a man. Despite the obvious danger—which was cut down sharply, they figured, since there were four of them—a man would be more likely to have a sense of humor about the thing, and wouldn't refuse to take them straight into town.

There were a lot of stars out.

The same sort of buttery light again began to crawl at their feet, along with the grumbling self-contained sound of a motor. The girls stopped; Margot took a step forward as the others took one back. She put out a cocked thumb, but her yellow coat was enough indication that she was there. The brights blinded them before they wrenched away their gazes, and the car pulled to what seemed to Serena a crashingly loud halt; without any hesitation (Was that good? she wondered) the driver threw open both the front and the rear doors on their side. Margot got in front while the rest of them got in back.

Safe; toasty; snug as a bug in a rug, and Serena didn't even look at the driver before the car started up again and they began to move. It was a man, anywhere from twenty-five to fifty, wearing a knitted watch cap. He turned to Margot and asked pleasantly, "Where you headed?" Maybe about twenty-seven, by his voice. But this was the first foul-up. Pamela, who had the most mature voice, was supposed to do the talking, but she was sandwiched in back between Serena and Laurie.

There was a moment's palpable hesitation on Margot's part. "Bethesda. We wanted some ice cream."

It sounded O.K., but she was going on: "We're from Bryan School. They're ridiculously strict; nine-thirty curfew—study curfew—even for seniors, like us. But we all just *had* to have some soft ice cream, so we broke bounds."

And then she said, "Maybe we're pregnant," and laughed, as did the guy.

Oh, God.

"All four of you?"

But he switched on the radio and they spoke about the British rock-'n'-roll invasion, he confusing his groups, until they got to town. He dropped them at the Dairy Freeze. "If you want, I can wait. Maybe we could hit my friend's house. He has a lot of good records."

Margot said (and Serena held her breath), "No, but thanks. I think we're in enough trouble already."

"There wouldn't be any trouble."

Pamela had opened her door, and they all slid out. Serena waved to the guy, who said, "Sure?"

"Sure," Serena answered and turned her back, feeling daring. She heard the car move and waited a minute to turn around and see it going down the street. "He was nice," she told Laurie, who was shaking from a mixture of cold and nerves.

They bought pints—Serena, chocolate chip; Laurie, rum raisin; Margot, pistachio; Pamela, cherry vanilla. They asked for a freezer bag, and—in an afterthought that made Laurie run back after they had left the window—spoons.

It had seemed to all of them that the street on which the Dairy Freeze stood was well traveled, but that was a daylight assumption. As it turned out, they walked a full block back toward the road to school before they saw a car, and it was going the wrong way.

"A woman—let's change it. A woman this time," Laurie anxiously pleaded.

"I hope this doesn't melt," Pamela said. They had decided

to pass the bag to one another every twenty minutes, allowing each of them to keep their hands in their pockets for an equal amount of time.

A bar was open at the end of the second block they walked; country and Western music rumbled from within. Margot pointed across the street, and they crossed over, a shared skittishness making each of their cold-quickened and fear-driven half trots fall in together.

Serena giggled.

"Oh, shit," Margot said as she almost tripped over a beer can lying in the middle of the pavement. Laurie gave a quick look across the street at the bar. The can rolled slowly to the curb, dropping into the gutter with a resonant *ungkgh*. A step or two more, and there was another can lying before Serena's snow boots. She kicked it lightly to the side; it felt heavy against her toe. She stooped.

"This is full!" she whispered.

"I think so was the other one I kicked away."

Serena picked up the can of Carling Black Label. "It's not only full; I think it's frozen."

Margot took a quick glance at the bar, which was now a half block behind them, and ran to where she had kicked her can. "So's this."

"Look for more."

Laurie found a can resting near a barber pole, Margot another standing upright against a newspaper-vending machine. The four of them moved to the doorway of the barbershop, each holding a can.

"What do we do?" Laurie wanted to know.

"What do you mean? We'll take them back. They're full!"

The new and added excitement brought all their eyes out to the empty street; the thought of safety in their rooms, with the ice cream and beer, grew more attractive with each succeeding moment. No cars.

"There's a cab phone across the street. See it on that pole? What do you say?"

"You think it would be all right? I mean, would a cab take us? What if he reports us?"

"I have a lot of money," Serena said. "We'll give him a big tip."

Pamela was already crossing the street, and with a point at the bar for the others to watch that a whole horde of drunken hoodlums wouldn't pour out of the place and abduct her as she spoke on the phone, she opened the box and her voice could be heard saying, "We're on— Wait, I'm not sure, but it's three blocks west of the Dairy Freeze, going out toward the Bryan School. No, no luggage. Thank you *very* much."

She crossed over to the others. "They said in three minutes. The cars have radios in them."

In just about that much time, the cab pulled to the opposite corner, and they ran to it and piled in. Each girl kept her beer in the pocket of her coat, and the one with the bag filled with the ice cream put it close to that pocket, trying to keep the ice cream firm.

"Bryan School, right?" asked the cabby, who hadn't moved a faint smile off his lips since he watched them get in the cab.

"Right," Serena answered softly, trying to sound kittenish. Pamela had to clasp the mitten that was not in her pocket over her mouth. "We had dinner at one of the teachers' houses in town, and I think we stayed a little too long."

"Uh-huh."

"Yes. I guess we're going to really get it when we get back."

"That ice cream?" He pointed back at Laurie, whose turn it was to hold the bag.

"Yes," Serena, the new spokesman, answered again. "What we get to eat there isn't exactly the greatest." Laurie, who didn't have a free hand to shield her mouth, began to explode softly. "I mean the school, not the teacher's house."

"I hope it's not soup by the time we get there. Maybe you girls should eat some of it now."

Serena grabbed the bag from Laurie. "Would *you* like some?"

"I can't get you girls back and eat at the same time. Very nice of you, though."

That did it. They all broke up, a big bang, and Serena almost had tears in her eyes, so that she couldn't see in the dim light of the moving car whose ice cream was whose. "This is pistachio."

"Mine!" said Margot, who leaned over from the front seat to take it from Serena. "And a spoon, please." She was giggling a regular blip, and when, not thinking, she began to pull her hand out of the pocket to open the lid, she really burst out.

The others caught it in a second, and as Margot tremblingly handed the ice cream back to Serena, everyone was laughing so hard that the car filled with a high vinegarish treble pitch that was almost uncomfortable.

"Changed your mind?" The cabby laughed a little, too, infected, which made the girls even more hysterical.

"We'll wait," Pamela answered, hardly able to catch her breath.

They asked the driver to stop a good hundred yards before the gate. Serena pulled out a five-dollar bill from her wallet and handed it up to him.

"There's change," he said. "Comes to three-twenty, even."

"That's for you."

"All right. All right. Good luck getting back in." His sketched smile blossomed.

"Thank you very, very much."

"Enjoy it."

Weaseling back through the hole in the fence, Serena concentrating in anticipation of the evergreen branch that had met her coming out, the girls now had it down perfectly. With their minds on taking a different route in—they had to go in the back door, since they were unable to jump high enough to grab the fire-escape ladder—they were suddenly mirthless, but what was left of their happy energy came out in excited, lung-curling breaths. Lights were on on the second floor, and as they crept up the stairs they expected the worst. But it was only Mim, Lettie, and Paula waiting for them. Serena pulled out her beer can and waved it at the other girls, which made Lettie gasp, "What!"

The seven of them pushed into Margot and Laurie's room, dropping coats on the beds after pulling the beers from the pockets.

"We found them in the street. They're frozen."

"Oh, it really is almost melted," Pamela said, opening the bag of ice cream containers.

"I have a bowl downstairs," Mim said, leaving. She returned in a minute with a large plastic salad bowl.

Margot put her can of beer to her cheek.

"It's thawed some," Serena announced. "I can hear mine sloshing."

"What about the ice cream?"

"Pour it all together in the bowl."

It was nice mixing it all in, four colors which rapidly went a dull pink.

"Yuchh!" said Pamela, the first taster.

Laurie picked up the bowl, looked around, got nods, and walked with it into the bathroom. The sound of the flushing toilet prompted some laughter.

"Put the cans between your boobs. That'll defrost them," said Lettie, who since the summer occasionally spoke this way.

Serena opened up her cardigan and stuck the bottom of the can into the top edge of her bra. "Too cold!"

The four escapees told the story in detail, amended constantly by each other. Margot interrupted Laurie's telling about the bar, then stared at the beer can under the pillow next to her. She pulled it out. "Come *on*," she pleaded, shaking it.

At twelve-thirty, they decided to let Mim go down to her room and get the Swiss Army combination knife—a present from her brother—that contained a can opener. They cracked open the cans in a row. Serena handed one to each of the adventurers and they settled onto the bed. Each took four or

five gulps of tooth-numbing, metallic-tasting liquid before let-
ing the other girls have sips.

Serena didn't take hers back from Paula. "I have cello early
in the morning. I'm going to bed."

"You have to finish it," Margot said, doing so with her own.

"I guess you're right."

Then they shook hands, wondering how they were going to
get to sleep.

It looked like: Pamela to Mount Holyoke; Margot to
Radcliffe; Laurie to Swarthmore; and she and Lettie to New
York, Lettie to Barnard, herself to Juilliard.

"Daddy and Trace are buying a house in Colorado
again, for the summer," Marcy said, passing around the white-
bean casserole.

"I know. She wrote me before I left school."

"See, it's not easy to shuffle around," said Bob, Marcy's
lawyer husband, sitting opposite Serena in their apartment on
Horatio Street, where she was staying while she had her audi-
tion at Juilliard. "The myth is that Americans are highly mo-
bile people, that they move around at will. If you looked carefully, I think you'd see it isn't true. Your parents are professional people; they have the advantage of the best of two
worlds—a house in Colorado and one in Providence. But I
wonder how many people relocate, find they can't adjust at
all, and just chuck the whole thing and move back."

"Not many," Marcy said. "That's an expensive proposition."

"But the other way is psychically expensive. It confuses the
sense of territory."

Marcy watched Bob carve the leg of lamb. "If the bone's
giving you trouble, cut half slices."

"Well," Serena said, tasting the beans. "Hey, this is good! Well, they had to go back. When they came to see me in school, I had the feeling that they—Trace, in particular—were unhappy. And the house in Rhode Island is nothing like the one we had in Littleton."

"Smaller. Of course, you have to remember that it's just for the two of them."

"Here." Bob put three slices of lamb onto Serena's plate.

"I haven't heard you practice since you got here," Marcy said, looking worriedly at the rarer slices of the lamb. "Aren't you unsure of yourself? I mean, don't you want to get a little more polish?"

"No."

"Hah-hah! At least she's honest." Bob looked at his wife. "You're no one to talk about polish." He turned to Serena. "Do you remember your sister as neat? Because if she was, she isn't now. We spent a whole weekend cleaning before you arrived."

"That wasn't necess—"

"Yes, it was. Otherwise this place would be the elephants' graveyard."

"Your brother-in-law," her sister said to her, "doesn't understand the difficulties of working full-time and cleaning and keeping a house."

"Oh, yes, I do. I do *both*, since you don't."

"I don't remember whether she was neat," said Serena. "I remember very little about her. She was so much older."

"You're both making me feel great," Marcy said, smiling. "Listen, if this is not well done enough for you, Bob can slice from the other side."

"By the way, Bob," Serena mumbled with a mouthful of meat, "I don't want to forget. Can you get me an apartment near Juilliard? That's if I get in."

"You will," Marcy affirmed.

"I don't see why not. I have clients who own buildings in Morningside Heights. You'll like living up there—very ex-

citing, a lot of interesting people. Been to Cambridge, Mass.?"
Serena nodded. "A friend lives there."
"Well, it's like that. A lot of students, bright people. Sure,
I can't see why not."
"Are you planning to live alone?" Marcy asked.
"I think so. Kate is; she has her own apartment. If she can,
I can."
"I guess so."
Bob said, "I'll drive you up to Juilliard tomorrow. Taking
that big cello on the subway's not a good idea."
"When she was little," Marcy said to her husband, "you
should have seen her. And it. Bigger than she was."
"My security. I fight off monsters with it."
"Well, there are plenty of those on the subway."

S.R.O.—Single Room Occupancy, Standing Room
Only. Bob said he'd try to do better, but apartments were not
as easy to get hold of up there as he had expected. But he was
still asking around.

At least she was in; classes starting in a week; the guy
downstairs a violinist; the rent only twenty-five a week. The
cello looked gargantuan in the tiny room, but maybe that
would serve to focus her attention. And Bob was right: it was
a great neighborhood—111th Street off Broadway. New York.

He talked approvingly, if a little bit over her head,
about Xenakis and "stochastic distribution" composition. The
only books she should be reading now if she was serious were
Schoenberg's *Structural Functions of Harmony* and Hindemith's *The Craft of Musical Composition*. He ridiculed Mr.
Tamoff's idea of pairing her with Tina Goldberg, his other top
freshman cellist, in De Boismortier's Sonata for Two Cellos.

What she should be learning, to acquire a good diversified, eclectic background, was the Britten Suite for Cello, or Elliott Carter's Sonata, or, most important, Webern's *Drei kleine Stücke*, Opus 11. If she was in the dark about serialism, she'd be lost and flailing in the attempt to make any music today. No one survives without learning the language, he warned her. Stuck in the bog of Bloch and Villa-Lobos and Fauré, she'd petrify. Did she even know who Earle Brown is? That he wrote a cello sonata? She'd begin to play herself out of touch, thinking that only the classics were there, ignoring the very essence of music: change. A past, a present, a future. There is no music, he declared. There are phenomena; read Webern's famous letter where he says just that.

Not to be too hard on her, he really did understand. There were only a limited number of means to gain access to new thought; it's why modernism is a declarative moment and then is lost, only to come back in the world of art to haunt and prod and insinuate until its tenets are almost unconsciously accepted. But having no idea—having, for that matter, no receptivity to the fact that there is a new music (not so new, really; fifty years old or more)—that wasn't possible for a serious student in the second half of this century.

She went to the movies, didn't she? She saw Godard and Antonioni, and she understood that, right? Well, place the same understanding in what she knew best: music. Begin to see what the syntax is there, in what moved her most deeply. Think: what did she have in Bach? She had emotion, she had feeling, and most of all she had faith, as he had, in the utter supremacy and reality of the music, right? Well, bring the possibility of faith to this music, have faith in tonal and harmonic essentials, have faith in the atomic structure of art.

What it came down to was much too humanistic a sense of art on her part. She believed in virtuosity, but only the virtuosity of the performer, like herself. Half the reason she was so good was that she believed she could be, that she could master the music. Well, the music must be allowed to master the player. The art, the reality, must surround the execution, the life. Otherwise there is no sincerity, only hubris. She'd be guyed—excuse the Briticism; he was, after all, English, couldn't help it—thinking that music was some lovely color to shade and deepen the experience of life. For music was a reality just as grand as life, and how in the world did she think she'd shuttle between them unprepared?

End of spontaneous lecture, and they got up from the steps of Low Library and walked off the campus, watching the Columbia boys and Barnard girls loaf through the first afternoon of spring. She knew he was brilliant and she knew he was attractive. And the most recent thing she knew was that with both these things there was no going back on his part—there was a rocketing inevitability about his youth and his prestige and his classroom presence—and that if he found her beautiful and wise, she could have nothing else pressing but to make those things be true. If not, it would be at the cost of his attention, which was like another life he lived with, something that if denied would shoot off easily in another direction, taking him with it, leaving her in its wake. That she was almost achingly and brightly a strawberry blonde; that she was mysteriously tan after nearly two semesters in cold and dark New York; that she was "feature-wise," and the only student he had cared to have coffee and a walk with in his two years of teaching at Juilliard since coming from London—these things were true only as he said them and, she felt, would corrode and vanish if ignored. It had never fully occurred to her before that there were people in this world made so much to be like music: complete in presence, nothing in absence except insistent bits of tune.

Three hours later, when he fucked her in his apartment on Riverside Drive, the bed pulled close to the window to get the sun's light and heat, when his smooth penis had her for the very first time flipped from pain to precision, she held his moving hips in order to confirm everything, to reassure her suddenly piecemealed self-possession that it was really herself that was being lifted before his poise, that she had the best seat in the house from which to see him.

She turned down dinner, having to practice her Kodály for the next day. On Sunday they went to Orchard Street, then Chinatown, crossed the Brooklyn Bridge and strolled the Promenade in Brooklyn Heights, came back into Manhattan, took the I.R.T. to his house, and slept there together until she had to get up and attend her first class, and he had to get up to teach his: the same one.

Kate sent her a letter from Chicago asking her to go down to 5 Beekman Street, The War Resisters' League, to get a booklet on draft resistance for her boyfriend Toby, with whom she was living. She didn't, under the circumstances, trust getting mail with that sort of organization's return address. Serena would've liked John to go with her, but he said he wanted as little as possible to do with the politics of America, either pro or con. The quote from another part of Kate's letter, which she thought unnecessarily snide at spots, came to Serena and she threw it at him, although it was originally meant to apply to herself.

"You know, when there's a war on, you sometimes have to choose between the ethical and the aesthetic."

"That's old rubbish. Just not true."

The next week, having obtained the booklet—*The Draft and Its Alternatives*—and sent it to Chicago, she attended her first peace demonstration, standing with three hundred other people in Duffy Square on a dog day of August, listening to Pete Seeger sing "Last Night I Had the Strangest Dream" and then introduce three survivors of Hiroshima and Nagasaki. John was three blocks away in the Public Library doing some research on Busoni.

. . .

They had been joking about it off and on for a week before the concert. He was to be Leslie Howard, serious and young and sensitive composer, and she Deborah Kerr or Vivien Leigh, sitting nervously in a first-tier box, waiting for the triumph to begin.

". . . and I stride onto the stage, resplendent in white tie and tails, my long black hair sleek and purposively combed. You hold your breath—you also hold your breasts, the knockings of lust already strong in you at the sight of me—and I walk slowly, slowly to mid-stage. And there . . . instead of a piano—the console! The audience hushes, socko excitement. Swinging back the tails, I seat myself, put hands to the switches, and then, instead of the Warsaw Concerto, out comes: BLINK BOB PHFTZZTIKK TONK BONK NONK BLINK ZOOT, et cetera."

The performance was the last of the season for the Columbia Group for Contemporary Music, and there were about two hundred people sitting in the theatre. A small after-concert party was held in an apartment on Claremont Avenue, at which different fondues were offered. John was pleased at the way it had gone, but "frankly pissed" that the program had misspelled in its notes about him his early piece as "Credo" when it in fact was titled "Crito" after the Platonic dialogue.

"Congratulate me," Serena said to him as they walked down Broadway toward his apartment.

"Congratulations." Then his expression rotted. "Preg?"

She had to laugh. "No. Oh, you're worried, huh?"

"What? Congratulations about what?"

"I spent all this afternoon sitting in the library, trying to get a set to listen to the Hindemith Sonata on, but I couldn't, so I just thought about the concert. I was petrified."

"So was I."

"No, for a different reason. I was petrified that I wouldn't understand the piece tonight, and then I wouldn't know what to say to you."

"But you've heard the tape at the apartment."

"I know."

"Well."

"I was just afraid."

"But you understood it."

"Right."

"Good for you."

"I understand everything. I saw why certain tonal things were balanced the way they were, and why there was that coda near the end. I really saw it all."

"No one sees it all. Even I don't."

"Well, I did. I'm the greatest authority on John Bellstone's 'Praxis' walking on Broadway right now."

"What about John Bellstone. He's on the street too. Closer to you than you think. Wait, look—he's walking right next to you, listening to your self-satisfied shit!"

No one had to know that they were having an affair. Not to be blatant about it, therefore, he gave her a B in the course.

All he managed to send her from London that summer was a postcard, which said he was spending a good deal of time in pubs, and a letter describing what a decrepit state his mother was in. After staying a week or so with her parents in Colorado, she returned for August, found Tina Goldberg, another maligned "virtuoso" who was taking summer courses, and together they went to parties, one on the lower East Side, one in Rego Park, another on Tremont Avenue in the Bronx. Most of the people went to the city colleges, and they were very bright, while not putting it on, especially one truly vital and fascinating girl.

"Taxman"
"Eleanor Rigby"
"Love You To"
"Here, There and Everywhere"
"Yellow Submarine"
"She Said She Said"
"Good Day Sunshine"
"For No One."
"I Want to Tell You"
"Got to Get You Into My Life"
"Tomorrow Never Knows"

Marilyn suggested Canal Street; the things they needed were always cheaper there. So one Sunday that's where they went, returning about three in the afternoon, time still left to do things, with heavy-duty cleaner for the floors, rolls of Contact paper, three sponge mops, brackets and standards for shelving, a large industrial-size box of Ajax, a hammer, two screwdrivers—one Phillips, one standard—an assortment package of nails and screws, four different-watt light bulbs, a large canister of Dro roach paste, and a small can of turps.

The night before was the first they had spent as roommates in the four-room railroad flat on York Avenue and Ninety-first Street that Bob had obtained for them at only eighty-five dollars a month; after they had finished their delicatessen sandwiches and a large bottle of Coke and taken down the garbage (something they made a pledge to be disciplined about—no more bugs than necessary), a half-work, half-new-experience sweat still dotting their eyebrows, they set about discovering who had what as they opened their respective packing cartons of records. Serena had, of course, all the cello music and, to Marilyn's delight and surprise, each and every Beatle album, while she herself had only two to duplicate. Marilyn's collection of folk music—every Dave Van Ronk album, all except one of Joan Baez's, two Judy Collinses, three Dylans, five Pete Seegers, a Greenbrier Boys, two Jean Ritchies, and a whole set of different Folkways—drew a compliment from Serena, who then cried out in joy upon pulling out by the familiar spine a good recording of *Don Quixote*.

"It's one of my few classical things," Marilyn said, smiling at her roommate's bright face. "But I've always loved it."

"I *knew* this would work out," Serena said, shaking the record sleeve up and down. "We're *perfect!*"

Now, while they both took turns with the one scissors, trimming the Contact paper to lay on the yellowing steel shelves already installed in the kitchen, they further impressed each other as they made up a tentative list of spices to buy in Gristede's the next day, in order to set up a fairly comprehensive basic pantry.

"Marjoram."

"Basil. Coarse-ground black pepper. It's better than the fine powdery stuff."

"Sure. Saffron, in case we ever make paella."

"Sage, curry powder . . . Oh, I just thought. You know what I forgot today? An extension cord. I need one to pull the alarm clock closer to my bed."

"It's better to leave it far away," Marilyn said. "Then you're sure to get up."

"Actually, I'm thinking that it doesn't matter. If we're both going to be leaving for school together, one can wake the other." They had talked about trying to get similar schedules at their schools, in order to be able to leave the house and take the winding trip to the West Side together, then meet at five or six at night and have dinner out or come back home and cook their meals in each other's company.

"Cinnamon. Paprika, for Hungarian food."

"You know how to cook Hungarian food?" Serena asked.

"No, but." They laughed.

That first week turned out to be a marvel of easeful organization. School hadn't yet begun; they had free time to fix up the apartment in the morning, explore the neighborhood in the afternoon. One day, they went to the Metropolitan Museum; another, they strolled in and out of the galleries along Madison Avenue. Their nights at home proved as relaxingly distributed. On Tuesday night, they talked about politics, meandering into a long exchange on civil rights that lazed toward the question of dating Negro men. At that they stopped, both aware in a crisp and fearless empathy that something like that should be included in a conversation about sex, an exchange they got to the very next night. On Thursday night, after sharing a pretty fair lasagna, they told each other about their pasts in earnest, if miscellaneous, detail, Serena close then to pitying tears at hearing Marilyn's quietly related horror story of a family broken apart when she was three, a neurotic mother, a distant and dearly loved and needed father, a world of girl friends in not much better straits, the summers spent when she was thirteen, fourteen, fifteen, and sixteen at a not so subtle Communist camp, where her life finally got a small chance to jell around a center of social concern and sensitive boys.

"I'm sorry I went on so after hearing about you," Serena said, getting up off the green couch they had picked up at the Salvation Army before moving in. "My story must have sounded like a lot of silly little postcards."

"Want to trade?"

"No."

"Listen," Marilyn said, "I meant to mention this to you. Practice whenever you want. I haven't heard you touch your cello since we've been here. I like it, and you're so good I like it even better."

"Ummhh." Serena hugged her arms around her chest. "Flattery. Nice."

"No, not flattery. Truth."

"Well, I haven't been in the mood. When school starts I'll most likely panic, and then I'll practice so maniacally that you'll look back on now and wish for the silence again."

Marilyn smirked. "O.K. Pick your record." They had set up the phonograph in such a way that it was approximately half-way between their bedrooms, and for two nights now they had each put a record on to listen to as they fell asleep. The turntable shut itself off at the end of the record, but Serena and Marilyn found themselves usually still awake, listening to the silence, thinking the calm, almost gorgeous thoughts of new and certain-to-be-fast friends.

She put down her package. "When?"

Marilyn said, "About fifteen, twenty minutes ago."

"I wonder how he got the number."

"He was very talkative. Nice voice, the accent. He said a friend of yours, Tina, told him the phone number. And then he told me that he'd seen you walking on 116th Street, but you hadn't seen him, and he called out but you didn't hear."

"He was playing on your sympathies, making things seem like accidents. That's called 'aleatoric.' I saw him, and I heard him, too. He knows that. Prick."

"Here's the number."

"Oh, Christ! Like I wouldn't know the number."

"He's playing it cautious."

"Still his rules, though. Fuck him."

They met one night and went to Barnard to see four hours of Flash Gordon serials, of which they sat for two. Marilyn was with Stuart, a boy in horn rims, studious from the neck up, then broken down into work-shirt and dungaree casualness over the rest of him. Serena had met him previously at one

of the parties. Twice, during some of the more absurd parts of
the movies, he let out a lasciviously timed, silver-clear whistle
that broke up the whole audience. The bashful, completely
faked smile he then tossed Marilyn's way served to keep her
and Serena laughing after the others had ceased. They could
only take so much of it; it was getting both too embarrassing
and too good to waste in the campy darkness. He stayed at
the apartment that night. In the morning, Serena woke early,
dressed, and went into the kitchen to fork open some English
muffins, throwing random glances toward Marilyn's room.

As she was rescuing the first two muffins from the unpre-
dictable heat of the oven broiler, Stuart came in, rubbing his
hands together. "Finally, finally. I seenk I haf done it."

Serena's eyes and grin widened questioningly.

"I haf found ze perfect brain. Ant now—" he turned toward
Marilyn's closed door—"she lize zere, my own creation! My
monster! Zoon she vill avake and roam ze lant in search of
ozzers who can be ust by me for ze same ents. And zen, and
zen . . . ah, findication! I vill show zoze lackeys and cowards
at ze Institut vat a real genius can accomplish. I vill rule ze
vorld. Hear? I vill! I vill!" He shook Serena's already shaking
shoulders.

"Would you like an English muffin?"

"Ah, yes." He sat down, still straight-faced. "English muffins." His expression turned moony. "One of my greater achief-
ments. Took many years of hart labor to break ze amino-acit
chain in order to create ze perfect English muffin." He took a
bite out of one that Serena had been in the process of butter-
ing. "Brinks back font memories."

"Is Marilyn still sleeping?"

"Zleeping? Ah, yes, she is ztill zleeping. But zoon, zoon she
vill arise. And valk! Hurry, butter up some more of zese de-
lightful Prussian buskins."

"Let your monster do it. I'm not your slave."

"But you are! Zoon everyone vill be: Margaret Mead . . .
John Lennon . . . Christian Dior!"

"Oh, great."

"Glat you aproof." Then he smiled. In a few minutes, Marilyn came into the kitchen, dropping uncomprehending, sleep-mortared glances at both of them, and Serena felt her envy top to a foam.

Moody. Finished with John and his amazing music machine. Listening to the Brahms F-Minor Piano Quintet a lot. It was probably very bad when she had written home— although she couldn't recall precisely—because of the response it had tendered. Not that she still didn't believe everything she had written, but the specifics of her feelings seemed to evaporate on contact with their expression, and that made her even more annoyed.

. . . *You haven't been very clear about what caused the reversal. Trace and I feel, and have felt, that considering your love for the cello and its music, Juilliard would give you the opportunity to be involved with it to a far greater degree than anywhere else. Now, though, you say you don't want to attend there any more, and you hint the cello has become less important to you than before. If you're in love with someone, a diminution in interest in all other realities of your life is to be expected. Yet I don't seem to get a feeling of love in your letter. It seems too despairing. I'll, of course, support you in whatever you decide to do, transfer to one of the city colleges or not. It does, though, seem a waste. It also increases both our fears—parents' fears, but still genuine—that you're not absolutely all right down there. Marcy and Bob have let us know that you've been to see them only three times in the last seven months. This disturbs me. Knowing you as well as I think I do, I know that just my declaration of that will give you pause. . . .*

She wrote back à la Kate, a letter tripping over itself to get at the next insult, remark, innuendo, damnation, and threat. As she sealed the envelope, she knew that they wouldn't believe a word of it, and that she was still safe. Emotional and brooding Eenie, still theirs—as, in fact, she was.

Cobbie's, a bar on Second Avenue near the house, turned out to be a pleasant place to have a drink occasionally when they returned from classes. There were a few weeks during which Marilyn didn't see Stuart at all—something about his suggesting she call her mother. And since she and Marilyn took a night course together on Thursdays, these nights guaranteed each other's company. One Thursday night during that time, two guys came in and began to talk to them. One of them, Rich, grabbed a quarter from his change on the bar and pushed the buttons on the jukebox to get a song that Serena immediately thought wonderful and funny: "Mellow Yellow." The looks she and Marilyn zipped each other as the hours went by made it clear that taking the guys back to the apartment was out of the question. But, unable to extricate—and not that eager to, anyway—they stayed there, drinking too much. Marilyn told her the next day that she had left her guy, Jerry, at the bar. But Serena herself gave up to the ambience, attending to her better sense only long enough to let Rich know that they couldn't go to her place. His was fine, and filled with piles of back-number *Scientific Americans*. A graduate assistant in Biology at N.Y.U.; not such an athlete as John, but satisfying. So said her sophistication.

It sat there, behind the brown leather shock-resistant case.

She had always made things her own. Her family—*hers*, not a group of separate people. Marilyn, John, Tina, Stuart, his friend David, Rich—*her* friends, unmanageable out of the sphere, safe and enjoyable within. And she had even made her own music; melodies she picked out brought on responses of satisfaction and achievement she was gunning for. Move the fingers and course the bow, and get from it exactly what you wanted. In a sense, she never even listened: she executed. A whole world of masturbation.

Only the city threw her. The sounds, the accidents, the faces, the meanness, the élan. To walk through strange neighborhoods and see newly perceived buildings was to break the narcissism. Only that was a clear invitation to *find*.

She was going to find; she was going to concentrate on being startled. She was going to try to be New York, and let the cello sit there until she'd take it out and be able to produce a sound and a feeling that surprised her.

She watched Rich watch Daddy, who was peering into the back of the Volkswagen camper, his eyes seeming to snare again and again on the two wine-colored bolsters that served as beds. Trace stood at the door of their new stone house, squared impressively in the middle of a copse of quivering aspen, watching Serena. If this was the way it was going to be . . .

But at dinner things seemed to improve. Daddy and Rich talked about life sciences, both of them discovering and underlining with gestures and repeated "Right"'s their shared swerve from clinical medicine. Daddy, taking a consciously "mature" tack, talked about his cynicism and destroyed idealism when in med school, while Rich spoke about research and cause as against cure and effect. Trace, with a calm tone that impressed and eased her daughter, asked, "Are you people going to spend the night here?"

In Ohio they had agreed not to.

"No, but thanks," Serena said. "As long as we're camping, we might as well get as much in as possible."

Daddy's face assumed an expression that looked like one he
had expected to need, and had rehearsed. "It'll be dark in an
hour. How are you going to find a campsite?"

"We'll stay in the bus," Rich answered. "Serena's told me
all about Colorado daybreaks, so I figured I couldn't miss
one."

"They're the same as the dawns you'll see in Canada."
Daddy's voice had darkened, almost against his will, since
his expression still showed some equanimity. Serena felt her
stomach begin to turn.

"Rich has a schedule. And God forbid if we break it," she
said to her mother.

"Of course," Trace replied. "You'll be back in two weeks,
anyway." She looked at her husband. "We can't be pigs
about it."

"I don't see why not." But then he lifted his hands, shaking
his head with a mild smile. "Well, of course. You go and
have a good time."

As planned, in two weeks she was back; but alone. Rich
drove her down from Alberta to a hurried, horrible scene a
mile from her parents' house, where she got out with her pack
and duffel bag and was told to walk the rest of the way, since
he didn't want to see them. They said goodbye to each other
numbly and in a way that made it look as if he had given her
a casual lift. He was off to San Francisco—probably dumb
enough, too, to wear the suggested flower in his hair. But at
least it was all behind her. Three-quarters of a summer, not
counting the four boring months in New York, spent with an
emotional cripple. Confusion almost left her immobilized on
the road, watching the camper-bus U-turn and ride off in
search of self-realization for its driver, but a bigger and more
compelling bitterness started to move her feet, pushing her
toward her parents' new and mostly unexplored, yet still completely home.

·   ·   ·

With friends, it was like a dance on some moonstruck ledge, everyone humming a well-known cherished tune that widens the blood, locks their eyes to each other, as the world below could turn feverish and crack—and still enough warmth. Better than love. The envelope of friendship that holds itself ready like a chair, a couch, a bed on which to rest and be yourself. To be each other's monastery, each other's rich golden place. It was such a clear example of grace: the unearned gift. It took so little effort. Better than love. Such a feast of understanding and support. No roll call, no inventory. No toting-up and no sour figure as the sum. Only reflection, diversity, a clear and bright concern at all times on call. To be taken as you are by those you take precisely the same way—and taken you really are, away from what only looks like your life to where it quietly and fully and actually lies. Among them then, among friends, the sky above a ceiling of certainty, undisturbed by flashy passions. One had only to guard against faithlessness; and perhaps even faithlessness wouldn't shatter it. A wonder. To be so amply cradled. To have so much life without needing to travel for it. Friends. Better than love.

She got off the plane in New York shivering with feeling; she could hardly make a fist to grab her bags.

One way to look at it was that her life was falling apart. Marilyn moving in with Stuart up in Washington Heights; John resuming a biweekly bombardment of half-insulting, half-pleading notes; her classes beginning to annoy her; a stuffy head she couldn't get rid of; the letter silence that followed her recuperating weeks with her parents. And David, Stuart's friend, who had all of John's intensity but none of his glare, getting married to what struck her as a very catty girl.

Another way to view it was as a lull, and it was deep in that view that she cut classes one day and went down to answer the want ad, just to see what kind of job she could get if she wanted one.

Even as Marge Silver explained what the duties of "teen correspondent" would entail, Serena was still toying. The hundred dollars a week would be nice; there was a goofy sort of prestige in writing a column for gullible adolescent girls; Marge and the other editor she was introduced to—Mike— seemed nice enough. She was all prepared to say that she'd think about it when, outside the window that Marge sat before, the air zinc-greyed into the chilled fog of autumn. A quick once-over of the office—issue covers in a row on one wall, the slightly seedy beige metal office furniture, the sound of the coffee wagon bell plinking in the corridor, Marge's sincere, not too serious face—and another look out the window at the prelude to one more New York winter, and she knew that if she walked out saying no, chances were better than even that the cold would take her, steal all her footholds, that, at wit's end, she might even go back home, which was no longer fresh Colorado but grimy Providence. She took the job.

Marge sent her off instructing her not to worry: it was a small staff, none of whom knew what they were doing. She had a choice of answering letters either with her own name or with the name that the girl who left had used, Jane Taylor. She took the pseudonym. Also, she could work out an arrangement by which she could continue school at night, leaving early three times a week. Marge said, "Congratulations," as she was getting her coat on to leave.

She felt gritty and high-strung all the way home, until she called Marilyn, who yelled "Great!" and put on Stuart, who made smutty and soothing cracks about the possibilities her new job brought to his "minty mind."

As Stuart watched the Mets game out on the terrace, she and Marilyn elbowed each other for space in the small kitchenette to get the food ready for the party, the first she'd had in the new apartment on lower Lexington Avenue; the guests

—half from the office, the rest from school—were expected in two hours for a late afternoon buffet. There didn't seem to be one knife that could cut neat slices of the peperoni.

In answer to Marilyn's last question, she said, "No. I don't think of it that way."

"Well, it used to gall me when you'd say 'a guy from Montreal I knew' or 'this guy from Washington I met in Providence.' " Marilyn put down the dishcloth with which she was drying the inside of the wooden salad bowl and spread her hands wide, waiting for Serena to turn around and look. "The whole world, and you seemed to know someone from every part of it. Unfair?"

"No. But I did know people, not from all over the whole world, but there are a lot of people."

"Well, in my closed little life it just seemed like you had too many options, more than anyone deserved."

"You learned."

Stuart yelled in the window, "Kranepool! A homer, with two on. Four–three!"

"What did I learn?"

Serena took the salad bowl from Marilyn and began to cover the bottom with leaves of romaine and chicory. "That your closed-in life was bigger than you could handle, and my big open worldly one was smaller than I could."

Marilyn walked to the record player in the living room and put on Judy Collins. "Did we do something about it?"

"I don't remember. I must have skipped that part."

"Me too."

Stuart came in from the terrace and walked to the serving table, filching a rolled anchovy. "We're winning, for a change. Something must be wrong."

Serena pointed at him for Marilyn's benefit. "Maybe *he* knows."

"Sure I know. Whatever it is, you can be sure I know."

Serena bowed low. "Tell us, O sage."

"We're winning four–three."

Marilyn sank into the only comfortable chair in the two-room apartment. "Speak for yourself."

Jim was handy and creative—even from the first, when he had started to send her up funny cartoons from the production department, to now, building all the storage chests and shelving to make their sharing of the admittedly one-person apartment possible. It was difficult not to take his wit and his wits for granted, and when she got around to introducing him to her friends she found that she was nonchalant and breezy, while, more often than not, Jim was totally left out. It was a situation that called for some mending. She put her mind to dipping him into her circle slowly, helping him beforehand and afterward with explanations and stories, hoping that he'd catch the gist of what made her so close to these people; and if he couldn't share that (which she was not yet going to concede), at least he'd have a leg up and not feel quite so like a Martian.

She talked quietly and somberly about David's very private marriage and his parents' death. Jim nodded. She mentioned that Marilyn, who was closer to David than she herself was, had the feeling that David was near a collapse.

"Is she anyone to talk?"

Without responding, she continued. The whole idea of this dinner party was a gamble by Joyce, David's wife, to shake him free of some of his more irrational fears. They were all asked to be as natural as possible, which was why they were bringing along the grass.

Jim seemed to understand, and the dinner that night went off nicely; a half ounce of pot, as well as a fifth of I. W. Harper, was leisurely polished off. Jim didn't mention the party again; he began a project to build a wall of bookcases. She wished to herself that she weren't like that, but something about his silent unconcern about the closeness between her and her friends grated on her and made her impatient. A problem was exactly what she needed least, but a problem it was becoming. When David called a few weeks after the party to tell her that he was leaving Joyce and going to Vermont to teach in an experimental college, she felt a relief she knew was brutal and wrong. Perhaps to do penance for that feeling, she resumed talking to Jim about her friends, mostly to the same result; he'd listen, she'd talk; she'd talk, and all the while new shelves, new work spaces, new lighting fixtures would emerge from his handiness. One night at supper, she started to reminisce about the night of graduation. She was dramatically sentimental—how Marilyn, like Pagliacci, had sung and then cried; cried, she was sure, for all of them together, out of fear and love; that incredible night, a feast of understanding and support. Jim's unconcern lay recumbent all over his face. The memory of that long-ago night, when the world and the people she most loved within it came so remarkably together to declare the stunning fitness of things, was in suspended inane contrast to Jim's blank expression. For a second her resolve was almost like a taste in her mouth, and charging right ahead, surprising herself a little, she said to him that, after a lot of thought, it seemed a better idea if they lived separately, still seeing each other if he liked. As she knew he would, he agreed.

"Sergeant Pepper's Lonely Hearts Club Band."

The first time she took it out, she was pleased at how little it had slipped out of tune. Very consciously, she held the Bach for last. Since she was playing for herself, and for herself only, she'd play as long as and whatever she liked. Finally she went into the beautiful, beautiful Suite, pausing mid-piece to play over parts that particularly exalted her. It was her life, after all, and who deserved the pleasure more?

SECOND

September 15, 1968

Dear Serena,

It is beginning to get chilly here. The summer was such an unorganized time for everyone: a lot about this place was only an idea in all our minds, and as people arrived it quickly became apparent that no one could teach, eat, or sleep in an idea. So, as well as setting up curriculum and organizational particulars, we also did carpentry. I'll stop speaking for everyone else now and say that the last few weeks have been the first time that I've been relaxed enough to realize that this is a beautiful place. When I first got here it was Eden, mainly because I needed very much for it to be Eden. So I never looked around. But now, with the leaves turning orange and yellow, sheer force of Nature has made me take notice, and I like what I see. In three weeks, things will begin to swing into action, the students arriving, etc., and I'm sure I won't take notice again. So, for posterity: this place is a knockout.

As well as hammering nails, much of the planning here was

*devoted to intensive sessions among the faculty. As I think you
know, most of us who are teaching are young, generally not more
than four or five years older than the students we're to teach.
There is one guy who's thirty-three and he's the director, but
mainly we range from about twenty-three to twenty-seven, which
is one of the points of the whole thing (we gave up calling it
an "experiment": too many seeds of doom in that word). The
often all-night sessions we held were meant primarily to bring
all the aspects of this out, as well as our own personal fears and
hesitancies about it. In a sense, I'm glad these sessions are over
for the time being. Having never been in psychoanalysis proper,
all this ripping and baring made me feel very uncomfortable, and
it was a distress that, unlike some of the other people, I'm not
all that sure I found worth it once the truth had sprung. But
that's not so important. What was important was that in talking
to people whom I really did not know, and trying to talk as if
I did, I was able to get reactions that were truly revealing. As
I'm writing I'm not sure how I mean this. Because really, the
reactions to what I said were all pretty superficial, but they were
fast and they were hard. And that I liked then and I like now—
two things that attract me. When I described my marriage and
what happened to it, one of the girls here said, "That was
quick." While that was an approving comment and she went
on to say that it's better for a bad relationship to fall apart
quickly, it was the first time I had ever heard such a final and
complete verdict applied to anything I'd ever done. First I was
hurt, and then, second, I was hurt, and third, I was hurt. I'm
still hurt. I guess that I've always thought that nothing in my
life has been able to be classified in terms of time, but instead
was a porous ache that would drip from stage to stage, changing
hosts but always the same visitor. And here she was saying "That
was quick," and being perfectly right. It's made me think. Certainly everything anyone does or is appears as just a fact or
personality quirk to those passing him in the street or meeting
him for the first time. They pass on, or say good night, with
the fact under their arm, and the person from whom they've
taken it knows nothing about it. The next time they see him,
they say, "How is your dog," or, "How is your job," and what
they mean is "How is that thing you revealed to us so completely*

and which you still don't know well enough to give a name, like Spot." And he says, "I'm sorry, I don't understand." And then goes back to his untitled suffering, ignoring its fame. The thing is, though, that if they would just say, "How is your suffering?" without being specific, that I would understand. And respond to.

The second week here, after the sensitivity sessions were well along, some of us decided to get up early one morning and get together to fix the insulation material in the theatre building. As we assembled in front of the cafeteria, we all broke out into smiles. We were, nearly every one, wearing blue chambray work shirts, jeans, and battered tennis shoes. It was the first time I felt at all at ease. I surprised myself. In New York, if I were with people who were all dressed alike, I'd feel uncomfortable. But here, up in the woods, it was as if, unknown to each other, we had brought our style. Maybe to save us. With everyone that morning, it was work shirts and sneakers; for me, all along, it has been panic. And just as it was not necessary to say "Gee, we all have the same shitty clothes," soon I think it won't be necessary to comment on the style of fear we each of us packed as well. No more sensitivity sessions that catalogue troubles about drugs and politics and sex, but a thick and darned band of shared fright that has and calls for no name. Our style. Some of the students have arrived early, and already, in talking to them, I can see that they are different from us, although only a few years younger. To me they seem like survivors of some terrible catastrophe that has jiggled them—maybe just growing up—toward specifics, certain salvations. But we, the teachers, are not survivors, and I think that most of us can't wait to get in line with those who are to see exactly what their catastrophe was that allowed them a recuperation so precise. They talk about the nineteen-fifties as being an apathetic time, those who had to grow up in it fully sunk in the void. But the sixties were no different, at least not to me, or to Stuart, or to Joyce, or to Marilyn, or to you. We got a big taste, but nothing to chew on, so we chewed on ourselves. As if the Rolling Stones didn't break my heart.

Our style. As I said, we're all so eager up here to be saved by those we're supposed to save that it diffuses a little, and there are more than enough times in which to think that everything is turning out O.K. But our style checks that. Which is the only thing we can rely on, that that will stay. All of this is probably enough reason for me to ask you to come up here soon.

I love you. I have always loved you since I met you. And while loving you I loved Joyce and married her and was apart from you. Style once more. When my parents were killed, everything went, and with everything going, that whoosh in my ears of breakdown, I was at home. In peace. And in the calm of general confusion, I was able to drop all the goals and appointments. I won't pick them up again—the style won't let me. In this I am in perfect relaxation. I love you.

David

THE MAN REPEATEDLY TOPPLED EACH OF HIS UNDER-
standably indignant sentences with an ending titter, and by
the time Marilyn put down the phone to look in her book and
then go downstairs to check the shipping records, she had
become surprisingly unnerved. When she returned to the
floor, the copy of the shipping bill in her hand—the package
had been sent—she didn't remember how she had been
speaking to the man a minute before. Settling on a voice
pressed even in understanding, she now read off the date of
shipment and assured him that if there was any foul-up, it
was in the mails, and was not directly the store's. The man
asked, "Three weeks to Detroit?" and Marilyn answered, "I
guess so. It's pretty unbelievable. If you like, we can ask the
post office to put a tracer on the package, and then get back
to you." The man giggled again, this time before saying, "I'll
be back home by then." Marilyn promised that she'd investi-
gate, and if the package seemed to be lost, she'd see about a
replacement. The man said, "Fine, fine, very nice of you," and

before she could double-check his address with him, she heard
the phone click off on the other end. She hung up herself, then
attached a note to the shipping form telling the stockroom to
trace shipment on the purchase. She brought the form back
down to the basement, dropped it on one of the shipping
tables, and waited there a minute, scanning the cartoons from
Playboy that were arranged on the large corkboards above the
tables. Footsteps sounded behind her, and she turned to see
one of the new book salesmen searching through the trafficless
stacks for a book that was not on the floor. She smiled to him
when passing, and he looked up, righting his title-searching
head for a moment. "A paperback, *The Spanish Armada?*"

"I work in the jewelry department," she said, shaking her
head.

"Ah. Figured maybe you'd know."

"Sorry."

As she walked up the stairs, she passed the time clock. It
was ten-twenty, about an hour and a half to go. In forty
minutes or so, it would get crowded again, the last brief business of the night, but on the floor the store was virtually
empty. She walked back to her station, passing the statuary
case she had straightened and dusted a half-hour earlier, and
toward the counter, where Celia and Lola were talking quietly.
Lola was describing her latest batik. Marilyn listened for a
while, standing apart from the other girls, straightening the
leaves and carbons of her order pad.

Lola turned to her: "We did go last night."

"Oh. Was it good?" A group of three had come in at closing
and taken Lola down to Chinatown for a late supper.

"Very. But those fried dumplings. I just love them. I must
have eaten twelve by myself."

"How do you have any room for the rest of the meal?"
Marilyn asked, putting aside her tidied order book.

"I manage." Lola bit her bottom lip, raising her eyes. "As
is apparent." She lightly moved her large brown hands over
her dumpling hips.

No sound could be heard, even from the far end of the store where the best-sellers were displayed. A cash-register bell hadn't rung in ten minutes.

"Your new batik came out all right, huh?"

"Very classy," Lola said. "You have to come down and see them."

"Have you ever asked Mr. Seiden about carrying them here?" Celia asked, moving a few steps to get closer to the newly widened conversation ring.

"No. I've been here long enough to know what they'll sell and what they won't. To be honest, I'm not sure I'd sell them here. The place is, after all, a bookstore."

Celia picked up a set of earrings that she had sold a few hours before and that she had yet to put into the dumbwaiter to send down to shipping. "Great books like these?"

"You know what I mean," Lola answered sleepily.

Celia looked at her watch and then at Marilyn. "Your break?"

Marilyn took the girl's wrist to see for herself. "Right. It's so slow I almost forgot."

Shoving her order book into a cubbyhole beneath the counter, she walked for the third time in twenty minutes toward the door that led down to the stockroom. As she pulled it open, a sliver of the store's bright-light silence rose airily to the top of her head, where it didn't quite mix with her restlessness but seemed to outline and deepen it. She went down the steps and crossed the length of the stockroom, reaching the small room to the left of the manager's office that was used by the sales personnel for ten-minute breaks. She opened the lockers where coats and pocketbooks were stored and removed her bag, which contained her book. In the last week or two, she had also begun to carry a small drawing pad, and it was this that she chose now over her copy of *Life Against Death*. Getting her felt-tip pen from deep in the bag, she opened up the pad and set down a curlicue. On top of that, slightly higher, she swirled another.

From the other side of the room, down past the stacks and shipping tables, she could hear a swishing that went unnamed in her for a moment, but then in a capillary of recognition she realized it was the bathroom floor being mopped by Jackie, the night porter. Hard on that, a slow tumbling of footsteps was heard coming down the stairs, stopping—probably one of the book salesmen searching for a Bible, since they were stock-shelved nearest to the stairs; did that mean there was some business again?—and then repeating its hard sound sequence, dynamics softening as he went back up the stairs. She rolled another spiral, this one horizontally crossing the others.

She looked at the clock. Six more minutes.

Jackie's pail rang against something in the bathroom, and then steps again—his—as he went upstairs for something. Marilyn lifted her pen from the paper. The new silence pushed lightly at that section of itself already embedded in her mood. The tight curlicues on her paper looked now more wincing than languorous. She brought her knee up beneath the table to hit it lightly, to make some sound. It wasn't sufficient. The vacuums of her inner ear turned up their volumes; she could feel the tom-toms of the pressure points at her neck.

Looking up from the pad, she danced her eyes around the room, walls tacked with break schedules and workmen's compensation bulletins. But, as she knew it might, the quick film that pushed back the world from her had begun to cover, coming in almost in an instant to yellow and hold from her the angles and lights and sounds. The hardening frenzy in her mind she now hated for two reasons: first, that it was happening again at all; and second, that it was happening here, now. She tried to focus out of the room at part of a shelf holding multicolored book spines, but this, too, began to inch back. It was here again, and as she strained her eyes, trying to burn it off by force of concentration, she nevertheless felt herself begin to be turned, pulled, and wrapped at the edges, getting smaller and the world fleeing backward, slammed abruptly into a tunnel of emptiness through which, as so often lately, she could see the workingness of life and sound and light and her strands to it all puff monstrously into great departing clouds.

There were still ways out: she jerked her head back up toward the clock. She had three more minutes, but that she didn't see. She saw only the clock face, and the revolving second hand, and beneath all that subtle movement was the electric hum of the works biting and spitting time, all the distance that had so brusquely moved between her and the world kept track of. The clock fuzzed its circle until it, too, was absorbed.

She could scream; it was the one last sharpness that might tear away the gauze. Marilyn opened her mouth, but all she produced was a slithering "eee" that crested and broke while still in her throat. She threw the pad and pencil down on the floor. They made no sound. All that she had now was the one thought, a chant stung through her so that it stuck and took control. She could hear it tapping: me, me, me, me, me, me. Her head was flung back and her fists hit once against the metal table. "Ohhh. *Ohhhh*," she moaned angrily.

Please don't leave me.

She put her head down. Sound returned with footsteps down near the bathrooms again. She heard it clearly. Trying not to look at things too sharply, she bent down and retrieved the pad and pen. She got up and began to walk. After ten feet, she could recognize the shelving and the books; she knew where she was, and that she was coming out. Thankfully, she noticed the bathroom door was closed as she passed it, allowing her a few more moments to piece together, unseen.

There was nothing she could do about her flush. Luckily there were a few customers walking through the aisles, Lola and Celia following at their heels, pointing out suggestions, supplying prices. Marilyn stood by the cash register. Her breathing had started to quicken—what had been separate and taunting before was now locking back together. The phone rang. She hoped it wasn't the man from Detroit.

"Jewelry and statuary. Miss Dissman."

"Ay. Ya know dem statoos dat dey got up on top a dat

choich in Rome, Saint Pete's" A squeaked, simpy voice. "All dem saints, done by dat cat, Buhnini? Well, me and my mom, we was wonderin' how ta get a whole set a dose—in minacha, mind ya, but still de complete set, ya know?"

"I'm not sure I . . ."

"Ain't you Catholic?"

"No, but . . . uh . . . I'm not exactly sure exactly what you want. We have reproduc—"

"All you dames generally do."

"Well, I'm sorry, it's very busy here now. Maybe you should call during the day; you'd get the manager, and—"

"Hey!"

"Oh, for Christ's sake."

"Faked you out completely."

"I'm in no mood for jokes."

"Clearly."

"So goodb—"

"Wait, hold on! I'm going to pick you up."

"Where are you?"

"On Forty-second Street. I worked late, until nine, and then I went to the movies."

"Good. I don't want to go home alone."

"You sound lousy."

"It's been very slow. And I got hassled by a complaint call."

"I thought all you did was rub thumbs over semiprecious stones, getting kicks."

"I have to hang up."

"I'll see you in twenty minutes."

While she was showing a woman a Mayan calendar pendant, Stuart strode in, wearing his three-piece suit and a raincoat. He stood by the counter, lifting finger circles to his eyes to sight her. Lola was just finishing a mailing order, and she began to talk with him, both of them speaking softly, so that Marilyn couldn't hear anything but Lola's occasional laughter. The woman she was helping decided just to browse and Marilyn moved off. She joined them at the counter.

Stuart said, "I've just been telling the night manager here. My name is Lovelace, Bureau of Narcotics. It's come to the attention of the Bureau that certain charm bracelets being sold in this establishment have been turned over to our labs, and under laboratory inspection we've discovered that one of the charms on the bracelet—let's not beat around the bush: it's the one of the little dwarf with the erection—when slipped under the tongue turns out to be pure cocaine. Now, the night manager here has been very cooperative . . ."

Lola gave out a great bark.

". . . and informed me that the only salesperson who has been consistently peddling these bracelets is you. Therefore, merely as a matter of procedure, routine, I'd like to ask you to divest yourself of your clothing, except your briefs—we're in a public place, after all—so that I can make a search for the evil little powder which may be secreted on your person."

Marilyn, unsmiling, turned to Lola. "O.K. if I go early? Could you punch out for me? It's only fifteen minutes."

"Sure. Go."

"The Bureau appreciates your cooperation," Stuart said to Lola. "Now I can take her down to headquarters and get a gander at her without the briefs that modesty would otherwise dictate."

Enunciating every word behind a large rubbery grin, Lola said to him, "You are abso*lutely* bananas!"

When Marilyn returned with her coat and bag, Stuart was browsing through an art book. She tapped his shoulder. He turned toward Celia and Lola at the counter and bowed from the waist. "Ladies."

"See you tomorrow, Mar."

"Bye."

Out on Fifth Avenue, after they had taken only a few steps without talking, she said to him, "Before we start to talk, I want you to be serious."

"Always."

"See. There you go."

"All right. Serious."

They walked a block silently.

"Where are we going?" Marilyn asked.

"I thought we'd walk up Fifth to Fifty-ninth, cut over, and take the A at Columbus Circle."

She nodded.

"I had lunch with Joyce Abrams today," Stuart told her. He was walking with hands planted deep in his pockets, the chill on the nearly deserted avenue cutting easily through the thinness of his raincoat. "She seems all right. Actually it was very interesting."

"I'm sure."

"What kind of bug's up your ass?"

"Nothing. I just said that I was sure it was interesting."

"Sure."

"Go on," she urged.

"You're pretty weird tonight."

"Go *on*."

"Well, of course we talked about David and about the breakup, what happens—you know. But in between talking about his parents and the accident and moving into that apartment, she would be saying things about her job like 'It began to be very hard for me to square the situation at home with what was going on at work'—something like that. She was dropping hints like crazy. So I asked her if she was seeing another guy at that time and she said 'Sort of.' " He turned to Marilyn for her reaction. She stared straight ahead, walking. "Then she said that she didn't think David ever knew. I don't think so, either. You remember that time when he came over and let it out a little? There was nothing about Joyce sleeping with someone else. I've thought about it all afternoon. I'm positive he didn't suspect anything. And then we both agreed that if he didn't know, it was, in a funny way, good. He didn't need another problem. And I think the ones he had were larger than adultery. That he could have handled. But not on top of everything else. She agreed. Joyce is shrewd."

"You bet."

"No, I don't mean it that way."

"Of course you don't. You're accommodating. Even though David is your best friend, you can still accommodate this bitch who messed up his life."

"His life was messed up already. Come off it."

"You're very pliable. Just tell you that this person is a friend, whether or not that's true, and you immediately find no fault."

They were at the corner of Fifty-seventh Street and they turned left.

"I realize what she did. I'm saying that it was something that had no bearing on what finally happened. It's unfair to make believe it did."

"Old teleological Stuart."

"But it's true."

"I would have spit in her face."

"I know you would," he said. "Because you don't know how to deal with people. You only know how to take worthless courses, work in some dumb precious job, and worry about yourself."

"I worry about you, too. You need it more than I do." Marilyn ran a few steps so that she was nearly ten feet in front of him, then walked hurriedly. He let her keep the carefully controlled distance until they passed Carnegie Hall. There he took his hands out of his pockets and jumped ahead, catching her in a few long lopes.

"You haven't been worrying about me for two blocks," he said, trying to get a hand on her arm, which she continually shrugged off.

"It's a finite essence. I wouldn't want to use it up on a dope."

Stuart put his hand into the breast pocket of his suit jacket. "I always carry around a small aerosol spray of it with me. Want to squirt me in the face?"

At the corner, stopped by a light, she hit once at his arm.

"Before you get joky, I just want to say something. I want to tell you what I worry about with you."

"Roll it."

"I worry about how you use your moments of recognition."

"Which means?"

"Which means that when you learn something, like today, something really important, having to do with the things you care for most, I worry about how you postpone analyzing it, waiting to see what it means. You may not know this, but I figure out my life constantly." She looked at him; he was staring up at the traffic light. "I know you want to ask whether I get any answers. I don't, but at least I respect the questions. You hide in your friends."

"They're a kind of answer."

"What about their questions?"

There was no desire in her for a response; he was kind or bored enough not to offer one. By the time they got to Columbus Circle and on the subway, the simple application of her voice, cold and dull as it had been in the late night streets, had been enough to reactivate the part of her that had a say, that had some mastery over the unreal wrench that had pulled the world out from under her down in the stockroom. She took Stuart's hand, which he gave easily.

At home, in bed—Stuart in the candy-stripe nightshirt Serena had presented him for Christmas, Marilyn wearing her slip—they played gin. Their different working hours had at first given them some problem: she couldn't get to sleep immediately on returning home; he found himself groggy and irritable about eleven the next morning if he stayed up with her. But since Marilyn had enrolled in the Decadent European Literature course at N.Y.U., which met in the morning, they woke up together, or close to it, and they both had figured out parts of the day in which to rest and revive. At about three-thirty in the afternoon, before layouts had to be photostated, he found that he could just sit at his desk and rest with no one bothering him for at least an hour. And Marilyn would put her head down about noon in the N.Y.U. library, or, in the summer, just sit for an hour with a Good Humor in Washington Square Park. Her father's checks had lately increased in size: he had got an after-school job in a community center in Morristown. Yet, despite their having more money to go out with, fatigue and habit were the tyrants they both easily submitted to.

Marilyn looked up at him after staring at her first dealt hand, dismayed.

"Trouble, huh?" Stuart nickered. "Doesn't matter. You can't beat the shark here." He had destroyed her quickly the last six nights they played. The problem with her playing was, he had lectured, that she didn't pay attention to the situations that come up; she was constantly giving up the card that gave him gin. Offense *and* defense, he had insisted.

"I spoke to Serena today on the phone," she said, snapping the waist band of her slip, which was crumpled into her skin.

"So did I."

"I can never give you any news! You're the one who's always telling me who you had lunch with, or who you met in the street. And when I get a call, you get one too. It's unfair." But she didn't really care.

"Did she tell you about that conference in Akron she may have to go to?"

"She invited me along—that's if she goes. It's on a weekend. I wouldn't have to miss classes, and I'd just take Saturday off from work."

Stuart gave her a long-cast eye. "But she's getting paid to endure that."

"Well, I never use my money. It would be fun: a plane trip, a hotel."

"Are you going to play with eleven cards? Drop already."

Marilyn held mostly a variety of low cards; she let go of a nine of clubs.

"See," Stuart said, diving for the card, "you don't watch. You should have *seen* I was picking up high clubs."

"But what do I do? I sit here and play cards with you. It might be fun. It would be a change. Maybe I'd even come back knowing how to play cards."

"You're going to learn in Akron? What kind of conference is it, Gamblers Anonymous?"

"I bet you almost have gin."

"You don't want to play any more."

"We'll finish out the game. I don't like to deprive you of the chance to humiliate me." But she felt too mealy, and put down her cards. "No, I don't want to play any more."

"You had a bad night tonight. I know it, it's the way you are."

Marilyn slammed her fist down on the mattress to reclaim Stuart's attention from shuffling and squaring the cards into a deck. "I had a *good* night."

"I don't believe you, but all right."

"Nothing I do you believe. My job, my friends, my money."

"What's all this?"

She got off the bed to go into the bathroom and shower. Pulling down her slip, she threw it behind her, hoping to hit him with it.

"I'll sleep on the couch tonight," he called to her. "That's what they say on television." He was confused again; her moods and moments had been isinglass since he picked her up; just as he held one and began to believe it transparent and understandable, it broke in two, changing.

"No. I want to make love." She was yelling from the hallway leading to the bathroom. Her scary primness, the definite sentences as if sheared from a ritual stone. Once she had said, "You're not going to leave this house," standing in the kitchen in the morning as he was getting ready to go to work. She had grabbed a steak knife, pointed it at him, and then put it to her own navel, point touching flesh, as she inhaled and exhaled luridly. Ever since that morning, he had paid attention, a bemused, quizzical attention, to the phrase "war between the sexes." Perhaps. But certainly there were none of the classic lines: no blood antagonism, no cunning strategy, not even the baleful victory or clattering defeat. Any fool could wiggle behind his lines and slam him—it was one of the things he liked about himself. Where on the field, though, was Marilyn? And how to attack her, less to destroy than rescue? He switched on the last few minutes of the Tonight Show, lying there and anticipating her return. "Wheee!" a girl singer on the show yelped, finishing off her account of a marvelous stint in Vegas. Stuart, the discombobulated soldier, found this strangely touching. No fright, no love—just "Wheee!"

DAVID HAD SHAVED BEFORE HE WENT TO BED; NOW he just had to put on his clothes and brush his teeth, then walk downstairs in the empty house—George had gone to Amherst with two students to hear Marcuse lecture, Sam taught his Visionary Painting course on Saturday mornings —which was neat and dustless from the cleaning he had given it using the school's borrowed vacuum cleaner. He had a glass of cranberry juice and would wait to have coffee in town. A partly opened window in the kitchen was bringing in the weather: a bird's-nest chill, delicate, strong, and somehow complicated. The smoky breaths he issued as he stuck his head out the window backfired vigor as they swirled in the stiff sunlight. He took his pile-lined coat from the closet and was reaching for his cap when he decided to go bareheaded; he'd introduce her to the change in himself gradually. The snow that had fallen during the night had dropped enough to pillow up against the back fender of George's car in a vampish slope that David put his gloves on to clear by hand. One of the students accompanying George to Amherst had taken him in her station wagon, so David had the use of the car for the weekend. The crack and cough of the engine when he floored, a sound he thought could never be more dramatic than it was here in Vermont—a dry, thinning rack breaking over the early morning fresh air—sung out the first announcement of the weekend, which, if it stayed as it was now, would be beautiful. When the motor was caught and humming, David got out to scrape some of the thin ice down off the back window. That done, he got back in, maneuvered through the drifts that had piled almost regularly around the front of the house, and came out onto the road, cleared by the county snow-removal equipment just hours before, by the fresh look of the Cat tracks grooving the sides of the road.

It was early enough not to have to pick up students hitch-hiking into town when he passed the school. He wanted this ride all to himself, the excitement he felt snapping at his wrists and neck too pure and distinct to be tamped by idle talk. The ice-cream foothills out and up from the smooth fields, once he was on the main highway, sparkled with last sleepiness, the torn blue air light and goading at their outlines. David opened his window. George had warned about accelerating over sixty—and that's if you were lucky—so he drove at forty, with no cars to pass and plenty of time before the bus came in. Two roan colts stood in the midst of a whitened pasture as if dropped there, bending their necks for anything they could find. David put an instinctive hand to the radio before remembering that it, like a half-dozen other laughingly termed "optionals," didn't work, including things not so optional, like windshield wipers. He pressed in the lighter just for fun, and in a few seconds, when it popped out, he depressed it once more and dug for his Winstons in his coat pocket. He looked down at his boots: they were weather-worn and the heavy leather laces were already thin. The wide-wale cords he wore, coffee-colored, and the heavy checked winter shirt. The coat, and the rough gloves on his wind-chapped hands. She was in for a surprise, one that must impress her and at the same time move her toward this new, more essential, nearly wiser him. He lit his cigarette and blew smoke out the window.

Though it was only ten when he got to the top of the hill that led down to the village, he could see more than the usual few people on the streets. The A. & P. was open, and already there were a number of husbands hauling boxes of groceries to the backs of their wagons, wives trailing behind, making last checks of the tab tapes they had stuck their hands out for, New England frugal, rather than let the clerks stuff them in among the purchases. Three cars were parked diagonally in front of the drugstore, which served as the bus depot. Two of the cars David recognized as belonging to students from the school, most likely waiting for friends who would spend a spaced-out, drug-hazed weekend with them, tramping through the woods, a soft turned-onness coming to flower as they managed large drifts and natural wonders. Such a group had wandered near the house a few weekends back, a low but growing collective chant of *Om Mani Padme Hum* spiriting out of their mouths.

He pulled into a space on the street. The unconscious smily look that had been on his face since he drank his juice at home brought polite nods and a raised hand from two or three of the townspeople he passed while crossing over to the drugstore. Once inside, he headed for the lunch counter, passing two booths that were occupied by the students whose cars he had recognized outside. Although he had intended to ask the druggist, Charlie, first, David went back to one of the booths and said to a girl sitting over coffee and what was left of a plate of scrambled eggs, "Comes in at ten-fifty-four, right?"

The girl nodded with a nice expression. "Want to sit down?" She patted the empty seat next to her.

"I'm going to have coffee first. Then I'll come over." The day's first lie, and behind it the day's first reason. Despite the fact that when the bus came in they'd all separate to greet their guests, David didn't want even the hint of an earlier contact to be noticeable to Serena. That he was completely alone was a premise of the whole thing; and that was, of course, true. It wasn't going to be modified by a cheerful half-hour with a group of students, who might, though it was far from likely, divert his attention. Besides, five months of actual operation had thrown out the starry-eyed brochure trips about the age similarity between faculty and students functioning as a natural bridge to community. The teachers were the teachers, the students the students, no matter that they both might still have a few pimples dotting their chins.

He drew a *New York Times* out of a pile and swung onto a stool at the half-filled counter, ordering coffee and a toasted corn muffin. A glance at the front page was all he could manage; as he got up and replaced the newspaper on the pile, he felt his nerves strain for the first time all morning.

Sam had been unclear about his plans for the weekend. His course ran till one; he hadn't said specifically what he'd be doing afterward. But he had assured David he wouldn't be back Saturday at all, giving them at least one whole day and night alone. Maybe it was the students sitting in the booths that had set him on edge. Serena might have struck up a conversation—the chances were good on such a long trip—with one of the kids they were waiting for. What would they tell her? Would she step off the bus expecting nothing, or arrive with tales of pot and sex and youth spinning in her mind? He lit a cigarette. He had wanted to make it clear to her early on that he felt estranged from this place, its strident communalism and trust, yet also convey his relief in being out of the city. Henry David Kierkegaard, as George had called him one afternoon.

Charlie, the druggist, came in from the back of the store lugging a carton of Modess. As he passed the lunch counter and the booths, he said with a voice high-wiring it between his native Boston and ten years of acquired Vermont accents, "Roads are clear all the way up. Should be here in ten minutes."

The girl who had invited David to sit with her and her

friends said loudly to one of her group, "Aluminum foil! We're all out!" The group got up, filing out the door after leaving money on the table and, as David watched, crossed the street toward the supermarket. When he looked back, his eyes passing over the remaining students in the other booth, he caught their smiles of understanding, to which he added his own. This precarious insularity that he, too, took for "us-against-them," the instant knowledge of what the aluminum foil would be used for, the presumed mystery it presented to the "straights" in the store. Up here, unlike New York, each instance of this sort of culture-nick grabbed his interest whole. It was the kind of distortion strangers took for solace. One of the remaining students got up and ambled to the mini-jukebox set over the booth that had just been abandoned. "Ruby Tuesday" broke the noise of banging dishes and ringing cash register, filling the store with a rottenly modulated but totally familiar sound. Sonya, Charlie's thirtyish daughter, who manned the counter, came over to take away his corn-muffin plate, mumbling as she did so, "Early in the morning. Early in the morning." She shook her head. David felt a flare of immediate sympathy for her, as he had for even the worst son-of-a-bitch of a cop, holding up and glaring into a car filled with long-hairs from "that college out on Twelve." The idea of residency, again so much unlike the way it was in the city, didn't have to be explained to these people: they *were* the town. And, like sitting ducks, they were there to be set upon by the students; there was no suburb to retreat to. What a traitor he was, laughing at the arcane meaning of the aluminum foil and willing, in the next moment, to share indignation at the loud rock music setting the shakes to the peaceful country store. A real Janus. He heard the door open and turned to see Charlie standing there with watch in hand. The kids at the booth got up to go out and stand on the porch. David dropped thirty-five cents on the counter and went to join them.

To no one in particular, Charlie said, "Good time. Roads must have been a breeze," as the large beige bus moved gigantically down Main, stopping for a light at the corner of Latimer, then making the last slow roll to stop before the depot. The smoke-grey windows didn't allow a clear look in. With some concern, David noticed that the sky had partially clouded. The driver emerged first, followed by a boy with his hair sheafed into a ponytail by a piece of braid, followed by someone's grandmother, who got a helping hand down by the long-haired kid, followed by a sailor who took a look at the hippies standing in wait before him and didn't know what to do with his expression, followed by another kid, this one bearded and carrying a rucksack, followed by—finally—Serena. She waved before coming off the last step. David walked to her.

"Hi!" she said. "I have to wait for the driver to get my stuff out of the compartment." She put her arms around his neck and kissed him on the mouth. Surprised, he returned the kiss with less force than he wished. "You look great!" She now held him traveler-style, with outstretched arms.

"You, too." She wore a crocheted cap that covered her head, excepting two spits of blond curl that fell over her temples. A ski jacket and flared orange pants. On her hands, snowflake mittens.

"Let's get your stuff," he said, taking her arm and walking her around the bus, where the driver had left on the ground the grandmother's suitcase and Serena's two round American Touristers. He picked them both up, but she slipped one out from under his left arm. "The car's across the street. Come."

She gave a little skip as they walked. "When did you get a car?"

"It's not mine. It belongs to one of the guys I share a house with. But we have it—the car *and* the house—all to ourselves this weekend. The other guys split." He took the bag from her. "This." He helped her in, opened the back door and shoved the luggage on the seat, then went around to the driver's side and got in next to her.

When they began to move, he said to her, "I bet you're bushed."

"You're not kidding. I thought I'd sleep, but I sat next to

a girl who got off a few stops before I did, and we were talking—mostly about Cuba. She'd been there. She told me things
I never knew before."

"You can take a nap when we get home. Then I'll make
some lunch and you can rejoin the living."

"Home! Isn't that nice, to say 'home.' It reminds me of
Colorado. Somehow you never say that in New York, and if
you do you don't mean it that particular way."

"I know." They were on the highway now. "It's nice country the bus goes through."

"Beautiful. Look at this!" She pointed at the flat glazed
fields, the farmhouses.

"It really is one of the compensations."

"What's your house like?"

"A rented archetype: stone, roomy, a fireplace. It gives me
guilty little thrills to come home to it. I half expect to see Nat
King Cole roasting chestnuts on an open fire."

"You mean it's sort of like the lower East Side."

"That's right. Just to be comfortable, I converted the out-
house in the back to a *bodega*."

Serena smiled.

"And then I worked out an arrangement with one of the
town good-for-nothings to have him come and rob me every
three months. Of course, then he gives the stuff back. Ole
Vermont verchoo."

"How does the town get along with the college?"

"The newspapers call it an 'uneasy truce.' "

"Newspapers? You get them up here?"

"In a way. A town crier comes every night, gathers a bunch
of people around, and reads the daily happenings off a piece
of elm bark."

"You sound like Stuart."

"How is he?"

"Don't you write?"

"No." He hadn't had the time to think of any other way
to deal with this.

"Marilyn's having trouble. It's very depressing."

"But how is *he?*"

"He's the way he'd be with Marilyn having trouble. He jokes, but nothing's going past him unnoticed."

"The school." David pointed out to the right at a collection of buildings, looking still very new on their dirt plots.

Serena looked closely, then turned back to look ahead, making no comment. "How far away are you?"

"Mile, mile and a half."

"I think I'm going to take a nap when we get there."

"Thata girl."

"Oh, you're right!" Serena cheered, and David's pride perked. "A record player, all these books—great shelves—and the fire . . . I bet you cut your own wood."

"No, we buy it in town. At the A. & P." They laughed together. "True."

He followed her around. "And this is my kind of kitchen," she said; "not too modern. Who cooks?"

"The chef. He's out in the woods with the trained pig upturning the earth looking for truffles."

"No, really. Who?"

"All of us. Most of the time I eat at the school. The food is awful but it's convenient."

"What do your roommates teach?"

"George teaches a course called Reason and Revolution, which is mainly Marcuse. And Sam teaches a lot of different art things, things like pottery and also Conceptualism."

"You?"

"I never told you what I'm teaching?"

"No."

"I teach Transcendental American writers—Emerson, Thoreau, you know."

"One course?"

"It's structured here so that one course is taught each semester for some people, but the course is intensive, meets four

times a week for a half-day, all morning or all afternoon.
You're really able to delve. Now we're reading science fiction
to see what kind of extension that sort of writing would be
from someone like Hawthorne, for instance."

She sat down on one of the steps leading up to the top
floor. "It sounds very dull."

"It is. But it's hip." He smiled at her.

"You look so great!"

"It's really just a groovier survey course," he continued.

"Are you lonely here?" She was taking off her socks, having
left her boots on the rubber mat by the door.

David motioned for her to move over on the step, and sat
next to her. "It's so different from anything I've ever done
before, anywhere I've ever lived—which has just been New
York—that I spend a lot of time noticing the changes. The
loneliness is something I can handle."

"Good for you, liar." She stood up. "Where is your room?"

"There's only a bathroom and my room up there. I'm
counting on you to make the distinction."

"Well, if you find me deep asleep in the toilet bowl, change
your opinion."

"I will. I'm going to make sandwiches. Tuna salad all right?"

She was almost to the landing above him. "Good."

David went to the kitchen, opened the refrigerator, and removed the mayonnaise and celery. He heard the upstairs door
close. He used the whole of a big can of Star-Kist, mixing the
mayo and the chopped celery into an orange plastic bowl that
he had purchased with the weekend food the day before.
Mashing the pink fish through the tines of a fork, he realized
how greatly he had depended on these domestic actions to
dock him against his own churn. If he could make lunch,
supper, set a fire, pour from the bottle of Hennessy he had
splurged on with pleasure, get the car started without much
trouble when they wanted to take a drive, he might also be
able to talk to her. He had already written that he loved her;
the props, smoothly constructed and fluidly used, would now,

he hoped, confirm it. When the salad was well mixed, he covered the bowl and shoved it in the refrigerator, checking the coldness of the beer there by grasping two cans. It was twelve noon.

He heard his door open. "Friend!" she yelled down.

He answered, walking to the foot of the stairs. "Friend?"

"Come up."

"Yessum. I'se a-comin'. I'se a-comin'."

She was under the quilt. The closet door gaped open a little, her bags open flat on a chair. He could see that she had hung some of her clothes on hangers, covering his own. "Hotwater bottle fo' yo' feet, Miss Serena?"

"How long have *you* been up this morning?" She had a flattened-down repose to her that made her look as if she were subsiding from some slight physical shock, like hiccups. For years, David had speculated—once, in who knows what kind of moment, even saying it to Joyce—that Serena would look most beautiful in bed; there was no doubt about it.

"Since eight," he said, moving one of her emptied bags off the chair and sitting down, his hands on his thighs. "You look very beautiful."

"Only morons tell me that."

"I figured. You know, you're really ugly."

"That's better, friend." She extracted a bare arm from beneath the cover to smooth her hair, her shoulder banded with a print bra strap. "Want to nap with me?"

"Sure." He got up from the chair.

She pulled down the quilt to her waist. "See, I'm in my ultra-chic unmentionables." The bra was tiny, lifting her small breasts to two rounded swellings above the V. "How's yours?"

"Not chic, but still unmentionable." He lowered himself to the bed.

"Come on. Show."

David stood up again, unbuttoning his shirt. He was wearing a quilted long-johns top.

"Very New England," she said, sliding toward the wall.

"It gets *cold* up here, what are you talking about?" He dropped his pants. He wore regular jockey shorts.

"How come you don't wear thermal bottoms?"

"I have my love to keep me warm." He got in next to her, slipping his arm beneath her head to cradle it. She moved her neck over the sleeve of the undershirt "Is that uncomfortable?" he asked.

"Not the arm. Just the shirt. Take it off."

He sat up, slipped the shirt over his head, and put it on the chair. When he replaced his arm, she put a hand on his breastbone. "I never had a brother," she said, the lolling arm on his chest an artifact of her relaxation.

"Me either. You had sisters, though."

"Um-hum." That low purr brought his arm down to her shoulders. "Have you ever had anything?"

"I'm not sure," he said. Her comfort was leaving his excitement in limbo. "Go to sleep."

"Right." She sat up, throwing back the cover. She unhooked the clasp of her bra, releasing her breasts, then took a little hop to slip her panties down. She rolled them in a fist and threw them at the chair. Then, in a quick movement, she hooked hands beneath the elastic of his underpants and pulled them free of his emboldening penis. Flinging them away as well, she lay down, slipping the cover to both their necks. "A kiss, huh?" and she nearly tucked her puckered mouth into his slightly yawning one. David skated a hand over her silky-cool rib cage until he came to a breast, chopsticking the hard pebble at the tip. Her mouth opened in his, the tangle acceding to his tongue which searched over the inside of her mouth, parry and thrust, touching her teeth. David felt her hand drawing at him. She moved her mouth away to kiss his neck. For a second, hand still exciting him—his own now down to her groin, paffling it with quick and tender touches—she stopped kissing and said, "I love you, too. I couldn't have written a letter like that. This is a good thing for me."

All he could say was "Yes," and then force the quilt up with an elbow so that he could slide to her. When they were in position, he threw the quilt back completely, looked down at his own hard curls hooking with her lamby ones, and put a hand on her thighs, moving them so he could better enter. The two diminutive "Davy"'s she oozed out pushed novelty— a more down-to-earth, less brittle one—in with him, and when first locked, double body-lava, he felt her heat and swelling muscles as a great home. They fucked with a greed that made David aware of his clenching sighs once or twice ready to give way to laughter so spooky that he had to control himself, moving that feather in his head away by grabbing her force-fully, often lifting her hips straight off the bed, popping the ounce of stickum that had rapidly formed between their bodies.

"Please, please, *please!*" And then her penultimate yows began, creased at first but growing in full sex to the point in which they soldered the air around them both with a mantling sleeve that harkened a burst. Her "David!" pried open the lighted end, and when he shot through himself to her he was left with a reward so little earned that he wished to repeat immediately. He timed her release by the gradual relaxation of her hands on his buttocks.

They dried themselves with the quilt. Without dressing, David ran downstairs and returned with his cigarettes. Serena had removed the cover and lay, legs spread, to let the air cool her body. The sun, which had re-emerged strong from the momentary cloudiness he noticed in town, slapped a large gild-ing splotch over the lemon down of her arms and neck. Serena motioned him to her and dried his back once more. The quiet, unbroken by words, reminded David of Saturday mornings when he was a child, a cataract of rushing pure light and tangled silence sidestepped to go out and play baseball. Then, for a moment, he also thought that it was never like this with Joyce, but knew immediately that that was not true. He stood up and dressed quickly. "Lunch," he said to her.

"Lunch," she echoed. As she sat up to receive the clothes

David handed her, her face appeared to clothe as well, expression starting to drape onto her heretofore blankly contented features. After she hooked on her bra, she took a step to him and put her head down on his shoulder. "Nice nap," she murmured. He gave her a quick kiss and left the room.

The sandwiches were on the table when she came down, along with two cans of perfectly cold Narragansett. "I didn't have breakfast," she said, taking two of the sandwiches and pulling the ring on the top of the beer can.

"You're starved, then."

"I spent the trip thinking."

"Buses are conducive."

"Of course you know what I thought about."

He nodded, taking a small gulp of beer.

"Your letter was so good, so complete. Even when I called you to tell you I was coming, there was nothing really to say. So what I thought about was when."

"And when did you think?" David asked, eating slowly, afraid to miss anything she said.

"I thought maybe tonight, after we had spent the day together, after we had talked. But now I realize we didn't have to talk and say a lot of things. The letter said everything. Even though it was you writing, it was me there, too. The act of writing just brought out what was there already." She began to eat her sandwich with true hunger. "You know . . . wait." She swallowed what she was chewing. "All through school, and the two colleges, I was always afraid that the rapport I naturally felt was only because the institution bound everyone together. And if that was the case, then it was basically artificial. But now that we've all been out a few years, I realize that the structure had more of a say than I thought, that we're genuinely close. You see, maybe it's that we've all been freed, with everything and nothing before us, so we just have to shine as ourselves. That self-assertion lets me know you better than I ever could as just a member of a group of friends."

"I never saw it as a group," David said.

"What, then?"

"I saw people who saw me. After a while, you develop a vantage point. But then we all quickly shifted."

"But we remain close."

"Except that I don't see them whole any more. I see how far they've moved, or not moved." David got up and took another beer from the refrigerator. "You?"

"I'm still working on this one," she replied. "But you still care; otherwise you wouldn't have written me."

"I wrote to you . . . It's difficult. I think I wrote to you because the picture that I was looking at had me in a corner, and you too. It's like Dutch painting. It used to be that we were all sitters for a big group portrait. Now we're those little specks of people up on the hill in a Breughel, trying to get closer, trying to get bigger."

"What's in the middle?"

"No one."

"But you just said there was once a big group portrait."

He smiled. "It never got painted."

"I'm not sure, David." She had finished her second sandwich. "We're all still around."

"Look at you—you must have been really starved. Take another."

"No. I'll eat too much and you won't be able to fit into bed next to me."

David picked up the dishes and glasses from the table and put them in the sink. "A drive?"

"Let's walk. But first sit awhile so I can let all the food I pigged myself on go down."

"Down where?"

"Key West."

He laughed and took her hand. "How do you do."

"Hello. Fine." She got up and went to turn on the water at the sink, to rinse the dishes. "Do you hear from Joyce?"

"Two cards. She's living with her boss, Don. The agency may move to Los Angeles."

"What about a divorce?"

"We'll see. Don't wash the—"

"Shh. I'm finished already."

After they had thrown each other in the biggest drift in front of the house a few times, David suggested that they forget about the walk and maybe go to his room and . . . Serena answered that she hadn't taken a five-hour bus ride just to lie in bed a whole weekend; she could do that in New York —and David heard the substantial proportion of seriousness in her voice as she said it. They could, he said, ride to one of his friends, and borrow the guy's snowshoes. But she liked the idea of taking their chances, and they started toward the woods, David chasing her, their steps clumsy and diverse as they pushed at the tricky depths of snow up to their knees.

"When does it finally all melt?" she yelled back at him.

"In about three minutes. You better have your scuba equipment." She turned and flung a large white clod that landed a yard in front of him. He caught up to her. "Why does this turn you on? You've seen enough snow in Colorado."

"That's why. Colorado." Her nose was running and she wiped at it with her mitten. "I'm home."

"Look what I have." He removed from his coat pocket an olive jar he had filled with Cognac for the lack of anything resembling a flask. She gave a mocking razz at the sight of it. "Laughing, huh?" he said. "Never tasted 'colossal-size' Cognac before? You're in for a treat." He unscrewed the lid and took a swig, then passed it to her. As she raised the jar and let a little of the brandy trickle down her throat, he said, "Watch out for the pits," and she sprayed out the unswallowed sip, staining the snow yellow.

"You bastard. Not while I'm drinking."

"I'm sorry. I thought I saw a budding alcoholic for a moment."

Serena tipped the whole jar empty. "Better safe than sorry." She pitched it into the trees.

"Look," he said to her, "I don't mind you wasting my Cognac—there's more at home—but that was my favorite olive jar."

"Family heirloom, huh?"

Somehow this poleaxed him. He had got used to the word "home," to talking about Joyce and the breakup, to thinking about the apartment on Cabrini Boulevard; but "family" meant that Carolina morning, those lumpy, still faces. Her joke was innocuous, but still a bull's-eye; it scraped away any easy comeback and left him silent. He couldn't be sure if she understood or not, but she quickly walked away. After a few seconds, she turned and waved him forward.

He tried to think of a funny thing to say, something to allay her embarrassment, which he feared and loathed much more than he did his own frozen reaction. He scooped up snow, balled it, and threw, hitting her between the wings of her back.

Serena turned. "I'm sorry."

Panicky, he blurted, "Aren't you going to defend yourself?"

"I'm sorry about that," she repeated. She stood still for him to catch up. As he came close, she smiled. "Did you ever make love in the snow?"

"With whom?"

"I don't know, with one of the girls here."

"I haven't made love with anyone since Joyce. Since you, I mean."

She blew air out. "I thought you forgot for a second. I was very flattered."

"Why, do you want to?"

"I don't think so. I hate a cold ass."

As David was skewering the tiny tomatoes, the green peppers, and the onions between the cubes of lamb, Serena stood at the doorway of the kitchen, watching him with a shaky grin on her face, partly the product of three Scotch highballs and partly a thought that had trailed off from the sleepy conversation they had shared in the living room with their drinks. "So O.K. There are philosophical anarchists and real ones. Well, you're a philosophical pessimist, but not a real one. Otherwise, if you truly had no hope, you wouldn't have marinated the meat."

He turned away from the table and smiled obliquely at her.

Serena stood where she was. All through the afternoon, their smiles had exerted a drawing power over both of them, steps taken to approach each other more closely at even the hint of a mouth dishing upward. "See, you admit it."

"I admit to nothing. This is going to be a classic shish kebab, and I would have had it even if you didn't make it up."

"I'm sure. This is good Scotch."

"You said that already."

She walked to the table and sat herself down. "I've said everything already. That doesn't mean anything. Could you get me another drink?"

He finished a skewer before answering her. "I have two things to say." The liquor had raised a siltlike cloudiness to his speech, and he talked slowly, savoring the husky individuality of each word. "First, deep down, you're patrician. A little service, and you think you're Madame Récamier."

"*Who?*"

"And second, what would the little girls who read your column and what you say about cosmetics and popularity— what would they think if they saw you now? Swilling debbil rum and loving it. I'll tell you. They'd think you were a fallen woman. A fallen woman. That's right."

"I wonder what they think anyway," Serena answered, tapping her fingers flat against the Formica table.

"What's your name again?"

"Jane Taylor. Teen Correspondent."

David started out of the room to get her drink. "I always mean to pick up a copy of the magazine. But I forget." He went into the living room and poured them both some more Scotch over the failing ice in their glasses. He brought the drinks back to the kitchen. "Madame."

"Thanks." She took a long sip, then perched her chin on her knuckles. She looked at him with a wavering intensity. "You know, I'm drunk."

David was down on his haunches to the broiler of the stove, turning the skewers. "It's because you haven't had much to eat today." He basted the skewers with a soup spoon filled with marinade. "But at least I know you're hungry."

"Everyone's hungry. The whole world is hungry. No one gets enough of anything." She stood up. "And I'm going to wash my face and brush my teeth." She left the room, walking heavily on her heels. David looked over his shoulder to watch her go.

He set the table, taking her highball and putting it on top of the refrigerator. He wondered whether or not to serve the wine, seeing what kind of shape she was in already from the cocktails. Apart from his own speech clumsiness—which he appreciated; it gave him time to tend to the cooking of the meal while not talking too much—he thought he was perfectly sober.

A run of doughy sobs issued from the bathroom upstairs, and David mounted the stairs slowly, thinking that she was vomiting. The door was open a bit, but before going in he asked, "You all right?" The sobbing got louder. He pushed open the door. Serena stood by the washbowl, toothbrush in hand, staring down at the enamel basin, tears all over her face, yet without the constricted flush of someone being sick. She didn't turn around as he entered. Her blond hair had been slipped from its bun by the despairing hands she ran through it. "What's the matter?"

"It's so *sad*," she moaned, still not looking up from the bowl.

"What?"

"It's sad. It's the saddest thing. Oh."

David put an arm around her.

"See?" She pointed down at the froth of Ipana swirling, water-dispersed, around the drain. "See how sad it is? It's all going *away!* Down. Down. Down." Her voice was cracking back into that of her childhood. Slivers of his amusement converged in David's throat into a laugh.

"Don't laugh!" she insisted, pulling her shoulder from under his arm, her voice still that of a five-year-old. "It's so sad."

David sat down on the lid of the toilet.

"It's the very saddest thing in the whole world," she said.

"You yourself are running a close second. Come on downstairs." He stood up. "Here," he said, taking some water in his hand, "wash your face." He wiped her pretty, stricken features with his wet hand, grabbing a towel with his free one to dry her off. Then he gave her a kiss, the taste of tears and toothpaste coming strong off her lips.

"You're very sturdy," she said to David as they were going down the steps. "Maybe you're too sturdy. You can't see how sad everything is."

Serena refused the idea of wine, so David didn't bother opening the bottle, contenting himself with a can of beer, just ice water for her. They ate in a foggy but enjoyed silence, commenting only on how well the shish kebab and rice had turned out.

After supper, she wanted only to sit in front of the fire. David had a Cognac, his arms beginning to melt. The silence was contained and kind to them. Twenty minutes of being bespelled by the embers and the flames, and she got up to walk, browsing at the shelves of books until she came to George's records and found a complete set of Starker playing the Bach Suites. She put it on.

It was clear from her stillness, legs tucked under her, arms hung over the arm of the couch, that the music was not blending into her but rather drawing from a fund of familiarity that cast her into shape, the shape of her music, her life. But the rich and dark virtuosity, the growling warmth of the cello played out in extraordinary confidence—we will return, the music seemed to say—snagged the peace for David. It was another perfect element, but it was the *too* perfect element, the one that brought the sticks down chattering, the straw and the camel's back a stew. He shifted and struggled with his body.

They listened to two sides and she was up to put on another when the night blasted apart outside, an evil booming followed by sharp reports scuttled in the trees. She paused and listened. There was another boom, something like heavy artillery fire, and then another, each followed by the brittle raucousness of the air recoiling in the thick forest.

"What?" she asked, putting down the record.

David opened the door and looked up into the slate sky. There was another muffled explosion and its attendant roar in the trees, and then, above the birches to the right of the house, he saw a quick light fly up, then burst into metallic needles of green. A brilliant weeping willow of tinsel that dropped, and dropping blew red and orange until it hung in the blackness like a sea anemone. He turned and yelled in to her, "Get my coat. Get yours."

Serena came trotting out and handed him his coat. "Watch up there," he pointed, as this time the gob of prickling light dismantled into long blue shoots, stripped off a paler middle like corn silk.

"What is it?"

"What it looks like. Fireworks."

"Who? Where?"

"I don't know." Two muffles and two fast points were lifted, these really spectacular, pushing forward, two twin bursting nebulae like the formation of the universe, rising in colorful abandon until they meshed and turned orange. "Wait, I know. I saw signs in the supermarket. There's a country club near here that borders on the school. It's their winter carnival."

"It's freezing out here," Serena said, grabbing his elbow with both her hands. "Look at that one!" This came up already full, a huge gout of white and purple rim. As it burned, each fleck seemed to shuffle back into the dark, into a farther, hidden night, one never to be seen. With each explosion, the trees held the shock.

Serena turned away from the display and walked to the other side of the house, near where the car was parked. She yelled, "IT'S TERRIFYING!" and flapped her arms.

"IT'S GREAT!" David responded. Their yawps added to the riot of color and sound.

The last rocket was bursting, a giant badge of blue. The launching stopped and only their mirth remained. Serena began to yell, stopped, then let out:

"MERRY WINTER. AND HO, HO, HO."

"THE POOR FOREST" was David's last shriek. Serena's laughter was clear and chilly; he saw her picking up snow and ran behind the door. The missile hit the side of the house.

She came inside, knocking snow off her boots. "Did you plan this?"

"What's a visit without fireworks?"

"It's too bad we didn't go to the carnival. No, this was better. The surprise. I'm completely sober now."

"I'll tell you a secret," he said, leading her to the couch. "It wasn't really a carnival. It's just this very strange thing that happens up here when you put Bach on the stereo. You should see how the heavens light up when you try the B-Minor Mass."

In bed, they exchanged verbal doodles. He told her about the fabled Giants team of his youth: "Young" Goodman Brown on first; "Doc" Rappaccini playing short; Ethan Brand —"a real phenom; went to his right beautifully"—at third; "Dimmes" Dale in left; Willie Mays where else but in center; Roger Chillingworth in right; Johnny Calvin calling the signals behind the plate; and Nat Hawthorne throwing heat from the mound.

He was falling asleep as she was saying, ". . . the way some ballet students lose their hymen on the first full split, so the cello student has to be very careful about setting the spike on the floor . . . a girl who wasn't . . . baby named Strad . . . perils of the pizzicato . . ."

. . .

They awoke early, caught in the extra quilt and pajamas they covered themselves with in the middle of the night when the room had grown chillier than it had been when they fell asleep. David was anxious to try out the waffle iron he had bought especially for her visit. Breakfast, Serena declared, getting into her clothes, was going to be her responsibility. They were in the kitchen, she mixing the batter, he splitting the cellophane of the bacon package with a knife, when Sam came in with a girl, a student David had seen him with before. She introduced herself with a smile as Lisa. They had eaten in town, Sam said, but would have coffee with them. Serena made more batter and put the whole package of bacon in the pan, and when the food was ready they all ate anyway.

"Catch the fireworks?" Sam asked both of them.

"You'd have to have been dead not to," Serena said.

"We were really close to it," said Lisa. "On campus. We were doing snow sculpture."

"Which all turned out very phallic," Sam added, looking tired.

Lisa yipped. "And we were so stoned! You have no idea what it did to us." She turned impishly to look at Sam. "We were having a good time when it started."

"What, the snow looking phallic or the fireworks?" Serena asked. Her eyes told David how little she appreciated the interrupting visit.

"The fireworks of course. Snow doesn't make me horny."

Sam put down his cup and, grinning, pointed to David. "Try him sometime. He's even colder. The Abominable Snowman. Not only is it hard to get him interested, you have to thaw him out first." David gave an agreeable snort to all this ingrown banter.

Serena paid attention to her plate, her hand fidgeting with her knife, rolling it in circles in the maple syrup. Finally she looked up at Sam and said shortly, "How do *you* know?" She paused, anger gelid in her stare. "Are you some sort of fag?"

David was ready to intervene when Lisa said delightedly,

"What a gas!" She looked at Sam. "*Are* you? That's too much."

Sam said, "Serena seems to think so. It's Serena, right?"

Serena nodded, her chin coming down sharply enough to cut stone.

"What did you do yesterday?" David took the opportunity of the pause to ask Sam something unrelated to the decaying conversation.

"I taught the class. Then Lisa and I drove up to Carrie's and we spent the afternoon there. Then we did the sculpture at night. I stayed with her in the dorm."

David looked down at his plate, saying to Serena without looking at her, "I guess that settles the fag question."

But before Serena answered, which from her furious concentration on the bacon it seemed she was not going to do, Lisa said, "That doesn't mean anything. Fags can make it with chicks."

David responded, "Let's forget all this fag stuff."

"But *I* didn't bring it up. Your girl friend did."

Serena flashed at her, "I'm not his girl friend!"

"Oh, are you a dyke?"

"All right, enough," Sam shoved in.

Lisa turned to him, sopping with the neutral expression that David, though accustomed to its infinite use by people at the college, now felt himself murderously hating. "There's nothing wrong—you're all hung up on sex distinctions—there's nothing wrong with being a dyke."

Serena looked up at Lisa. "Look, sweetie"—which sent a voltage through David that nearly made him jump—"why don't you go fuck yourself, since you're so wrapped up in that?"

Sam stood up. "We're going into town. Need anything?"

David shook his head, catching a look at Serena's fastening beam on Lisa. He stood and began to gather plates, feeling pressed and giddy, a feeling unusual so early in the morning.

As Lisa was walking out of the kitchen, she said to him, "See you, David." She turned back to Serena. "Bye."

David's back was to her. Serena might have answered the goodbye with a wave which he couldn't see, but he didn't hear her say a thing. The front door opened and closed. He began to run the water. "Sam's taste in women leaves something to be desired. Just some dumb little girl." He spoke quickly. "You handled it right. I wouldn't let it get you upset. She was trying to be 'with it.'" Shaken by her bitchy retort to Lisa—justified as it was—he was trying to say all that she might say before she could herself.

"Well, it upset *you*," Serena finally said.

He reached for the dish towel. "No, no. I'm used to it. Everything is supposed to be very casual here. A lot of bad manners get out easily."

"She was a little prick."

Her anger—very much like Joyce's. Worse—very much like his mother's on the phone that terrible time. His thoughts began to fiddle: go away, go. He put down the towel after wiping his face with it. "To change the subject. When is your bus?"

She sat very quietly. "Are you trying to get rid of me?"

"For Christ's sake!"

"I'm sorry. Four-fifteen." She got up to view the clock. "But it's only nine-thirty. Let's take a drive. Can you get a *Times* up here?"

"That's an idea."

He helped her into her coat. She put her hand in his as they walked to the car. "I lied to that girl," she said, looking ahead. "I can say I'm your girl friend."

"Damn straight," David said, although he was almost sure he was lying.

They drove around the better part of the morning, the Sunday *Times* untouched on the back seat. At about twelve, they pulled into a Holiday Inn and had hamburgers in the restaurant.

He promised to write Stuart.

Serena began to worry about the time. Driving back, David took a small road that seemed to lead nowhere.

"Where does this go?" she asked. She had never completely recovered from the kitchen scene in the morning, and her whole manner retained a brittleness that had begun to excite him over lunch.

David pulled into a small clearing in the woods, the closest thing around them a deserted barn fifty yards behind. "I want to have time for a last talk. Let's go in the back seat."

She flung the paper up to the front. As she was pulling her slacks down, she asked, "This is a Volvo, right?" David nodded, preoccupied with his own partial undressing in the cramped space.

"Does Consumers' Union rate cars for this. Back-seat length?"

He put a hand gently on her mound. "No. Why don't you do something like that in your column? Girls would be interested."

They went slowly. The job now was to release each other from a grip of tense misgivings, and when their muscles obliged, David let his own moans, unusual for him, mix with hers.

Neither of them had a desire to rest in each other's arms afterward, so they dressed and drove. She smoked four of his cigarettes before they reached the house.

"Did this go O.K. for you?" David asked her as they sat in a booth in the drugstore. Charlie had told them that snow had started upstate, but that if it wasn't really coming down heavy the chances were that the bus would stay ahead of the storm all the way down to New York.

"You know it did." She was turning over in her hands the paperback Simenon she had bought for the trip back.

"Now I'll have to take all this wilderness alone."

"You've managed up till now. I have faith in you."

The drugstore was empty but for them. The kids who had

come up on the bus with her had probably either secured rides back or decided to stay an extra day. "I love you," he said. "It's very important for me to know you know that."

"I never told you this," she said, "but when you got married I was really miserable. I didn't know you very well, but I was immediately attracted. Once you were with Joyce, of course, there was nothing else to be but a friend."

"You could have stolen me."

"No. Absolutely not. Everyone was too close."

David saw the bus. "Well, here we go."

Serena looked around, then stood up, going for her bags. They walked out into the cold afternoon, the sun only freckling the Sunday-empty streets. After she had given her bags to the driver to stow in the baggage area, she walked to the door of the bus with David. "You're going to write me, right?"

He gave a small laugh. "Probably tonight."

"And you're going to come down in a few weeks and stay with me."

"Right."

They kissed. When she was up the steps, she turned back. "And remember, write Stuart."

David nodded. He was happy that she hadn't thanked him for the weekend.

As he drove back, he had the strange but settling thought that she was basically very religious. He probably loved someone like that.

Dear Ichabod,

Well, what happened, the hoarfrost begin to melt up there? Nine months! Why should I answer the questions of some yussel who goes north to ice his rocks? I think I'll just throw some of my own questions, lamentably home grown, like:

Name me the ribby champ in the National League, circa 1954, and how many?

Who hit four homers in a game on June 10, 1959? What innings?

How come you're so good to your friends?

Let's have the N.B.A. all-pro team for 1960.

Who was the poor schmuck Joe Louis got a shot at on March 29, 1940? How long did it take for the guy to become pea soup?

Judge Himes, Elwood, Agile, Sir Huron, Pink Star, Stone Street, Wintergreen, Donau, Meridian, Worth, Donerail, Old Rosebud, Regret, George Smith, Omar Khayyam, Exterminator, Sir Barton, Paul Jones, Behave Yourself, Morvich, Zev, Black

Gold, Flying Ebony, Bubbling Over, Whiskery, Reigh Count, Clyde Van Dusen, Gallant Fox, Twenty Grand, Burgoo King: Derby winners or rock groups?

Give the years of ascendancy for the following "Flinch" champions: Jamie "the Geek" Gordon; Billy "I Gotta Go to Hebrew, I'll Play Later" Sandowitz; Serena "Don't Fence Me In" Carlyle; Stuart "The Hindu Champ of Foster Avenue" Lapin; David "It's Too Cold to Remember Anything" Abrams.*

Get five out of seven and judge yourself "amenable." Any less or any more than five, consider yourself far from or too close to cure.

Getting laid a lot up there? How about sports? The college got a "Four Horsemen" backfield yet? "Macro" Biotics still the coach?

Enough.

I'm having a tough time with this. I was just getting angry with you for not sending word of your gambols when you did. Please, none of these surprises.

Not much is new. Whatever is you probably know already from Serena. As a matter of fact her hick concern is stamped all over the tone of your questions about Marilyn. Sure Marilyn's a wreck, but when hasn't she been? We get on—sort of like the Andrea Doria *and the great god Neptune. Yes, I know and understand that you worry about us all, even when there's nothing to worry about. Get with it, kid! Hasn't that hip school taught you nothin'? You're a generational card carrier— you're supposed to flee responsibility as fast as you would a rhumba. I'm not only joking now. You put your greedy little guilt right in the middle of the arena before you even know whether you're going to face the lady or the tiger. You end up precipitating (high-school chem word) your own chaos, klutz.*

When catastrophe strikes, I'll be sure to call you and Allstate, in that order.

Listen, I'm sorry. This is a snotty, stupid letter. I'm counting on you to ignore it on the strength of the cross you really do bear: the long time you know me. I'll write again in a few days when I can be more human.

* Answers:
Ted the Klu—141.

Serena tells Marilyn that you've been dangling before our very large noses the prospect of a visit by you to our homey little metropolis. In case you forget how to get around here in the the Apple, just remember this: keep the West Side Highway to your left walking uptown.
O.K.

Stuie

Colavito with Cleveland. In the third, the fifth, the sixth, and the ninth.

Because you're still a good little vontz, even if you have learned how to eat store cheese and drink hard cider.

Pettit, St. Louis; Baylor, Minnesota; Chamberlain, Philly; Cousy, Boston; Shue, Detroit.

Johnny Paychek. K.O.'d in two, right here in the city.

Horses. Each now has the honor of being the name of a high-grade marijuana.

1964; 1956; 1965; eternal; who knows?

B IG-DEAL UNIVERSE.

She had a mother. A divorcee, a haberdasher. About now she'd be decorating her windows. One for traditional grey and tan: suits and sports jackets, poplins, lightweight cottons. One for sports clothes: greens, blues, whites. The small window on the side street for ties and underwear and robes. A mother who touted men's fashions to her daughter like fillies: "I give Continental a year, if that; Ivy League, something on that order, modified, I can see coming back and staying." "Men don't want to look like sailors. I carry some flares, but I refuse to junk my whole slacks stock for something that'll be gone in six months." A mother who was constantly out for the "angles"; lately also, Betty told her, active in the local Democratic Club.

A father, fifty-six years old with a new girl friend. With also a little more money now: nine-to-three math teacher, three-thirty-to-five playground counselor, summer camp director. Maybe he'd use his extra money to leave the dump he lived in. Surrounded by spanking-new suburbia, and he in what was actually nothing more than a shanty; not even one of those old, solid, haughty houses. A piebald scratch of lawn, uneven walls papered ludicrously, a broken-up driveway for a Plymouth, asthmatic and shot. The only regular improvement was a woman, a new girl friend. Fifty-six years old. A new Cheryl, a Martha, a Pauline, a Suki, a . . . a Joanne. "Oh, Phil, she's *dear*, looks just like you!" as he painted squares of epoxy on the bathroom wall to anchor his gift of a towel rack. "We all have to get together," Joanne would effervesce, not venturing far from the bathroom door near where Phil toiled. "This is a wonderful apartment. Something to really get your hands on and work with." But goodbye, Joanne. The next visit, at the next apartment, would be with Martha, or Suki, or Cheryl. "This is a wonderful apartment!" And another towel rack. Fifty-six years old.

Flee. Flee . . . on the milk-white steed.

The essence of comedy is surprise. She didn't recall: either Bergson said that or maybe a comedian getting serious on a talk show. So it would be comedy if her mother rang up in two minutes from now and said: "Baby? I have good news. Daddy and I have talked. It took us twenty years, but we finally did. We figured it out. We realized that we had become, in those years, bitter people. Once you're that, it's no easy thing to change. The bitterness grows and grows, and you get harder, and your attitudes, too. All that actually happened was that, when you were a baby, your father and I wanted different things out of a family. What we seemed to have forgotten was that most of all we wanted a family first. We forgot that, and we destroyed the family. The baby with the bath water. But, as I say, we've talked now. We're older—you, too. It'll be different, it'll be better, a family. Daddy's moving back into the apartment in a few weeks. We'll get married again; oh, my sweet baby, do you realize you'll be a witness to your mother and father's wedding? Let your friends top *that*. And your room I'm decorating so that it will be comfortable for

you. We'll have a new car, trips to the Bronx Zoo, those real
old times. Betty tells me you have a boyfriend, which is wonderful. You'll see him a lot; he'll go places with us all. I have
the Castro in the living room where he could sleep if sometimes he stays over . . ."

". . . *and Lord Arlen's wife lies in his arms asleep* . . ."

It would be, then, comedy. Stuart would be especially well
attuned, and if there was any hesitation on her part, he could
be counted on to start: a smile, a grin, a giggle, a laugh, a
veritable thunderclap of hilarity. Come along with me down
this perfectly hilarious path, his eyes would dance.

Run away on the milk-white steed.

All she wanted was for everyone to be still for a moment.
Just long enough to have one thing said to them, a thing she'd
think of at her leisure, assured that they wouldn't be scrabbling
around once more, drifting here and there. She was a sensitive
person; ask Steffie's father, who had seen her sway to the lovely
tunes of *The Fantasticks*. She wanted things equal and poign-
ant and motionless. As if we were all drowned.

Only then let everything buzz that still felt the need to.
Then let the colors speak, the city rip forward with its business, and there, by the shores of the Hudson, we drownings,
quiet and absorbent.

Even the fuddled roaches frozen and listening.

Marilyn put the needle back to the beginning of "Matty
Groves."

Only Joan Baez will be saved. Only Lola and Joan Baez,
because they have no problems.

Milk-white steed.

Charge into things. Get interested in Wagner. Go to Bay-
reuth. Get interested in natural childbirth. Have one. Get interested in gravestone rubbings. Rub some.

Wander through the stately pleasure dome and find a bed
there. You can't move your arms or your legs: when Stuart
comes and finds you, he says, "That's natural. Don't get into
a state about it, huh? It's perfectly natural."

Someone's supposed to save you when you're miserable. Supposed to come on in and lay on unnatural, sweet, still hands. And without permission. Without you saying a word, someone's to pop with realization, shut up for a moment, and disentangle you. Matty Groves.

But instead a Stuart. A Stuart and a Marilyn, mannequins in her mother's windows. Armless at times, headless at others, often just a trunk. They wouldn't even drown; they'd float off across the watery state line sunk into the Hudson and knock up against the shore in Jersey, its piebald lawns, Sukis and Paulines and towel racks.

The essence of comedy is hate and death. Drownings and Joannes. "Angles" in the summer windows filled with dacrons and worsteds. And endless laughter hyena'd in the pleasure dome while the roaches and I are stuck and fuddled.

Time.

When the record ended this time, she let the arm go back and the changer click itself shut. The house, when she left, would be without trace of her. The bathroom, then into the bedroom to find her shoes. As she was closing the window in the kitchen that faced out onto the fire escape, she glanced at the cleared table and felt like spitting on it, leaving the glob for Stuart to find when he returned. She put on her sweater.

She purposely didn't double-lock the door.

It was a warm afternoon, with the greeny growth of spring on the Palisades across the river knitting a tiredness into the streets of the Heights. Marilyn stood on the steps of the apartment building for a minute, then went back upstairs. She called in and said that she'd be late, about seven.

And sit. To rearrange, just a little, the dome. She slid her coat off her shoulders and onto the back of one of the kitchen chairs.

Poor tenderness. Americans don't name their children Desdemona. Spit.

She held it in her mouth, then swallowed it back, looking at the clock in the living room.

Basically because there was no supporting line. She got out her pad and pen. Off and down went the line to turn and stop at an angle. That line turns hard and razorlike because it is afraid of an eternal plummet. Her mother caught (caught) in the crucial degree, the very cornice of the most fearsome literal isosceles. Struggle, push.

Actually, no. Not the owner of a clothing store. What's in it for me? Pushing the sides of some figure? Stuck in the pad was the airplane-route map Serena had given her when they were thinking of going to Akron together. Marilyn studied the maze of intersecting flights. Who sleeps beneath the grid?

The songs save (the songs save). Nothing but the locomotives killing the brave sweet lads who drive them, the murders by the banks of murky marvelous rivers, the love sealed and torn by the silver dagger.

Never been in a sleeping bag in my life.

Her (her) father: jigsaw teacher, potter. From him the emotion and respect for rounding, for the smooth whirl.

". . . *and the grass is as high as an elephant's eye, and* . . ."

She stopped murmuring the song when she heard the door open. Quickly, before Stuart would come into the kitchen, she sucked up the insides of her mouth and deposited a trickle of saliva onto the table.

He was carrying a bag from the supermarket. She turned to look out the window.

"Hello! What's this, you're not going in? You're all dressed. Jesus, if I'd have known, I would have bought supper for you, too."

She turned around to see him remove a package of lamb chops from the bag. "You eat pretty well when I'm not here."

"Lamb chops? It's all right, but I wouldn't say it was—"

"You have vegetables with it?"

"Sure. Here . . ." He pulled out a package of fresh spinach from the bag and then made a Popeye muscle.

"Could I have two leaves of spinach?"

Stuart put his hands on his head. "You're making me feel

terrible. I'll go down and get more lamb chops." He grabbed
for his coat, which he had thrown down on a chair.

"I'm going in."

"Late?"

"Right, late. For my own reasons."

Stuart replaced the coat on the chair's back, returning to
the kitchen counter to fold the emptied bag. "Like?"

"Like I was depressed, and I'd rather be depressed here."

"That's what we pay rent for."

"Stuart, I want to tell you something." She waited until he
looked at her before she turned away from him, watching what
was out the window once more. "Get the fuck away from me."

"What is this?"

"Nothing. I just want you to get away from me."

"No, no. *This*."

She turned around. Stuart stared at the table, at her spitball,
separated by now into a bubble-shot translucent string.

She bent down close to it, picking at it with a fingernail. "I
coughed. I can't help it if I cough and some phlegm gets out."

Stuart left the room, grabbing his coat. Marilyn could hear
him changing his clothes in the bedroom.

"I'm going now," she yelled.

"Go!"

Before she left the kitchen, she opened her notebook and
tore out a page. Very neatly she wrote: YOU'RE AN ANGLE—OF
SHIT and left it directly over the spot on which she had spit,
discoloring the paper under the word "YOU'RE."

Whatever there was, there wasn't enough of it. She got on
the subway thinking about apple orchards.

Go back.

Because she had been reminded by a car on Broadway filled
with country-bound luggage and father, mother, two kids.
Farther back, because she had thought of her father trying to
get his piebald scratch of lawn into shape. And that because
she had seen rhododendrons on sale at the florist's near 168th
Street. Because before that . . . what?

Milk-white steed. Take off with the wind chilling your teeth. Fly with the pale moon up front; dark corridor roads; fear. Who, of all the people in this train, will save me? Who'll open their heads to make a little room?

But truly heads of plush and ticking (ticking, ticking). No brains, but soft cotton. What's wrong with that? Big deal.

When she got to the store, she was proud that she hadn't paid attention to anything on the street.

"For the benefit of Mr. Kite, there will be a show tonight . . ."

No carnivals.

"I thought you'd be coming in later." Lola.

Who also said, "Celia called about ten minutes after you did. She has terrible cramps, so we're going to be short. I was going to try to get one of the book people to work back here."

"No need." Marilyn opened the door leading down to the stockroom, then halted. "Hey, could you go downstairs and get my book and hang up my coat?"

Lola rolled fat eyes.

"I don't want to go down there right now," Marilyn said. "All right?"

"Mar, there are customers."

"It'll take you a second. I'll take care of up here."

Lola took the coat from Marilyn's arm. "I can see what kind of night this is going to be. Try to compensate by being extra helpful, O.K.? Get that guy by the statuary. I think he's looking for Degas ballerinas. It may be a sale; he's been looking carefully." She descended the stairs.

Marilyn walked over to the man—young, with an expensive straw boater on his head. "Excuse me, you're looking for—"

The young man gazed at her with complete puzzlement.

"I'm one of the sales personnel. Miss Lathem told me you were interested in Degas reproductions?"

"Miss Lathem?" His voice was light and thin; Marilyn hated him.

"The other girl."

"I'm just looking." His glance swiped at the Rodin "Penseur" as he began to walk out of the section.

Marilyn called after him, "The girl who helped you will be here on the floor in a second."

He didn't turn around.

She told Lola when she returned that the guy wasn't a buyer. Lola shrugged and went behind the counter to check the tape in the register.

Marilyn handled an earrings sale and one for a LOVE plaque. It was seven-twenty, dark already, and the greater part of the after-work browsers had been through and gone.

"Did you have your supper?" Marilyn asked Lola.

"Supper? Who had time? There are two of us, remember. Maybe about nine, when it's empty. You had yours, right?"

"No."

"Didn't you eat at home? I figured since you were coming in late you ate at home."

Marilyn didn't even pause. "I forgot. Sure, I ate. I had lamb chops and spinach."

"That's one of the talents I'd love to have. To forget if you've eaten or not. Listen, what was that last sale you handled?"

"The LOVE plaque. Fortysixninetythree."

"I thought so. There are no more on the floor. You better go down to stock and bring up—I don't know—three'll be enough."

Marilyn turned away. "Later."

All of Lola's making-do fossilized. "Later? What's the matter with now? What's the matter with *you?* Oh, shit, this is going to be fun tonight."

"Don't get excited," Marilyn answered, grabbing the feather duster and walking toward the aisles.

Two sales in two hours.

Lola called to her from the stockroom door: "I'm taking my supper break. I spoke to Tony, in books, and he'll stay with you."

Marilyn nodded. She showed Tony the keys for the locked display cases. He didn't look very attractive tonight.

"I saw you around N.Y.U. yesterday," he said. "You were in the library, by the window. I was passing."

"I take a course."

"Same. I'm in law school."

"It's a lousy place," and she laughed for no reason.

"The law school?"

"The library. I sleep there."

"Really?"

They had customers immediately after Lola left the store. Tony walked over to Marilyn to ask her the price of the "David" without base and when delivery could be expected.

"I don't know."

He squinted sourly at her.

"Tell her to wait. Or come back later when Lola is here."

"You tell her."

"I'm busy."

"You know," Tony mumbled, "I'm staying here as a favor." He walked back to his customer, raising his opened hands to begin an apology.

The old woman Marilyn had been helping finally moved off without buying, saying that she thought she was on safer grounds with something like a cookbook. Marilyn joined Tony behind the counter. When he began once more to talk about law school, she decided to go down to the stockroom for the plaques.

Inventory the week before had rearranged a large part of the stock. Marilyn stood at the front of one of the aisles, trying to remember what was where.

To be careful. To be slow, and get done what had to get done. A salesgirl replenishing stock—an object among objects. Just to be sure, take hold. She had time later to lap the track. Just let Marilyn (Marilyn) get done what had to be done. She went to the packing tables for a shopping bag. She smiled.

With the packing knife lying on the table, she split a length of wrapping ribbon so that it curled away from itself and over her hands. She pulled another arm's length of it and slashed it down the middle again. Gaily (gaily) decorate. Who ever saw her like this? Did her father see her splitting ribbon? See, see, easy, so very easy. Lazy, superfluous beauty. And the milk-white steed, that's silly as well, lazing in beauty. Only alone did she find the things she needed, like the ribbon. One thing, maybe two, but exactly the right things. Stop the flow of junk offered. Law school. Maybe it would help to take the private finds and show them off: these are (are) mine.

Marilyn walked down the aisle, an inch of ribbon ringed around a finger, watching for the stock numbers. The plaques were boxed in deep purple cardboard; she'd look for the color. In the middle of the aisle was a toppled carton of earrings, which she picked up, stuffing it back into place. About to walk on, she took a step backward and grabbed for the replaced box. The earrings were small: teardrops. She smiled. She put two sets of them in the shopping bag, her eyes catching the purple plaque boxes as she bent down to punch flat the bag's bottom. Lola had said five—three. Marilyn took the well-packaged plaques off the shelf and dropped them end-up in the bag next to the earrings. Things that she needed; things she picked by herself. When she heard the door open up by the floor, she walked quickly into the ladies room.

If left in the cotton of the boxes, the earrings could go into her bra. She opened the first three buttons of her blouse, watching herself in the mirror. Silly, superfluous face. Not what they wanted. She knew. They wanted chisels; they wanted angles that split (split) and cleaved other people.

Presumably to hurt. But she knew. The strong, the personalities—they were vials of poison kept in wait for the big moments, then grabbed to hurt yourself. How much Stuart loved her when she was in pieces. Silly face. She buttoned her blouse up without stuffing the wadded earrings in her bra, putting them instead back into their boxes, and the boxes back into the bag. Why have secrets when there is nothing to tell?

Most of the books she took for no particular reason. The

large Skira *Matisse* she couldn't resist, but the others she took
as much for the jacket designs as for their titles. As the bag
got heavier, she, too, felt herself weighting. A treasure, an
offering to herself (herself). What I have chosen. What I have
cared to say in pick, picking. It was no robbery to possess the
things that hold you.

Marilyn brought the bag back to the lockers at the other
end of the stockroom, opened her own locker, and rested the
bulging bag inside. Like going to a soft leaking sleep—what
she wanted and what she had chosen would wait for her. She
looked at the Frightening Clock on the wall—nine-thirty. Two
and a half hours in which what she had taken would wait for
her, in the dark—in the dark—dark greenness of metal. In the
unknown secret.

No, no secrets.

She put her coat on and dropped her pocketbook inside the
merchandise-filled bag. Each step she took toward the door
leading up to the sales floor made a nice sharp pound, a declaration. Who knows me—who knows me—who knows me;
and she couldn't stop smiling all the way up the steps.

It was all still there. A blur of hurry—Tony signaling relief as
he caught sight of her.

She walked on. Maybe it was by the reference-book section
that someone from behind the counter finally said something:
"Closing up shop back there?" Her smile kept a course, her
feet described its outside curve.

When she reached the guard at the Fifth Avenue door, she
could feel nearly all of herself widened, the walk across the
length of the store having stretched her large enough to all-
encompass.

The guard's smile was puny compared to her own.

"Early night, huh?"

Soft and Declared.

". . . to see your sales slip. Lot of birthdays, huh? . . . The
sales slip . . . I can't let you leave without me see—"

To be Absolute. And find. Oh, dear, Marilyn, found.

". . . Better wait here a second. Mr. Seiden!"

Heavy Motes.

"Hold it, let me understand. These are your purchases. He just wants to see the sales slip."

Silly face. How else to deal with Lord Arlen's men?

". . . isn't a joke. I mean, you were walking *out* with these things."

Lola walking back In. Her smile: she must have had a Nice Dinner.

". . . won't say a thing. Look what she's got in there. A hundred, hundred and fifty dollars' worth of merchandise."

If they only knew what they were doing, holding back the milk-white steed. Only her father knew it nipped.

"Marilyn, what, what's the matter, hon? Marilyn, what are you . . . what's the matter? . . . No, wait, Mr. Seiden, don't call them. Look at her, she's all out of it. Don't call them. I'll call her boyfriend."

Of course They flutter.

". . . and he's walking the beat. Just go down the three blocks and look on both sides of the street. Tell him it's a shoplifting."

She didn't like the touching. No need to rein the Steed and be off. She punched.

"Jimmy! Stan! You want to help me hold her?"

Lord Arlen Himself. She watched the dark blue uniform separate from the night as the window lights brought him into focus. She took a few steps backward, under the hands of the Others at her shoulders.

". . . can take her in if you want me to. But if she's a sales-girl, maybe you just want to . . ."

"Her boyfriend'll be down in twenty minutes. Wait to give her to him, Mr. Seiden, please. Look at her. Something's wrong, you can see that. Please wait."

". . . to book her anyway, since she hasn't taken it out of the store. I agree with this young lady here, she looks like she has enough problems without me taking her in."

She could hear the Bag being slid away, over to the counter.

Taken from her. Why not? Why not? How they messed up the Song. Didn't they know that it finishes, that the words are all written down?"

"All right. We'll wait for the boyfriend. I'd like to take her down to the stockroom, though. This is disrupting business."

From here to there—no, from there to here. They were curling It back. The hands on her shoulders: she went down under them. They were moving her away from the door.

". . . for your boyfriend. You can sit here and rest. The police have left; there's nothing to worry about. Now, come on, please."

A Clash: nice, soft, and sudden. She liked It. Breathing coolly and with pleasure. Accepting their chair. There was something about the fluorescent Light that was stealing their talk from their mouths. Close to it, she could already feel the ripples of a large lake lying placid down the Slope.

". . . not to worry about this, hear? You should never have come in. It's plain exhaustion. Don't you think there are times when *I* think I'm about to split? Look, here he is."

His look: disturbed and shitty—disturbance the flap, shit what it covered.

". . . have the taxi outside. We'll go. I had a feeling when I came home. Come on. The taxi's right out . . ."

They were driving up West End Avenue. Silky Night of Monsters. She smiled as he told her.

It would only take a Minute; then she'd remember to blank. Her mother was standing in the lobby, waiting.

In the elevator, very directly, her mother told them she'd pulled strings and a bed would be available in Gracie Square Hospital about two the next afternoon.

In the last pocket of the night of Relief, she slept with Stuart in her old bed, in her old room, and in the morning, before Stuart left to go and get her clothing from the apartment, they had pancakes and sausages and her mother's tears, which meant nothing and were just fine.

H

OW OFTEN DID ANYONE GET THREE PERSONAL letters in one morning's delivery? David opened Joyce's first.

. . . calling you and calling you. It wasn't something I wanted to do without telling you, but the arrangements worked out so that, finally, there was just no time. I'm sure you understand—I know you do. I was in Chicago and had to go to L.A., so when I heard from Michaelson that the papers were all done up and all that was needed was to go down there, I did. I took a plane to El Paso, got a cab directly to Juárez—that's a story all in itself; someday I'll have to tell you about it—and it took maybe four hours. Then I flew on to L.A. You'll get the papers in the mail.

David, I'm not going to mix something as serious as what all this means and has meant with merely the cold news of it. I'll write to you next week and it'll be a decent, long letter, I promise. In our letters to each other this whole last year, I think we have been very straight, recognizing how much we owe one another. Now that it's officially over, I, for one, will not lose this. This is the spot in which to say "No hard feel-

*ings, right?" but I'm not going to be that cheap and flighty.
I know there are hard feelings. On both sides. But we can remain close, despite them.*

*Please write to me at the office when you get this letter, or
you can wait until you get the papers, which you'll have to sign
anyway.*

So keep well, and know that I'm thinking of you.

Stuart's letter told about Marilyn's breakdown and hospital-
ization in enough detail for David nearly to decide to forgo
opening Serena's, which commanded that he cut the crap and
come back and live with her now, when everything was falling
apart.

THIRD

HE HAD BEEN WARNED, SO HE SHOULDN'T BE SO shocked by it. The very idea of someone dropping nails from fifteen stories up was frightening enough. The justification—that here were these poor slobs working forty hours a week in a belt factory for eighty dollars, and here you were stretched out on a chaise longue on the terrace attached to Serena's apartment, a place far too expensive for any of them ever to hope to live in—well, that sat nicely as long as it was just talk. But David, turning over the sharp nail weighted with two turns of masking tape that minutes before had landed three feet from where he had been lying, felt only rage. His hands had gone to his eyes as he heard the nail drop, but he stayed where he was. If they were watching from any one of the hundred windows surrounding the terrace, he wasn't going to give them the satisfaction of seeing him run. Nor did he look up to find his bombardiers. He lay still for a full five minutes, got up, walked to the perimeters of the terrace, and only then went inside, holding the nail. The bastards.

He put it on the kitchen table, next to the box of Cap'n Crunch and the glasses with a little milk left in them from breakfast. Serena was lucky; she left the house before the kids got up, before the chaos. And Kate obviously didn't give a shit. And the kids were kids. That left only him to squirm at the filthy faces that they never washed before they came to the table, the wet pajamas untouched until after the meal, Kate's bovine indulgence when the kids—especially the little one—would crumble an Oreo and blow the pieces all over the table. There was nothing specific he could do; generally he found himself becoming sarcastic, saying things like "Where are the croissants this morning," or, "Tell me again how much it cost you to put the kids through finishing school." But Kate would laugh—she dug put-ons. The morning of his third day there, his annoyance at Tira's mess-making with the oatmeal almost brought his hand up to knock back her gooey arm, but then he realized that Kate might think that out of sight, too, and it would be nothing but a wasted effort. Within a week he knew his only recourse, and it wasn't much. He would whisper to Serena in bed, would say that contrary to what her sister thought, the house was not Drop City, and he for one was not going to help her transform a far too small apartment on Lexington Avenue into a commune. To say nothing of the situation you had upon walking in on a scene in which a mother passes a hash pipe to her four-year-old, or says in front of that same little boy that all people need and should be happy with are air, water, fire, and, for a woman, an occasional big cock. What kind of behavior was that? And no, he wasn't being bourgeois. And even if he was. Serena's reply was a request to make the best of a bad and unexpected situation.

David took the glasses and put them into the sink, next to the plates speckled with toast crumbs. He was alone this morning; Kate had taken the kids over to the West Side to get brown rice and a few other particulars of a diet David first regarded with amusement and then revulsion after he got a half meal of it. He washed the glasses and plates and cleared the worktable of dried utensils, stacking them up on the shelf and closing the folding doors around the kitchenette. Kate had said something about returning for lunch, and with this in his mind he worked quickly, the extra perk of adrenaline left from the nail incident earlier in the morning now put to some use.

The trick was not to look at all the three cots jammed barracks-style in the tiny living room, but to make them up individually as quickly as possible. He stripped the urine-heavy sheet off Tira's cot first, wrapping it into a ball and dropping it on the floor. Then the same with Liam's. There was no need to change the sheet on Kate's bed, unless she had also peed, which, by the way she drank Gallo burgundy all through the night as she sat and worked her awl over the latest leather miniature she was making, he wouldn't be surprised one morning to find. He went into the bedroom and removed two fresh sheets from the low-lying chest of drawers that Serena's old boyfriend had ingeniously built beneath the bed. Before he put the sheets on, he remembered to take a damp sponge and once-over the rubber pads that protected the children's thin mattresses, lest the build-up of ammonia smell get too potent in the small space. A storm of crumpled tissues fell from beneath Kate's pillow as he made a few perfunctory punches at it, and these he picked up and dropped into the wastebasket in the bathroom. When David returned to the living room, he thought it looked all right, though nothing could alter the suggestion it offered of how he thought a flophouse would appear. He went into the bedroom, sat on the bed, and smoked a cigarette.

It was June and hot—he took offense at both. From the dressing table he picked up Serena's already read note. He read it again: "Escape tonight. Dinner out. Come to the office at five." Kate's arrival, unexpected and two days before his own, had robbed him and Serena of pliancy. "Escape." Two weeks already, and he felt as if they had been in plaster casts the whole while.

As he rolled over on the bed for the minutes of extra rest he had tried to take on the terrace, he felt in his pocket the keys to Kate's mini-bus. He sat upright again. He had forgotten to ask her about using the bus today, although he had no particular destination in mind. It was chancy just taking it; most of her and the kids' possessions were stored in it; the four or five times he had borrowed it there was invariably a funny moment when he felt like the storied Jewish peddler, the department store on wheels. It was a ridiculous-looking thing, the paint nearly wind-blasted off the sides, the cheap curtains on the rear windows barely hiding from view the piles of chintz, diapers, laundry bags, and canvas lumped in the back. He had never got the story straight enough to feel real sympathy—which was perhaps the problem—but it was in this bus that Kate and her children had weeks before driven to New York from Colorado, fleeing the mountain commune of sleazy but earnest geodesic domes in which Toby, her husband and the kids' father, was in the process of freaking out.

The slow sputtering of footsteps in the hall told David he hadn't got out of the house in time. He sat up and was walking into the living room when the door opened. Liam came in first, grinning sweetly, followed by Kate, who held Tira under the knees and by the shoulders, folding the little girl into a chubby V that pointed her bulging bottom toward the floor.

"Was the store closed?" David asked the little boy.

Liam merely pointed at his sister, then ran to his bed to jump on it.

"Tira shit in her pants," Kate said, dropping her daughter, stomach down, on Liam's bed. "Just as I almost had a cab." Tira's forefinger was making expeditions in her nostrils.

"I'll get a diaper," David offered.

"Yeah. Man, this city is crazy. Until you get a lousy taxi." Tira's ankles were now being held up, her soft round baby rump smeared a light yellow.

David handed Kate the fresh diaper. "Why don't you train her? Liam's trained."

"What does 'trained' mean? Train, like an animal? When it gets uncomfortable enough for her walking around with a load of crap in her pants, she'll stop. That's what happened with Liam."

The little boy, realizing he was being spoken of, stopped stepping up and down off his pillow and smiled. "I make shitty."

"There." Kate slipped the rubber pants over the new diaper and pulled Tira's faded pants back up to her waist. When Kate bent down to grab the befouled diaper from the floor, David could see her large unconstrained breasts push languorously against the bib of her Mother Hubbard.

"Cap'n Crunch. Cap'n Crunch," Tira called, getting off the bed and running to the doors covering the kitchenette, putting hands to the knobs.

David spoke to Kate in the bathroom. "Can she have?"

"Of course. She's hungry."

David turned around to Liam, who sat on the bed quietly now, testing the muscles of his neck by craning it up and down. "You, Liam?" The boy paid no attention.

David took down the cereal box from the shelf and told Tira to open up her hand. He half filled it.

"More," the child demanded.

"That's enough for you now. Give some to your brother if he wants."

David turned around to see Liam opening the door to the terrace. He put down the box and rushed to him, holding him by the shoulders. The child squirmed vigorously, but with the small shrivel of a grin on his face.

"Let him go," Kate said. She stood brushing her hair in the middle of the room.

"No, I won't. I want to show you something." David released Liam, who immediately achieved his goal by slipping outside. David turned to him. "Liam!" He turned back to Kate. "Look at this." He held up the nail for Kate's inspection. "Liam, come in here. They threw this down from one of the factory buildings as I was lying out there about twenty-five minutes ago. Liam!"

Kate didn't move closer for a better look. "They won't throw it at a kid."

Balancing her fistful of cereal, Tira was now maneuvering the crack of open door to join her brother.

"Why not?" David heard his voice close to breaking. "They're maniacs!"

Kate sat down on one of the cots. "In Colorado, the ranchers, just to harass us, used to drop dead prairie dogs in the cars and trucks at night. Occasionally they would shoot into the air and whoop. Scare tactics. They just want to establish presence."

"Kate, these people are fifteen stories up. No one can see them. They're not interested in establishing *presence*. I mean, they're crazy people! They could kill someone! Liam, Tira!"

Kate left her brush on the bed and walked slowly to the terrace door. "Children, come in. David's into this paranoid trip, and we don't want to gross him out. Come." She waited there till the children re-entered the house. Liam gave a little innocent laugh; Tira hopped onto her bed. "You have the keys for the bus?" she asked him.

David removed them from his pocket.

"Good. Well, listen. A guy who used to be with us split a few months ago. I was thinking of looking him up. He's somewhere—I have the address, I guess in the bus—where? Something like B Street, B Avenue. That sound right?"

"Avenue B. I used to live around there. But I'm warning you, it's a lousy neighborhood."

Kate smiled, keeping whatever thought that prompted it to herself. Then she said, "Well, none of us have any money." Kate's "us"—specific as it was, meaning always her fellow communards—was at first annoying to David, but he found he was getting used to it. "Maybe you could take the kids for a ride, and I'll go over there for the afternoon."

Natural politeness started to lift agreement to his lips, but he quelled it. "Sorry. I have things to do."

"What?"

Liam was off the bed and inching toward the terrace again. David fired, "My own thing."

Kate shook her long hair, her small mouth pasted together. "Oh, Christ, where's *your* head at. I ask a simple question and you come on to me. You go and calm down." She watched Liam open the door and skip out to the terrace. She said nothing.

David put the keys down on Tira's cot. "I'll see you later." He left the house, a film of fatigue stuck too early all over him.

He planned to use the day up traveling in a generally downtown direction. Taking the Lexington Avenue local, David decided at Union Square to pass up the Village. He then considered Wall Street, but let the station go, finally getting off the train at Battery Park. He strolled a few park lanes, but there was almost no breeze off the water and he quickly felt stalled. He made his way to the ferry terminal, dropped a nickel into the turnstile, and went up the escalators, not sure yet whether or not he'd take a boat.

The cheap frankfurter he had at a stand-up lunch counter coddled his hunger but not his aimlessness. He tried to be interested in an elderly couple who came in the store and ordered two coffees, retreating then next to him at the Formica ledge, where they sipped their purchases and ate the piece of honey cake the old lady unwrapped from a rectangle of waxed paper kept in her pocketbook. Through the signs pasted to the window of the lunch counter David saw the boarding doors open as a ferry arrived, discharging a boatload of passengers that eddied into the people waiting to get on. He walked quickly and joined them.

There were days—but not this one—when the lameness of his schemes to amuse himself acted as the very amusement. As he stood by the guardrail at the back of the boat and watched the water chock around in grey-green eruptions when the ferry began to move, he felt more essentially than at any time since he'd returned from Vermont that he was going about it all wrong. He had nothing to do; he knew no one in the city, *his* city, where he had spent all his life. And rather than face it, he shoved his time into places to go and things to do that did nothing but confirm his placelessness. Yet somehow the minuses were too obvious: Marilyn in the nut house; Stuart and Serena working; Joyce—where was she? his parents gone; no place of his own to live. And he worked at uncovering even smaller ones: going to Shea Stadium alone for a day game; wandering down St. Mark's Place to see which stores weren't there any more; walking and nearly mugged in Fort Tryon Park on a Wednesday morning.

When the ferry docked at St. George slip, David followed the six or seven people taking the round trip around the terminal and back onto the boat, finding himself a place at the front with no difficulty. On the trip back, he watched a long, cream-white, beautiful tanker—the *Hoshiba Maru*—sidle toward the docks in Brooklyn, and noticed that the Battery's skyline had changed.

Back on land in Manhattan, he sat on a bench for a while, then walked north to the financial district, stopping for lunch at a seafood restaurant whose hostess was plainly not too crazy about his tielessness. He ordered a bottle of Heineken first and sat sipping it from an ice-fogged mug until his fantail shrimp arrived. He ate slowly, but not slowly enough. He left a big tip.

As he entered the stationery store on Nassau Street, David saw that, twelve-thirty already, he had killed over two and a half hours. He handled with some interest a silver mechanical pencil for ten dollars, then bought it, asking for a small card to put inside the box, and writing: "Dear Jane Taylor—in appreciation for your helpful letter about my falling hair—Dora Jean Descartes."

He was really pushing it—he had to smile to himself—buying a ticket to a tour of the Stock Exchange. The plain girl who led the tour, Miss DeLiso, took the six of them—a family of four from some G.M. town south of Knoxville, an old man in a smartly pressed but ancient seersucker suit, and David—

onto the balcony overlooking the trading floor. All of them stared with a lack of comprehension at the flurry beneath them: piles of discarded paper haplessly shoved at by sweepers with brooms and no chance of success, a stew of hundreds of men mumbling numbers, the whole casserole covered with a gaseous yellow light pulsing off the electric tape boards. By that time there was nothing even faintly wacky about the expedition any longer, and he took the two feet of complimentary ticker tape from Miss DeLiso at the end of the tour without a smile.

When he got back outside, he found a candy story in which to make phone calls. The receptionist at Youthcept Magazines told him Serena was in a meeting. And Stuart, when he was called, couldn't talk right then; he had layouts that had to go out that night. David called Serena's office back and left a message that he might be there earlier than five. He bought himself three thin Jamaica cigars, a Clark bar, an early-edition *Post*, a disposable lighter.

If he could be sure that Kate had taken the kids to her friend's place on Avenue B, he'd go back to the apartment and nap away the time until five. As it was, he returned to the park, slightly cooler now, to sit for a while.

He was thinking of the idea of doubling as, later, he walked to the subway station. Doubling: going back on the ferry; eating dinner at the same restaurant where he had lunched; taking the Stock Exchange tour once more. Echoes of action that twice cast might send themselves back arranged, a pattern made visible. Wasn't it just possible that, forgetting specifics, there could be a ruse, a con committed by and for the kind of person who had spent the sort of day he had, a time illusion—back in the city, Marilyn and Stuart apart, he and his parents separated, another hot June—that let him think for a quick and quiet moment that it was four years ago? Large chunks of time cleared of particulars, and there before you is an ageless plateau on which, revived and comforted, change was a beautiful joke. A method of staying sane, certainly. David bought a subway token, thinking that Marilyn, for instance, had missed the ruse: she had let the specifics on, like an overcharitable driver picking up questionable hitchhikers. With only the back of a trusting head to her passengers, she had been stabbed repeatedly. Someone or something with isolate wisdom had had the good sense to push her out of the car before any more violence occurred.

At Serena's office, David had to sit for forty-five minutes in her cubicle before she appeared, a pencil stuck pygmy-fashion in the hair at the top of her head.

"My knees ache," she said after kissing him and going to sit behind her desk. "That idea I told you about, of doing something on alternative high schools—well, it's going to run. Since ten this morning, all of us have been on the floor of Marge's office looking at pictures. Oouuhh."

David removed the box containing the pencil from his breast pocket. "The receptionist asked me to bring this in. It was left at the desk."

Serena opened the box slowly, reading the card. "Thank you," she said with a sigh. "But you gave it to me at the wrong time. I'm too tired to be properly appreciative. You should have got me a nice sharp letter opener—something to tempt me on days like today."

"Your sister . . ."

She shook out a few mock-whimpers. "Don't tell me about Kate. That's something else that'll make me cry."

David was enjoying this. The weariness filing at Serena's voice, rather than making her vulnerable, left her only distant, her softly slurred words to him like the noise of an unseen animal left alone in dense woods.

"Nothing bad." David picked up a couple of unopened letters from Serena's incoming box. "She may not be home when we get there. A guy she knew from the commune is on Avenue B, and I think she took the kids with her to see him."

"Maybe she'll stay there the night. Pray, pray."

David grinned. He looked at the return addresses on the

envelopes: Bradenton, Florida; Davenport, Iowa; Livonia, Michigan; Cadiz, Ohio. "Do you ever get letters from girls in the city?"

"Not too often. Sometimes from Brooklyn or Queens, which I guess is not really the city."

"Oh, yes, it is."

"But from this area, mainly places like Long Island. And for some reason those letters are always about cars—whether it's all right for a girl to drive her boyfriend to his after-school job; should the hostess of a party offer to drive her guests home afterward. Like that."

"And the ones from Cadiz, Ohio?"

"Oh, I don't know any more. I'm too tired to think even."

"Probably"—his voice rose to falsetto—" 'I'm so confused I could die. Our local Methodist minister gave me a sex-education lesson three weeks ago, and I can't face going to Sunday school since then. What should I do?' "

"Thank God I haven't see that one yet."

"It may be the one I'm holding." David returned the letters to the box. "Tell her to become a Zoroastrian."

"See if anyone's passing by." She stood up and raised her skirt to adjust her panty hose. "Let's get out of here. I can't take any more of this *office*."

When they were in the elevator, David found the ticker tape in his pocket and waved it at Serena. Her weak smile, Sahara-empty, made the decision for him not to talk about his day.

They took a cab over to Chelsea and a steakhouse they wanted to try. While they waited at the bar for a table, she said, "This is good. An early night. All I want to do is take a hot bath, maybe watch television for an hour, and then sleep, sleep." She chewed briefly on a pretzel nib.

"Can I say something?"

"Of course you can say something. Please, as a matter of fact. Say something other than 'This picture'll go well with the text block' or 'Can't have two features back to back.' "

"I wasn't intending to."

"Go on." Serena took a sip of her Rob Roy.

"I thought about Marilyn today as if she were dead."

"You should let me know when you're going to say things like that before I give you permission to say them. What am I supposed to say to that?"

"I didn't mean it as a blinding revelation. Haven't you thought that way?"

"Plenty. It makes me feel terrible. Maybe that's why I can't go to see her. I'm her closest friend, and compared to you—you go every couple of days and you're linked really by Stuart, once removed—compared to you, I'm terrible. And now I'm going to be worse and make us change the subject."

"That's what the hospital is trying to do. Change the subject."

"If you're going to be sickeningly literal, I'm going to be sickeningly silent."

They went home directly from the restaurant. Serena pointed to lights on in the apartment. David looked at his watch.

The small light over the sink in the kitchenette was on, but the rest of the living room was dark, the children's blanketed forms irregular lumps in the summer night. They both tiptoed to the bedroom, where behind the closed door Kate sat watching the tube. She was wearing Serena's robe.

"They went to sleep early, huh?" Serena asked her sister as she slipped out of her dress.

"They had a good day."

"Did you find your friend?" David asked.

"Sure. We all had a nice day."

Serena passed before the television on her way to the bathroom. "Anything good on?"

Kate didn't answer, only shrugged. Her eyes were small green gimbals floating in the sockets. David could see she was as high as the Empire State Building. When Serena was out of the room, Kate took his hand in hers and tried to sit him down next to her on the bed. "I have something to ask you."

"All right." He slipped his hand from beneath hers.

Kate looked at him waveringly. "See how you are. Maybe I shouldn't ask you."

"Ask."

"Well, you have to sit down next to me and hold my hand. *Relax.*"

David stood where he was. But when it became clear that she wasn't going to speak until he did as she asked, he sat down and let her take his hand again.

"That's better. Now. Grady—the guy we went to see today —is packing up to split to the country, up near Woodstock. They have a house and some land. The kids and I are having trouble hacking it in the city, so we're going to take off with him. Now, you're going back to your college in the fall, correct?"

David nodded.

"Well, you should come with us. Serena could come up on weekends, and you could see her. But staying in this city, man! And another guy up there would be helpful. Liam and Tira dig you, you know that. So come with us."

"I have things to do here."

Kate raised her head to the ceiling. "Things to do. Things to do. Things everyone does, digesting, evacuating, making love, breathing. Things to do."

Serena came back into the bedroom wearing a blue nightgown. She pointed at the television again. "So what's on?"

"We're not watching," David replied. It must have come out short, because Serena's refreshed face crimped around her eyes.

Kate stood up, pushing at David's back for him to do the same. "You go to sleep or watch, Eenie. David and me are going out to rap."

Serena threw herself on the bed. "O.K." She grabbed pillows to fashion a loaf on which to prop her head.

It was a choice between Serena's fatigue and Kate's fluffy

importunings. Silent himself most of the day, and not as tired as Serena, he felt the prospect of half an hour on the terrace, even with Kate, in her high-flying queer imperative mood, wouldn't be too much to handle. He followed her outside. As they were pulling the two rusting garden chairs to the railing of the terrace, the light in the bedroom flicked off and through the window only the ghost light of the television screen afforded a changing glow. David removed his shoes and socks and rested his feet on the rail. Kate lit a cigarette that spread a small halo over her in the greyed, still, urban night.

"She's tired," David said.

"So what about it?"

David angled through the darkness to take the cigarette from Kate's pudgy fingers. He inhaled deep and twice, liking the even paler smoke layering above their heads in the breeze-less evening. "I don't think so. It's a nice idea and all, but I came in for the summer for specific reasons."

"Serena." Kate retrieved the cigarette.

"Not only Serena. Marilyn—this friend of ours is in the hospital. I want to see her. And, well, also this is where I live."

"Here?"

"The city."

"Wait a sec." Kate rose and went inside, returning with the jug of Gallo and two glasses.

David drank some wine, and continued: "I wouldn't have come back at all if I didn't feel some responsibility for what goes on with the people I'm closest to. You understand that. It's the same thing in a commune."

"What about your responsibility to me?"

David blanked. Sinuous, expanding, enfolding, even a little dangerous—a bushel of meanings in that. He chose not to understand rather than pick out what she implied.

"That's right, to me. See, I know a lot about you. You're all confused when it comes to distances. Who you're close to and who you're not. What you have to learn to do is take immediate responsibility for everyone, not only people who you feel safe with. That chick in the hospital—sure, she's had a bad time. But what about the people who are still going? Those are the ones you have to feel for, have to extend yourself for. Even Serena. Look, you know her for a few years and she's sort of a fact. Dead."

David laughed nervously. "No, she's only tired."

Kate drank down the wine in her glass, then refilled it. "Facts don't matter, man. One day they just bow out and then a guy like you falls apart. Life matters."

"Life matters, right. But life is people and what you've done to them."

"Where the hell do you come off 'doing things' to people. You're not Vishnu."

David felt matters settling onto a more abstract, manageable shelf. It was strangely pleasant. "Come on, Kate. Don't you do things to people? Don't you influence your children?"

"Only to the extent that I'm me."

David's shirt was soaked under the arms. After a few minutes of kneading the wet fabric, he got up. "I'll be right back. I'm going to put on a T-shirt."

Serena lay horizontally spread-eagled across the bed, her adenoids laying a tiny undertone beneath the situation-comedy dialogue and laugh track on the TV. David stripped off his shirt and, trying not to make too much noise, extracted a T-shirt from the chest of drawers under the bed. He left the room without turning off the set.

Kate had moved her chair closer to his. The glasses were filled again. When he was seated once more, she leaned over and took his hand. "I know from Serena all the hassle you've gone through. I've had it, too. And that's the point. Life has certain shapes to it. When you realize what the shape is at any particular moment, you have to *jive* with it. You don't go around changing the shape because you feel it's not the one you like. Right now, for you and me, it's a circle. We've been riding the bottom edge, and we have a chance to go full around." The burning tip of Kate's cigarette described her concept like an acrobatic firefly.

"I never passed geometry."

"Don't joke." Her hand fell to his thigh, her body leaning from the chair toward him. "This is serious shit. It's your life in relation and in responsibility to the greater life, the whole thing. You could be stuck forever on the ledge."

"This terrace?"

Kate moved her body off the chair, resting herself against David's involuntarily stiffening knees, knees that were in a second to support the two richly aureoled breasts Kate freed from beneath her robe. "I want you to make some contact, that's all," came from the mouth above her chin rubbing against his thighs. The hand he intended to use to push back her head fell instead on a breast, and stayed there, molding around it. The mass of nearly silent movement on his lap was joined by a hand that snapped open the metal button of his jeans, lowering them and his shorts as it would changing Tira.

The contact was simple. He wanted to have his eyes stay open, but they shut the instant Kate full-mouthed him. He wanted, too, the assurance of Serena's snores from the bedroom, but he could only hear the television. His mind shrank from the thought; his penis warmed to the treatment—neither one stronger yet than the other. But soon this earthier version of Kate's circle of responsibility took over, and his own rebuttal was wrecked. David put hands to her unshaven, sweat-dewed armpits to draw her further, acceding, agreeing, giving in, letting go, making up for it, trying something new, getting it all together, living it up, cutting it loose, driving in, throwing away, rinsing.

He delivered in her mouth and also with almost a kick at her shins, which he apologized for with a few strokes at her breast. Kate came up from the maelstrom with a look of argument-winning satisfaction. A shudder built in David watching her point with a finger at her mouth, till he realized she was asking for her wine. They clicked glasses, but David did not drink from his until he pulled his pants back up. Kate closed her robe and returned to her chair.

"Come share my cot," she said, and they both laughed. It

was a tidying remark, and because David knew he wouldn't
be able to say another thing and wouldn't try, he was happy
just to be able to keep his expression locked pleasant. He drank
down his wine and got up.

Kate said, "Good night . . ." and he walked away wincing
in fear of the next word, a "lover-boy," or, God forbid, a
more serious "baby." But it was just "Good night." He turned
at the terrace door for a farewell smile. Kate nodded, also
smiling.

He got in next to Serena, moving her vertical on the bed.
After a minute or so, he heard the door to the terrace open
and Kate's steps into the living room. The light in the kitchenette was turned off. Consolation winked out from the thought
that a great deal had to do with the city: the sprawling various
place where a young man's sprawling various life gets knocked
into shape, or becomes even more sprawling, more various.
Given enough complications, eventually they form a downy
nest, and all I really want to do is to lie down.

DAVID AND SERENA, THEIR HANDS SWEATING, AFRAID to ruin the red swirl gift wrapping, passed the package back and forth every few minutes. Kate had said nothing about the instrument—a dulcimer—how old it was or how it was to be tuned, but only that it was in tune. It was her goodbye gift as she packed the children up and left for Woodstock, with pleas for Serena and David to come up often. Serena had strummed the dulcimer for hours that night, the soft and buzz-furry tone delighting her one minute, and frustrating her the next because she didn't know how to play it. Stuart's call suggesting that they go to the hospital together that Friday night, July 4th eve, gave David the idea of bringing the dulcimer as a gift. Serena polished it, using the stuff she did her cello with, and swathed a bold-patterned paper over its curious shape.

Stuart was already a few minutes late. Watching the train-catchers rush into Grand Central behind them was pleasant for no longer than a few minutes, and since David and Serena had met early and had been standing in the heat for twenty minutes now, each second that Stuart did not appear swelled eternally. Serena's legs got appreciative stares that for a while were nice but soon became intrusive on David's thoughts. The first thing to do was to ask Stuart whether the hospital would allow Marilyn to keep the dulcimer. If not, they wouldn't even bring it up to her, but would leave it at the desk. And Serena had warned that if that happened, given her fragile state for this, her first visit, she might be so upset that she wouldn't be able to go up.

A hand from behind put the screws on David's shoulder, the accompanying unseen voice whispering, "Got some tickets to Ebbets Field. Tonight's game. Want?" As David began to turn, he saw Serena looking at the mysterious scalper and smiling. She said, "We expected you to come up Forty-second."

Stuart, wearing tan chinos and a blue blazer, gestured behind him with his newspaper. "I got off early and walked up Fifth. So I came down Vanderbilt." He put an arm over Serena's shoulders and began to walk.

"Do we eat first or go up and eat later?" David asked, at the same time pulling the newspaper from under Stuart's arm and scanning the sports headlines on the back page.

"We have time to eat. So, how's youse?"

Serena slipped her free arm around his waist. "Fine. Hot. Where should we eat? There are a lot of places around. . . ."

Stuart pointed across the street. "The Automat. We don't have that much time and it'll be quick. All right?"

"Sure. David?"

"Fine with me."

When they were taking silverware and napkins to put on their trays, Stuart said, "Try the Glorious Fourth Special. It's meat loaf that on the second bite explodes in your face."

Serena balanced the dulcimer on her tray, next to the plateful of vegetables that was all she was going to have—what she dubbed a "conscience meal" in response to David's mocking expression as she had the lady behind the counter spoon beets, spinach, and carrots onto her plate. The three of them found an empty table near the window up front.

Returning from the coin windows with rolls for each of them, Stuart asked, "What's the package? Are we going to liberate Marilyn by blowing up Gracie Square Hospital, a private institution for the emotionally disturbed?"

Serena pushed her roll back to Stuart. "Not for me. I'm going to lose some weight. It's a dulcimer. For Marilyn."

David asked, "Will they let her have it?"

"I don't know. They could think she'd hang herself with the strings. Where'd you get it?"

"My sister gave it to us when she left for Woodstock."

"Along with six pounds of brown rice," David added.

Serena put her hand out for the previously rejected roll. "I'm sorry. Bad habits last."

David stopped cutting his veal cutlet and said to Stuart, "She's not really suicidal, is she?"

Stuart grinned. "If she eats too many vegetables, who knows?"

Serena laughed.

"No, really. Marilyn."

Stuart shook his head. "I don't think so. The last few days, in fact, she looks so well and sounds—well, better, that I spoke to the doctor about maybe getting her out."

"And?" Serena asked.

"He wants her there for at least two more weeks. The problem with that is her mother. I know that that's what Mar hates most about being there. She doesn't particularly mind the quiet and the rest and the lack of demands. What she minds is her mother coming almost every day. She says she feels like she got stuck on a piece of flypaper, and a bigger bug has the unlimited chance to pester her."

"Does her father come?" David asked.

"About four times, so far. What a creep! But she loves to see him. Of course, her mother is never there then." Stuart pushed his empty plate to the side of the table. "Now I'm going to have watermelon. Youse?"

Serena hesitated, but finally shook her head no. David said, "A Coke, if you can."

Serena and David were silent in Stuart's absence. When he returned, Serena said, "Can't you speak to her mother, tell her to lay off a little?"

Stuart began to salt his melon. "Marilyn's mother sees this completely differently from anyone else. All the years that they didn't speak to each other, she considers as time spent building up poison. Now it's the boil broken, the healing process under-way, and soon everything will be hunky-dory."

"Last time I was there," David said, "Marilyn said she had a lot of plans. Which was a good sign, I guess."

Suddenly Stuart looked tired; the enameled sheen of the summer twilight coming through the window was mean to his features, especially his eyes, which behind his recently acquired wire rims were no longer even faintly animated. He looked at his watch and announced, "We should get up there. Finish."

They ran down the steps of the subway station two at a time and caught the last car of a local. The few blocks to the hospital, once they emerged into what was now night, were taken silently. David held the dulcimer in one hand, Serena's hand in the other. As they were entering the lobby, Stuart said, "Don't be surprised if she doesn't look or talk too much to me. I said something to her yesterday that she took offense at." Serena shivered; David felt the tremor in his hand; she blamed it on the air conditioning.

They sat on a couch while Stuart called from the desk to find out from the floor nurse if the dulcimer could be brought up. He returned two minutes later shaking his head. "So since only two of us are allowed up at a time anyway, one will keep it down here. You two want to go up first?"

Serena settled with an almost violent push onto the couch. "No. You go up with David. Tell her I'll be up in a minute. You know what I mean, whenever you come down."

David stood up and started to walk toward the elevator with Stuart.

Serena called out to them in a stronger voice, bumpy with trembles, "David, you come down. I don't want to go up there without Stu. . . . I'd rather Stuart was there. Is that all right?"

David and Stuart nodded.

In the elevator, David asked, "Is her mother there?"

Stuart rested his head against the back wall. "No. Since we were coming, I told her not to."

Walking down the corridor to the day room, they heard a tripping bark of firecrackers come from the street below. Stuart frowned.

Marilyn sat alone at a card table; the other patients were scattered at the sides of the large room, some talking to visitors, two playing checkers, one solitaire, another dreaming out in a dry gaze that David wanted to try not to cross. Marilyn wore a peasant blouse, red dungarees, and sandals. As they approached her, she stood. "I thought Serena was coming." Her voice was hoarse.

David took a seat opposite her at the table. "She's downstairs. You have a cold?"

Marilyn put her hand on David's wrist. "I was screaming this afternoon. There was nothing else to do." She turned quickly to Stuart and then just as quickly away. "See how upset that gets him," she said, shaking David's arm.

"Why?" Stuart asked.

"I'm joking. It's the medication. They gave me more last night." She withdrew her hand from David's arm and stuffed it under herself. "In the tushy." She brought a laugh from far away and wrung it out.

Stuart left the table to go to the coffee urn. David asked Marilyn, "What does the medication do, other than make you hoarse?"

"A horse? The medication doesn't make me a horse. But wait." She galloped her fingers around the corner of the table in a circle. "Maybe it did! How do you like that!"

"How's the food?" David didn't have time to think, and he knew if he tried he would only sink into a silence that might prompt even stranger reactions.

"Cooked."

Stuart returned with two cups of coffee, putting one in front of David, taking the other for himself. "My sister's coming to visit you next week."

Marilyn turned an upright index finger in the air.

"And your aunt called me at work this morning to see if you needed more clothes. Which I said you didn't."

"No, I don't. You picked the right answer. You get a prize. How would you like a horse? I'm a horse."

"Cut it." Stuart said it while David was drinking his coffee, his relief, he hoped, hidden by the rim of the paper cup. Stuart continued, eyes straight at her. "Why did they up the medication? Dr. Lentol say?"

Marilyn grabbed the wooden stirrer David had put on the table in front of him. "He doesn't say anything. No, he says something. He says, 'How are you doing?' Which is *really* interesting. Not 'What are you doing?' but 'How are you doing?' Shouldn't he say 'How are you doing *it*?' That's more correct."

David fumpfed a laugh.

"At least," Stuart said, "he doesn't say 'How are *we* doing?' Because if he ever says that, just lay into him. '*You're* doing great, Doc; I'm the one who's a mess.' "

"I once saw a cartoon in *The New Yorker* like that," David said.

"Sure you did," Stuart replied. "I've never said I was an original thinker."

Marilyn turned to David. "Tell me about *The New Yorker*."

What he wanted to do was look at Stuart, the translator, and dump it in his lap. But he said, "I'm sure you've read it. You forgot."

Marilyn shook her head vehemently, consistent in her excess.

"They publish a kind of classic funny cartoon. It's—the whole thing—considered the nth of sophistication."

Marilyn hummed. "The nth. Do they publish literary criticism?"

Stuart cut in sharply, startling David. "No, they don't. Forget it."

Sheepish, with a look that would have been burlesque-funny anywhere else, Marilyn looked at David. "Doesn't he"—she cocked her head toward Stuart—"make you un-com-fort-able?"

There was no more coffee in his cup. Robbed of his refuge, David changed the subject. "Is it cool during the day?" As he said it, Stuart got up, taking David's cup to refill it.

Marilyn's tone of voice whopped down to a whisper. "Why, *why* do you feel that you have to completely change what we're talking about? I have a very acute sense of time, and I can measure how long you stay on a subject. You've been shuffling every few minutes. Why can't"—her voice not only soft but chillingly definite—"we talk about one thing and keep it going, and going, and going, and going, and then—foop!— let it just die out on itself?"

David's face brightened with his rescuing thought. "I'd fall asleep."

Marilyn threw her head back and growled loudly. It was her most extreme reaction—yet, to David, strangely her most reassuring. The bonds of humor, God bless them, the bonds of humor.

Stuart returned with the refills and motioned to the clock on the wall. "You better go down and send Serena up. Twenty more minutes."

"To extinction," Marilyn appended. "Then everyone leaves and the whole place becomes sane." She laughed to herself. "This whole place is an experiment of the N.Y.U. drama school."

David stood up. "All right. Look, I'll see you again early in the week. Take care."

Marilyn rose, as she had when he and Stuart entered the room. She put a hand into his, then, surprisingly, shook it politely. "Nice to see you. Send up the next lambie."

"Cut it," Stuart said once again, the last thing David heard said as he left the room.

As he waited for the elevator, Marilyn came out of the day room and from down the hall yelled to him, "Wait." Stuart followed behind her. He raised a hand for David to stay where he was, then walked to him. Marilyn disappeared back into the room.

"She's still bugged with me. She wants you to stay and Serena to come up. I'll go down and get her. You go back in." Stuart put a hand on David's forearm. "Ten minutes, at the most. You can cut it shorter if you want. I'll be downstairs."

Suspended between the expectation of Marilyn coming out to the corridor and beckoning him back once again to the day room, and the wait for the elevator bearing Serena, David stood near the nurses' station and watched a nurse prepare medication cups. The nurse smiled; the elevator arrived.

Serena scowled, working hands flutteringly down her skirt as they walked toward the day room. She stopped him before they reached the door and asked, "Am I being a big baby?"

David didn't know; he walked her on.

Marilyn's back was to them as they entered: she was watching the two men who were playing checkers reconstruct the nearly game-finishing multiple jump one of them had just lucked into. David led Serena to the card table and was going to the coffee urn—the oasis of distraction—when she held his arm tightly, not letting him go. Marilyn turned and saw them. She walked very slowly to the table, no greeting on her face.

"Hi!" Serena said.

"Hello. Hello, David."

"It's been years, Mar," he said.

"What's new with you?" she asked Serena.

Unexpectedly, Serena bubbled, a suddenly gelatinous beauty, the glimmering of her nervousness, sparked up tiers and tiers of thin, snappy sentences. "Everything. The magazine's going haywire, but in a good way. They're finally facing up to the

fact that adolescent girls may be just as interested in the world
as in their fat hips." She threw whizzing glances around the
room as she spoke. "So we're all getting relevant, for a change.
It's really good. We're going to do an issue on counterculture
education and other things. I have to send you the next issue,
which'll really be good. And I'm going to write a few features,
beginning two issues from the next. You know, my sister came
to stay with us for a week and a half, with the kids. Who are
fantastic. I mean, you think *we* know things, you should watch
these kids when they grow up. Already they're so attuned to
different life styles—"

"Like being brats," David interjected.

Marilyn had said nothing after her greeting and what's new.
She was letting her eyebrows do oppressive things to her eyes.
"Go on," she declared simply.

"Well, they're both something else. Whatever quarrels I
have with Kate about the way . . . it doesn't matter . . .
well, anyway. Oh, yes! This I didn't even tell you, David. I've
been speaking to this woman in the building who's a member
of a group made up of neighborhood people from the area—
lower Lex, Park Avenue South, Gramercy Park—who formed
this organization that has liaison with the city about services,
like garbage collection and sanitation. They're going to have
a block party on Twenty-fourth Street to raise some money
to keep the committee going and get people involved. I said
I'd be on the planning thing for that. I mean, because even
though it's a fairly affluent area, the streets are filthy, you
never see a cop—things like that. And the point is, of course,
that we're all New Yorkers; this is *our* city, and we should
have some sort of say in how it's being run. It's not too much
to ask. When I first came here, I was so sure that people in
the next apartment didn't care at all about the neighbors, and
vice versa. Didn't even know who they were. But we really do
care. Each neighborhood is a community. And sure, as New
Yorkers, we're all very blasé, but still who needs the streets
all crapped up, and that you can't go out for a pizza after

seven-thirty because you're afraid to be attacked? Man! But these people from this group are really sharp, and the main thing is that they're friendly."

"Sort of like me?" Marilyn asked.

Serena blinked.

"Go ahead, cry."

"Marilyn." David tried to be stern.

"Don't say 'Marilyn' to me. You're not Stuart. Only he can say that. You know why? Because he's the walking pacifier." Her brows had now fashioned themselves into two angry diacritical marks above her shooting eyes. "If she wants to cry, let her, poor lambie."

"I don't," Serena said, chuckling her confusion.

"Yes, you do. You *can*. Us 'New Yorkers' cry whenever we feel like. You have a lot of fucking nerve. New Yorkers cry, they do, I'm telling you." She looked David's way. "I just know, I *know*, that under the table your knees are twitching and in two minutes you're going to say, 'Well, we gotta go.' Am I right?"

David turned his head away.

"Go ahead, cry. All chicks from Colorado cry over the dog doody in the street. I bet you don't cry when you see cow pies in a field. Go ahead. Pizza pies and crying all together at a block party. Ever since I met you, I knew you were a crier. How come you weren't weeping when you came in here—into the sanitized—the sanitized day room? Boy, you're so full of shit. And also I love you. Boy, they gave me a lot of medication."

Serena composed herself enough to say, "Does it make you feel lousy?"

Marilyn nodded like a puppet. "True, true, true, true."

David said, "You know, Serena's sister was on an organic-foods diet."

"Yes, I know. Colorado. Oh, fancy, faaancy magazine. Ritzy —Gramercy Park—ritzy neighborhood. Organic foods; that's nice." Marilyn put her hand on Serena's wrist as she had on

David's. She abruptly stood up. "You're going to go now, I just know it. Wait here, I have to give you something to give Stuart."

David assembled the empty coffee cups on the table immediately on seeing the start of irrigation in Serena's stunned blues. He dropped the cups into the plastic-lined pail beneath the coffee urn, then arranged the sugar bowl and the cup of wooden stirrers. He heard the chairs at the card table move, and only then, with Marilyn back in the room, did he return to Serena.

"Here." Marilyn stuffed a piece of paper torn from a spiral notebook and folded tightly four times into David's hand. She turned to Serena. "Both of you listen to this, so in case one of you forgets, the other will remember. Tell Stuart that this is the covering letter for the *Othello*. Tell him to type it up *neatly*—make sure he does it neatly—and send it along with the paper. O.K.?"

They both nodded. Serena stood up and made half a move to Marilyn. She stopped herself. David bestowed the numbed kiss for both of them. They left the room, David waiting until he was in the corridor out of Marilyn's sight to slip the paper into his shirt pocket. He looked at Serena as they waited for the elevator.

"Did she sit back down after we left, as we were leaving?" she asked.

"I guess so. Why?"

"That's what I didn't want to see. Her sitting back down."

She started to cry in the elevator when David pressed the button for lobby and said, "Don't you think she has to be left?"

Serena put the back of her hand on her forehead. She sniffled tautly. "I don't want Stuart to see me crying."

Stuart stood by the front door in the lobby, looking out to the street, the dulcimer under his arm. He got a picture of Serena's face as they walked to him and he said, "Tough?"

"I want you to forgive me," she said, and then let it all

come. She wept for a block as they walked toward Madison and Stuart's bus, separated by a few steps, her revolving sobs a continuo to their brisk echoing footsteps. David waited with each step taken for her return out of misery, her return to him, to Stuart, to the reality of refusal he now understood to be the composer of Stuart's face in the Automat. Under the entrance lights of an apartment house, David pulled the paper from his pocket and handed it to Stuart.

"I figured she'd give it to you," Stuart said, stopping for a moment, as did David. Serena walked on, gaining strides on them.

"What is it?" David asked. They began to walk again.

Stuart sent a stream of breath through his lips. "A letter. She's decided to send more of her Shakespeare papers she wrote in school to magazines. She wants me to send the one she wrote on *Othello* to *Life*, and, if they reject it, to *Look*. She thinks that there's a new interest, a popular one, in Shakespeare and that the term papers she wrote are jazzy enough to be published in *Life*. In *Life* magazine! I just don't know where she is."

The hand David put on Stuart's arm was half to console and half to lower his voice out of range of Serena's hearing. But she had stopped, her long blond hair swizzled over her shoulders as she turned around to face them and raise a sharded voice. "Don't shut him up! David, don't shut him up! I heard. What am I going to do?" She swung back around and kicked into a run, the run of a prep-school girl coming onto the field-hockey lawn, the run of a young professional trying to get to Bergdorf's before closing—but now the clipped run from mistake, from the very contrast of Stuart's and David's hauling walk, a walk of a grief so utterly familiar that, likely as not, they could blame it on the muggy night.

The last they saw of her for a while was her dangerous canter across Park Avenue, the traffic a phosphorescent run all itself. Stuart put the folded paper in his wallet.

"You're going to do it?"

"What else can I do? It's what she wants, it's her fucking *plan!* And I just can't kill it; I'm not that strong."

Serena stood in the doorway of a Gristede's when they both reached Madison Avenue. She waited for their approach, then stepped forward and put her arms around Stuart's waist, her chin resting in the niche of his shoulder and neck. "We have all these cots," she whispered, "left over from when my sister came. Come spend the night with us. I have a reason."

She felt Stuart's no against her chin.

"But I have a reason!" She moved off him. "Why are you all so dumb! Why don't you see? If you don't come and stay with us tonight, we're never going to see each other any more! Don't you understand that? I mean never!"

The Number 4 bus was a block south. Stuart walked out toward the curb, raising the hand which held the wrapped dulcimer to catch the bus driver's notice. "I'll call you to-morrow."

Serena yelled to him as he was climbing the steps onto the bus. "Don't! You better not!"

David had spotted a lone cab coming downtown and he stopped it, holding a flat palm for it to wait. He took her arm and led her across the street.

The cab got them home in fifteen minutes. Serena switched on only the light in the bedroom. David's move toward the switch in the living room was aborted by an angry "Don't" from her. He went into the bedroom to join her.

She looked at him fiercely. "You stay in here and close the door. Understand? You keep this fucking door closed!" She walked to the corner of the room where her cello rested. In a fluid, instinctively graceful motion, she swung the case horizontal by the handle and walked out of the room. "Now close the door."

He did as she commanded, sitting for a moment on the bed, hearing metal clasps flicked open and the hollow sound of the case dropped to the floor. He undressed and lay naked on the bed, listening.

As if it were her true voice, the cello faltered for a moment, then caught the undertow to produce the deep and muscled tones that David always pictured as planks of expensive mahogany. The tones went surely to the destination of rest, then elegantly turned into explanation. Bach.

It went on and on. He could hear an occasional "Shit!" as she missed an effect, but mostly it continued with irretrievable progress. In a few minutes, he would sleep to the music, to the nothingness which had finally splattered and become truly shared. Or maybe not sleep at all, but loll on the obliteration as one would on a dune. This was the true waiting—not for something new, but for the very soul of distress to cuddle in a downy nest of numbed arms.

He must have slept, because now Serena was in the room, placing the cello back in the corner. She was nude. Saying it was five in the morning, she got into bed, keeping distance.

David was nodding even as she began to tell him that she was no saint. Maybe even a sinner, to live that long on what she thought were good memories. But when it got this bad, saint or sinner had to get out. She had her whole life ahead of her. He could stay with Stuart for the rest of the summer; he'd need him more than she did. Did he understand? That maybe she'd even leave New York? That she had herself to think about first? They could make love once more, to at least finish all these years with something nice.

PRACTICE. PRACTICE. THE ESSENCE OF CRAFT."
Stuart grabbed one end of the stripped mattress, David the
other. "UP!"

With his foot, Stuart knocked away a chair and a wastebasket, sandwiching himself between the wall and the now-
upended mattress. He slipped out and they both arranged the
old Sealy so that it leaned slightly and would stand by itself.

"All right. Now I hope I can find it."

David followed Stuart out of the bedroom, walking to the
kitchen for the next six-pack. He got a glimpse of the empty
cans in a neat row on top of his two suitcases in the living
room, and had to smile.

From the hallway, head in the closet where he was rum-
maging, Stuart yelled, "We still have?"

"Plenty. Two more sixes. When did we stop keeping track?"

The voice among the winter clothes answered, "After one."

David extracted two cans from the cardboard holder and
opened them both, knees down on the living-room floor. He

turned to look down the hallway before returning to the bedroom. "Got it?"

"I see it. It's just a question of . . . wait. Shit, all of this
junk. There must be fifty sketch pads up here, filled with
Marilyn's quote unquote art. Wait . . . I . . . all right, I
got it. We're in business, Charlie."

David watched Stuart get off the chair on which he had
been standing. From the murk of the dark hallway came the
greyed softball, seams ripped all over it, but still intact. David
caught it and flipped it up once or twice.

"How old is this?"

"I stole it when I was in high school from the dean of boys."
Stuart took a sip of her beer. "Mr. Furber. 'All right, you
faggots, I don't want you to die. Now push-ups. I want to see
daylight between your fat bellies and the floor. Enough. Now
laps.' "

David spit into his hands and was about to rub up the ball
when Stuart snatched it away from him, in the process spilling
some of his beer from the can. "Fuck up my ball? Get outa
here."

David pulled the ball back to himself. "Me first. How many
for each of us?"

"Ten." Stuart went over to the mattress. "Ten to start.
Now, look." He bent down. "From this button over here"—
he raised his pointing finger about two feet—"to this one
here"—he moved the finger to the left about a foot—"to this
button here, and down to this one. That's the strike zone." He
straightened up and moved back.

David retreated to the far end of the bedroom. He put down
the ball for a second and picked up his beer.

"Soft at first," Stuart warned. "I don't want you to break
any windows."

David tried a cutting glance, but two days of steady drinking made it nearly cross-eyed instead. He picked up the ball.
"Get back. Koufax returns." He brought his arm up and
around, repeating the process, which was frankly making him

a little dizzy but was the right way to do it. Another turn, and another, and in the midst of the fourth and final revolution, Stuart yelled, "No windmilling! You'll break one of the fucking windows. Soft."

David stopped his motion. "Bad form to disturb a consummate artist while he's doing his thing."

"Go on. Now, soft, soft."

David brought his arm around again, letting go of the ball with only one turn. Speedy, but it hit the right-hand corner of the mattress near the floor with a muffled *vump*.

"Koufax, huh?"

"Shut up and throw the ball back."

David dispensed with the windmilling this time, and, relying only on a quick snap of the wrist, underhanded the ball so that it reached higher on the mattress, just a little out of the strike zone.

"Better, better."

"It's all in the wrist motion."

"But hair begins to grow on your palms."

"The ball—come on."

The next pitch David threw was perfect, high and inside, hitting one of the buttons with a dull little pop. He took a congratulatory pull on his beer. "I've proved my point. I don't need ten. You throw."

Stuart didn't move from the desk where he had positioned himself to watch the exhibition. "One more. Just so we know it wasn't lucky." He flipped back the ball.

David wasn't concentrating, and his next whizzer missed the target completely, landing against the lower drawer of the desk, inches below Stuart's hanging feet.

Stuart jumped off the desk and got the ball. "The prosecution rests. Now me."

Without a windup, Stuart let go of the ball and made it fly slowly through the room's space and land exactly in the middle of the strike zone. It made almost no sound as it hit.

"Yeah," David said, lips wet with beer. "But you know how far a guy would slam that ball? You'd find it in Rahway."

"Jealous. It was a strike."

"Against a paraplegic. To anybody who could even hold a bat it would be a home run, and you'd be off to the showers."

" 'The showers,' huh? This your old Nazi inclinations blooming forth?"

David flung the ball back.

Stuart wound up this time, the ball at first homing normally, then falling away left six or seven feet from the mattress to wing close to David's chest. Dropping his beer in order to save a window, David dived for it. He looked at Stuart while lifting the wet fabric of his pants off his leg. "That was just great."

"This is no substitute." Stuart approached the mattress, gripping the top with one hand, a side with the other. "Help me get this back on the bed. This is all bullshit."

As they moved the furniture back to their original places in the room, Stuart said, "Change your pants and we'll go down. Whose idea was this bullshit?"

David went into the living room and cleared the empties off one of his suitcases, removed a pair of fresh dungarees, and put them on after slipping the wet ones off and leaving them on the couch. "Are you going to take the ball?" he asked Stuart, who waited at the door.

"No." He surveyed the disorder. "We should clean up here later."

They had some trouble going down the stairs. The last time they'd been out was ten the evening before, and now, eleven the next morning, they were considerably less sure of their balance. It wasn't even something to laugh about any longer, just to endure.

There was going to be rain, and with that in their minds, they hurried up Fort Washington Avenue. When they arrived, they could see that half of the L-shaped schoolyard was empty. Entering anyway, they walked around to the other part, in which, on one of the concrete diamonds, eight or nine kids were playing stickball with bases and outfielders.

Saying nothing, David and Stuart walked to the ledge where the kids waiting their turns up sat. The one at the plate slapped a sharp grounder down to third, and they all watched his progress as he rounded first, gaining ground against an inept left fielder who had let the ball skip by him.

"This a game?" Stuart asked the kid sitting next to him, who wore a who-knew-how-many-times handed-down Davy Crockett T-shirt. The kid shrugged, but the one next to him said, with a low Spanish-accented grumble, "Yeah, man."

"Hey, Nacio!" The kid who had reached second base on the cheap hit ran from there to them, hands waving. "What the fuck they want?" He was obviously the one to talk to.

Nacio rolled the bottom of his shirt—the rock where Davy Crockett defiantly stood—around his fingers. "They wanta know is it a game."

"Yeah, it's a game." The leader kid, who wore a poplin jacket over no shirt, his yellow-brown skin shining with sweat, walked toward David with a bravado that turned all the kids' attention to him. He put his chin up. "Why?"

David looked him in his brown eyes. He didn't like the kid being so close; he didn't want the beer on his breath to jeopardize their chances. "Well, we just thought if it was a game— you know, if you got room—we'd like to play."

The kid who played first base ran toward them. "Julio, man. You can't let these cats play. They're grownups! Fuck up the whole fucking game."

Julio turned to the meddler with the noblesse oblige he exuded from each pore along with his sweat. "Shut up." He turned back to Stuart and David. "Why'd'you guys wanna play with us guys?"

Stuart began to hiccup.

The first baseman snorted, "Man, they're drunk."

"Ain't you got friends of your own?" Julio pressed.

David shook his head. Stuart, taking the cue, shook his as well.

The kid in the Davy Crockett shirt said, "Come on. It's gonna rain."

Julio studied both of them once more, pulling the zipper

of his jacket up and down. "Yeah. O.K. But, man, you're really sad cats." He took a playful step backward, his whole face a taunt of disdain and mastery.

David stood up. "Where do we play?"

"Outfield."

David motioned to Stuart to stand.

Julio added, "You're not gonna bat, but you'll field for us."

The kid in the T-shirt jumped up. "No fair, man. No fair."

Julio turned and ran back to his base. Stuart and David, unsure exactly what their duties were and when they were to perform them, loped out to the outfield against the school wall.

The outraged T-shirt yelled out, "They're gonna fuck up the whole game. Let 'em fuck up their own game."

It didn't much matter, anyway, because before they even got a chance to try for a ball it started to pour.

NOTE ABOUT THE AUTHOR

Ross Feld was born in 1947, in Brooklyn, New York. He attended public schools and the City College of New York. He has published poetry and prose in numerous literary magazines, including *Poetry, For Now,* and *Grosseteste Review.*
He is married and lives in New York City.

A NOTE ON THE TYPE

This book was set in Electra, a Linotype face designed
by W. A. Dwiggins. This face cannot be classified as
either modern or old-style. It is not based on any
historical model, nor does it echo any particular
period or style. It avoids the extreme contrasts
between thick and thin elements that mark most
modern faces and attempts to give a feeling of fluidity,
power, and speed.

Composed, printed, and bound by
H. Wolff Book Mfg. Co., New York, N.Y.
Typography and binding design by
VIRGINIA TAN